リリカル・バラッズ
Lyrical Ballads

ワーズワス・コールリッジ
抒情民謡集（英文）

序文と詩文選

高 瀬 彰 典 解説・註釈

ふくろう出版

は　し　が　き

　ワーズワスとコールリッジの最初の出会いは1795年頃であったが、その２年後にワーズワス兄妹がオールフォックスデンに移り住み、コールリッジが近くのネザー・ストウイに住むに至って両者の親密な交際が始まった。ほとんど毎日のように会って交わした詩や文学上の対話から実り多い友情関係が生まれて『抒情民謡詩集』を共同出版する計画が考えられた。1798年の初版は部数にして僅か500部のささやかなもので著者名もつけられなかった。コールリッジは名作「老水夫の歌」をはじめとして４編の詩を寄稿し、ワーズワスは「ティンタン僧院の上流で書いた詩」など19編を入れた。初版が案外に好評だったので、ワーズワスは初版を改訂し、さらに１巻の詩集を加えて２巻として、長編の「序文」に本格的な詩論を書き、新たな詩の改革とその実験的意義を世に問おうとした。この詩集は1805年の第４版まで版を重ねて、その間に多くの改訂や補足がなされた。第２版では詩の配列が大幅に変更され、当初巻頭にあった「老水夫の歌」が巻末の方にまわされ、ワーズワスの詩の特性を簡潔に表明した「諫めと答え」と「反論」が巻頭に据えられた。コールリッジの詩風が自分の意図するものとあまりに相違するため、詩集の巻頭を飾るにふさわしくないと彼は感じたのである。ワーズワスは自然の事象の美しさや静けさによって喚起された快感の影響力によって強められたものが詩的想像力であると信じ、コールリッジは人間の想像力が主体となって、自然界の不動の事象にひそむ生命力をひき出し可動性を与えると考えていた。しかし、いずれにしても、ワーズワスの卓越した現実観察からコールリッジの超現実的な世界に至るまで、両詩人の詩に存在する現実とヴィジョンとの間の根本的な緊張関係こそ、この詩集に一種独特の特質を与えているものである。

　初版の「綱領」から発展したワーズワスの「序文」は、真の詩の判断基準としての詩的快感について考え、古典主義文学の情熱の欠如を指摘し18世紀的な詩の素材や形式を否定して、人間の情熱の精髄において感じ考える詩人のあり方を考察したものであった。今日、この詩集が文学的革新をになうものと受けとめられ、ロマン主義復活の画期的な記念碑と考えられている背景には、すでに18世紀中頃から後半にかけて、ドライデンやポープの古典主義に対抗して、グレイ、コリンズ、クーパー、バーンズ、ブレイクなどの前期ロマン派の詩人達が憂鬱の心情や自然美、神秘的な想像の世界を歌いあげて文学上の革新の機運が熟していたことがあった。そして、『抒情民謡詩集』出版は、単に古典主義に対する英詩の革新を宣言するということばかりでなく、それまでの文学が人間の生命の根源的深層に触れる詩の出現をも意味し、偉大な２人の天才的詩人の出逢いによる新たな自然観や人間観の表明として意義深いものがある。両詩人の基本問題は、いかに内在的で抽象的なものを外在的で具象的なものによって表現するかであった。内的ヴィジョンと外的媒体との緊張感から象徴的イメージが作り出され、永遠の特質が有限な事物を通して詩人の心の眼に見えてくるのである。彼等は詩を高級な娯楽とする18世紀古典主義の詩語への反発から、詩には宗教にも匹敵するような偉大な力と価値があるという認識を深めていた。詩は人間精神に内在する不屈の崇高な力の発現であり、自然世界に存在する偉大で永続的な事物と呼応するものである。

この詩集の題名として用いられた「バラッド」という言葉は、当時では一般大衆の出来事を素朴で簡潔な手法で、写実的に物語を進めていく一連の短い節によって構成される詩という意味であり、今日使用されているような音楽と詩による物語歌謡という厳密な定義とは異なっている。そして、この詩集は当時流行していた土俗趣味、懐古趣味や抒情を求める大衆の要望に合致していたのである。しかし、バラッドと呼べるものは、「老水夫の歌」、「グディ・ブレイクとハリー・ギル」、「茨」、さらに、「サイモン・リー」、「私たちは7人」、「最後の羊」ぐらいであって、その他の多数の詩は抒情的小曲や瞑想詩というべきものである。また、実験的なバラッドよりも、「マイケル」や「兄弟」のような無韻詩が悲劇的情感を効果的に表現した秀作であるし、ワーズワスの原体験にかかわる深い喪失感はルーシー詩群によく示されている。「老水夫の歌」や「グディ・ブレイクとハリー・ギル」、「茨」、「放浪する女」などの詩は、極限状況にある人間の姿や異様な心理を題材として取り扱った作品であり、極限状況の中で究極的な人間の姿を凝視することによって人間性の根源的法則を示すものといえる。また、大人の合理的思考よりも、子供の率直な感性の方が一層、真実に触れるものがあると説いた「私たちは7人」などや、呪いの詩ともいうべき「鹿跳びの泉」がある。

　この詩集を通して両詩人が主張することは、人間と自然とが心を通わせうるという素朴な信念である。そして、極限状況にある人間は、普通よりも一層、自然の生命に近づいており、人間性の根源的な法則が自然全体に通じる法則であることを示している。美しい湖水地方の深い広がりの中で、自然との深い交感の神秘的体験を語って有名な「ティンタン僧院の上流で書いた詩」や、自然の中で孤独に生きる美しい少女を一種の精霊のように扱って深い喪失感を歌ったルーシー詩群などはワーズワスの傑作とされているものである。ワーズワスの感情の礼賛と自然的なものの探究が、感情の称揚のよって単なる誇張表現や劇的メロドラマにならないためには、力強い感情が静寂のうちに回想されねばならず、情熱的な感情がさまざまな要素によって制御されて、感情を伝えると同時に抑制するような客観的相関物としてのイメジャリーが駆使されねばならないのである。人間の情熱を愛して内的生活の本質に多くの喜びを見いだし、また自然宇宙の営みを観照して、それに相似した人間性の根源的法則を見いだすことができない場合は、習性として自らそれを創り出すことを課する人間こそワーズワスにとって真の詩人であった。このような人間の根源的法則を表現するために、素朴な田園生活に取材し、詩の言葉として日常生活において人間が実際に用いる言語を選ぶことなどを彼は「序文」の中で自らの詩論として述べているのである。しかし、共同責任者であり鋭敏な批評家でもあったコールリッジは、ワーズワスのこのような議論を問題視し、論難の対象として後年、『文学的自叙伝』の中でかなり多くの点で賛同できない点があるとして、ワーズワスの詩論を詳細に分析批評しているのである。この両者の討論の相違については、INTRODUCTIONにおいてさらに論究することになる。なお、本書では1805年の第4版をテキストとして使用し、便宜上、詩作品の配列順序を独自に組み替えて構成したことをお断りしておく。

　　　　　1987年8月30日

　　　　　　　　　　　　　　　　　　　　　　　　高　瀬　彰　典

ヘルヴェリン山上のワーズワス（晩年）

S.T. コールリッジ (1799)

CONTENTS

INTORODUCTION

Preface to Lyrical Ballads ·· 1

The Thorn ·· 16

We are Seven ··· 21

Hart-Leap Well ··· 23

'There was a boy' ··· 28

The Brothers, a Pastoral Poem ·································· 28

Expostulation and Reply ······································· 39

The tables Turned ··· 40

Lucy Gray ·· 40

Poor Susan ··· 42

Ruth ··· 43

Nutting ·· 49

The Ancient Mariner ·· 50

The Two April Morning ·· 66

The Fountain, a Conversation ·································· 68

Michael, Pastoral Poem ·· 70

Love ··· 79

'Strange fits of passion I have known' ·························· 82

'She dwelt among th' untrodden ways' ·························· 83

'A slumber did my spirit seal' ································· 83

'Three years she grew in sun and shower' ······················ 83

Lines written a few miles above Tintern Abbey ·················· 84

Goody Blake and Harry Gill ···································· 88

Simon Lee, the old Huntsman ·································· 90

Lines left upon a seat in a Yew-Tree ·························· 93

The Female Vagrant ··· 94

Lines written at a Small Distance from my House ················ 99

The Foster-Mother's Tale ······································ 101

Lines written in Early Spring ································· 102

The Nightingale ·· 103

The Last of the Flock ··· 105

NOTES

INTRODUCTION

I have said that poetry is the spontaneous overflow of powerful feelings; it takes its origin from emotion recollected in tranquillity: the emotion is contemplated till, by a species of reaction, the tranquillity gradually disappears, and an emotion, kindred to that which was before the subject of contemplation, is gradually produced, and does itself actually exist in the mind.

W. Wordsworth

The poet, described in *ideal* perfection, brings the whole soul of man into activity, with the subordination of its faculties to each other, according to their relative worth and dignity.

S. T. Coleridge

　ワーズワスが『抒情民謡集』に付した1800年版の序文は、(1802年版に加えられた章節を含めて) 詩の言語に対する彼の実験を正当化するために書かれたロマン主義理論の一宣言であった。ワーズワスの序文の中の詩論の背景には、18世紀末から19世紀始めのイギリス社会の変動、すなわちフランス革命や産業革命の影響を受けた当時の社会的意識が存在していた。当時のイギリス社会の変動を経験したワーズワスは、新たな社会的意識を持って、単に美しい自然の姿をうたう詩人としてではなく、自らの田園生活の体験を土台として、自然の中に生きる農民の素朴な生態、その喜びや悲しみに注目した詩人であった。フランス革命を現地で体験し、当時のイギリス社会の変動を経験したワーズワスにとって、グレイ、クーパー、バーンズの様な過去の自然詩人達の田園詩とは異った見方で農民の姿を表現することが何よりも必要な事であった。この様な新たな社会情勢の経験と観察を、どの様に言葉が適確に表現すべきかを考察したものが、詩の主題と用語に関するワーズワスの詩論であった。

　1790年以後のワーズワスは、湖畔地方での幼少年時代以来、精神形成において最も重大な時期を迎えた。グラスミアやウィンダミアでの幼少年期の単純な喜びや本能的な恐怖の描写に知的要素や社会的意識が欠落していたのは事実であり、フランス革命がワーズワスの知的生活に与えた影響力は、ケンブリッジよりもはるかに大きなものであった。フランス革命による政治的興奮を情緒的感性で受けとめていたワーズワスは、当時の革命的な精神活動の基盤を抽象的理性におこうと望んでいた。この時期のワーズワスに指導的役割を果たしたのが、ウィリアム・ゴドウィンであった。ゴドウィンの何物にも妥協しない理性的確信と明解な論理は、情緒的にゆれ動くワーズワスに確固たる足場を与えたかに見えたが、革命が恒久的理想となり得ないのは当然の結果であった。ワーズワスが革命に期待したものは、すべて失望と恐怖に終ったのである。フランス革命の苦い経験は、ワーズワスの精神的成長に重大な衝撃を与え、深刻な道徳的情緒的危機となった。この様に革命の衝撃と幻滅に苦悩していたワーズワスに新たな希望と光を投げかけたのがコールリッジであった。コールリッジの知性と広範な学識は、ゴドウィン以上にワーズワスの精神に豊かで変化に富んだ知

識を与えたのである。コールリッジの芸術哲学は詩的暗示性に豊み、深い思弁的特質を持っていた。ワーズワスの序文に見られる真の人間性に対する創作活動への精神的な革新は、ワーズワスの自然観照がコールリッジの理想主義的知性と深い連携を持つことによって、詩人ワーズワスの独自の哲学的志向が確立された事を示すものである。

　『抒情民謡集』序文におけるワーズワスの目的は、詩を特定の人間の特別な趣味から解放し、人類の中で普遍性を持った詩人像を確立することであった。このために、詩人は誰よりも人間性に関する広範囲の知識と力強い感性に恵まれていることが要求された。ワーズワスにとって、詩は特殊な技巧や用語によって、少数の知識人の知的自己満足のために存在するものではなかった。したがって、つつましい田舎の生活の中から素朴な主題を選び、日常的な会話に人間の真実の言葉を求めたワーズワスの態度は、詩の主題と用語に対して意図した平凡さと簡潔さの正当性を力説する意識的挑戦なのであった。ワーズワスが田舎の生活に注目したのは、特定の階層の人間や地域性に目をむけたわけでなく、素朴な主題があらゆる人間に共通の熱情を最も自然な形で伝達し得る表現形態を意識的に模索した結果であった。人間性の真実や永遠の相が、田舎の素朴な人々や羊の群れの中に見出されるならば、それは同時にワーズワスにとって、人間の真実の言葉を考察する場でもある。この様な真の人間の言葉が、ワーズワスの詩の言語となるべきものであった。田園生活を営む現実の人間の言葉の忠実な再現が、詩中において人間の真実の言葉として表現される時、読者を一層深く感動させることになり、詩人は描こうとする庶民の感情にできる限り近づくべきだとワーズワスは考えるのである。コールリッジの様に直観的認識を論理的に説明する哲学的手法を持たないワーズワスは、最も平凡な生活から一般論を導き出し、自分の基本的な詩作方針を次の様に記述している。

　　Humble and rustic life was generally chosen , because, in that condition, the essential passions of the heart find a better soil in which they can attain their maturity, are less under restraint , and speak a plainer and more emphatic language.[1]

ワーズワスが田舎の人間の素朴な言葉を詩の用語として選択した事は、田園生活の中で生きる人間の姿に最も自然な真の人間性を見出していたからであった。詩的直観によって経験した詩人の感動は、最も自然で無理のない形で読者に伝達されるべき事をワーズワスは詩的信条としていた。田舎の人間の素朴な言葉に深い意味を認め、田園生活の様式を詩の主題と用語にすることによって、ワーズワスが表現しようとしたものの本質は、自然の永遠の美と人間の熱情との融合であった。ワーズワスにとって永遠なものの探求とは、自然を熟視し、自然の意味を問い、自然に従うことであり、人間との最も基本的にして不変の均衡を追求し、"the primary laws of our nature "[2]を把握することであった。創造性と普遍的魂を持つ詩人が、他の人間に不可視なものの美を認識し、歓喜と共に詩作するのは、自然の中に生きる人間存在の " the primary laws of our nature "

を深い神秘性を湛えた鋭い直観的認識によって突然把握するためである。素朴な日常生活の中に見られるこの様な " the primary laws of our nature " こそ、田舎のつつましい農民の生活を詩の主題として設定することによって、ワーズワスが描き出そうとしたものであった。

　ワーズワスは序文の中で、田園生活に密着した詩の主題と用語が低俗であるとか、詩作の常識に反するという当時の批判や非難に対して、自ら弁護し反論を試みている。18世紀の思想的背景となった機械論的唯物主義や無味乾燥な科学的抽象に対して、ワーズワスは自己の具体的経験の普遍性によって独自の精神主義を宣言したのである。当時の精神的覚醒の先駆者として、自然と人間の相互作用を誰よりも深く見つめていたワーズワスにとって、詩は前時代に見られる技巧的イメジャリーや不自然な装飾のための単なる娯楽や特定の知識人のための趣味ではなく、力強い感情の自発的な流出でなければならない。

> 　I have said that poetry is the spontaneous overflow of powerful feelings :
> it takes its origin from emotion recollected in tranquillity : (3)

自発的に流出する力強い感情をどの様に言葉が適切に具象化するかという問題は、特殊な語彙語法や伝統的詩語を排斥するワーズワスにとって重大な関心事であった。" emotion recollected in tranquillity "とは、詩人が溢れ出る感情と適切な表現を求めて深く長い間考え続け、いく度も推敲をくり返さねばならないことを示すものである。詩人によって深く長い間考察された感情と言葉は、詩中において感情が言葉を生かし、言葉が感情によって独自の詩の魅力を発揮する魔術的な力を生み出すのである。詩における感情と言葉の理想的結合の可能性を模索したワーズワスは、18世紀的な詩の作法に満足せず、むしろ農村の日常的な言葉の中から新たな詩の用語をひろいあげようとしたのである。このために、静寂の中の瞑想活動が平静さを伴った深い感動を呼び起こすことが、ワーズワスの詩心に不可欠であった。5年前に訪れたワイ河の回想を述べた『ティンターン寺院賦』に見られる様に、以前に自然から受けた生の感動は、時間の経過によって平静さを伴った深い感動となり、ワーズワスの沈思黙考はかつての詩的ビジョンの体験に集中し、自然と人間精神との相互作用に目を向けていくのである。

> ───── that serene and blessed mood ,
> In which the affections gently lead us on , ─────
> Until , the breath of this corporeal frame
> And even the motion of our human blood
> Almost suspended , we are laid asleep
> In body , and become a living soul :
> While with an eye made quiet by the power
> Of harmony , and the deep power of joy ,
> We see into the life of things .
>
> 　　　　　　　(ll. 41 - 49)

ワーズワスの自然の積極的意義は、感覚的に身も心も自然と完全に融合することによって、詩人の生きた魂に実現されるのである。自然によって瞑想活動へ導びかれて、ワーズワスは静寂なる宇宙の美を一種の恍惚状態の中で感じとり、事物の中心に存在する聖なる静けさを感和する至高の瞬間を神の示現として受けとめていた。自然の美しい風景が与えた印象の道徳的意味を考え、倫理性を湛えた場面の数々を回想する時、精神に落ち着いた静寂と同時に高揚した感覚的喜悦を与える崇高な神の存在をワーズワスは独自の汎神論的認識によって自覚するのである。

　詩の用語として現実の農夫の話し言葉の諸相を再現しようとするワーズワスの主張は、日常使用されない言葉をすべて詩から排除することを意味するものではなく、18世紀の古典主義的詩語法に対する詩の革新を意識しながら、農夫の生活に見られる素朴さの中に真の人間性の基本を求めることによって、異常な事件を渇望する様な時流文学の弊害を改め、平凡な事件の中に不滅性を見出すことによって、本来あるべき健全なる文学の姿を提示しようとしたものであった。ワーズワスが当時としては革新的なこの様な詩作方針に強い信念を持つに至ったのは、幼少年時代に過した田園生活の体験のためである。ワーズワスが幼少年時代を過したウェストモーランドのグラスミアの湖や村は、その後も常に純粋な愛情の対象であり続けた。とりわけ、湖水地方の中心部の荘厳な静寂は、彼の魂に不滅の魅力を与え、郷土に対する熱狂的な愛着は終生変わることがなかったのである。幼少年時代の印象や体験は、ワーズワスの人生における豊かな知識の源泉というべきもので、『序曲』の様な偉大な思想詩を生み出す基盤となり、晩年の思想の最も深遠で重要な中心的観念を形成するものとなったのである。『序曲』には、自然と人間との絶ちがたい連帯が示されており、ワーズワスは人間の精神形成に対する自然の道徳的倫理的意義を幼少年時代の直接的体験の思い出の中で述べている。日暮れどきに、他人の小舟に無断で乗り込み、湖の岸辺から勢いよく漕ぎ出した時の不思議な出来事が次の様に述懐されている。

the huge Cliff
Rose up between me and the stars, and still,
With measur'd motion, like a living thing,
Strode after me. With trembling hands I turn'd
And through the silent water stole my way
Back to the Cavern of the Willow tree.
There, in her mooring-place, I left my Bark,
And, through the meadows homeward went, with grave
And serious thoughts; and after I had seen
That spectacle, for many days, my brain
Work'd with a dim and undetermin'd sense
Of unknown modes of being;

(BOOK I, ll. 409-420)

ワーズワスは独自の原始的自然観の中で、畏怖の念と共に無意識的な倫理感覚を身につけていたのである。この様な少年時代の恐怖の体験が回想によって再び内感の中で捉えられる時、詩人の先鋭化した意識は、自然の中に " unknown modes of be ing " 「存在の見知らぬ様式」を認識し、自然と人間精神の深い合一を再現しようとするのである。そこに描かれた自然は、もはや18世紀の巨大な機械ではなく、人間の魂に必然的なかかわりを持つ存在である。自然の道徳的影響力を見つめるワーズワスは、自然の観照によって神の意識へと導びかれていく。平凡な出来事にすぎないけれども、最も思いがけない時と場所において、ある巨大な不可視的存在との出会いによって得た神秘的な直観的認識は、ワーズワスの一連の作品の根源となった原体験であった。幼少年期の強烈な印象や連想は、自然の道徳的影響力を受けながら、深くて正しい永続的な形象を人格形成に残すことになる。直接的な感覚的印象がいたずらに空想的なものに走らず、自然の道徳的影響下で精神が受動的に受けとめたものが、人間性の根本的原則を深く把握することを、ワーズワスは『諫言と答え』の中で「賢明なる受動性」という言葉でも表現しているのである。ワーズワスの日常生活の言葉に関する理論は、この様な直接の感覚的経験に対する強い信頼を前提として、詩は対象となるべき素朴さを大胆に取り扱うべきだという信念を述べたものであった。いかなる知的要因よりも直接的経験への信頼を詩の源泉としたことは、ワーズワスの詩心の大きな特徴である。しかしながら、コールリッジも指摘している様に、ワーズワスの意図が十分に詩に発揮されなかった場合には、ワーズワスの詩の長所はそのまま短所となって、素朴な田園生活の描写は単純な虚構にすぎないものになってしまうのである。また、ワーズワスが精神の皮相的局面から作品を書いた場合、内容の空虚さが目立ち、陳腐な教訓と致命的な平板さに陥っているのである。コールリッジはこの典型的な例として『白痴の子供』や『茨』をあげている。要するに、人間性の全的反応を求めながら、自然の諸相の中に道徳的教訓を見出そうとするワーズワス的な信仰は、その意図があまりに露骨になった時には、無駄な饒舌と単純な虚構性の印象を読者に与えかねないのである。コールリッジは『文学的自叙伝』において、ワーズワスの記憶や回想が単に機械的な感覚的印象だけに終始している場合や、その受動性が単なる空想だけに終っている場合には、きびしい批判を下しており、序文に示された詩論にも綿密な考察を加えているのである。ジョージ・ワトソンも序文に対するコールリッジの強い関心に触れて次の様に述べている。

Coleridge's *Biographia Literaria* （1817）, hastily written in the summer of 1815、 is a summary attempt to marshal objections against the preface that had been growing up in his mind over the past fifteen years, and to provide criticism with a systematic basis of its own. (4)

ワーズワスの序文が提出した問題によって、コールリッジは詩の創造的精神の構成と活動について独自の考察を進めていたのである。『文学的自叙伝』におけるワーズワス批評は、コールリッジの14年間にも及ぶ思索の所産であった。1800年に序文が出されてからわずか2年後の1802年7月29日附のロバート・サウジー宛の書簡で、コールリッジはワーズワスの序文が半ば彼自身の頭

脳から生じたものであるにもかかわらず、詩論に関する根本的な点で両者に大きな見解の相違が見られると述べているのである。コールリッジは『文学的自叙伝』第4章の中で、ワーズワスの序文が不必要な誤解を生み出した結果、『抒情民謡集』が反対攻撃の的になったと述べ、第17章において論議の曖昧な点や論理の矛盾を指摘し、不十分な説明を訂正しているのである。コールリッジは詩作における最も普遍的な諸原則を導き出すために、ワーズワスの詩論を分析し、提起された諸問題に対して哲学的な考察を加えたのであった。コールリッジの論調はワーズワスよりも論理的で分析的なものである。コールリッジは田舎の農夫の言葉が他のいかなる言葉とも異なるものではなく、ワーズワスの主張する無技巧と素朴さの長所は、実際には最もすぐれた詩句の中には決して見られないものだと断言している。ワーズワスは当時の時流文学の動向を批判し、前時代の古典的な詩の作法から脱却するために、当時としては大胆な詩論をとなえたが、実践において必ずしも理論通りでなく、18世紀的な婉曲的表現や難解な言葉を使用していることも多いのである。コールリッジはこの点を指摘して、ワーズワスの詩論の行きすぎを批判し、序文で述べられた詩の様式をあらゆる種類の詩にひろげようと主張している様に思われる箇所に反対を唱えたのであった。コールリッジは詩の創作が自発的な感情の力強い流出によってなされるのではなく、熟考と内省を伴った技術であるという立場を取り、"The best part of human language, properly so called, is derived from reflection on the acts of the mind itself."[5] という見解を強調している。また、コールリッジはワーズワスが意図した詩の素材が、韻文で書かれるのに十分な正当性を持ち得るかどうかについても、つつましい田舎の生活がそのまま真に詩的衝動を与え得る偉大さを持つものか、それとも非現実的な空論にすぎないものか、実際の詩作品と詩論との矛盾を指摘しながら詳細な検討を加えている。田舎の農夫の日常生活から言葉の最良の部分が形成されるというワーズワスの主張に対しては、教養と知性による内部的活動によって導びかれる内在的法則、すなわち想像の過程にこそ人間性の共通の威厳が示されるのだと反論している。事実、『サイモン・リー』や『グーディ・ブレイク』の様なワーズワスの作品のいくつかには、詩論の行きすぎによって生じたと思える退屈な表現や無駄な饒舌が用いられ、構成自体も単なるエピソードに終始しているものがある。グレアム・ハウもワーズワスの序文における明白な意識的挑戦に付随する議論の弱点を指摘して次の様に述べている。

　　It is completely without the conscious literary artifice that we associate with pastoral poetry, and free from the trick of using rural simplicties to light up some sophisticated situation.[6]

牧歌的光景を意識的な文学的手段として、田園的な単純さを詩の構成要素とした時、本来あるべき無意識的な存在様式は虚構に陥りがちになるのである。最も単純で本源的な人間の絆や情愛、道徳的義務を自然との位相の中で表現してみせた『マイケル』や『兄弟たち』の様なワーズワスの田園詩の最良のものには、この様な問題は発生しないのである。これらの作品では、意識的な主体たる詩人が、田園の無意識的生活に対して、素朴な感情的興奮と想像力の共感を示しており、ワーズワ

ス独特の隠やかな手法によって、簡素で深い感情を伝達し、人間生活に与える自然の偉大な影響力が表現されている。ワーズワスの詩的精神の最良のものは、瞑想や回想が単なる経験の再創造に終るのでなく、神秘的喜悦の瞬間が具体的な直接的体験として精力的な創造へ或長発展したものである。ロマン派詩人の中でも、ワーズワスは賞讃すべき自己信頼と自己抑制から生じる落ち着いた詩風を堅持し続けた人物であった。ワーズワスが他の詩人達よりも、はるかに地に足をつけて自然に対する純粋で真摯な感情を、突然訪れる崇高な啓示の瞬間に昇華させて、作品全体に広がりわたるひとつの落ち着いた親しみ深い普遍的感情として描写した時、作者自身にとっても説明不可能な巨大な不可視的存在が暗示され、日常的な出来事をいたずらに取り扱うことに終始する態度は自ずと放棄されているのである。

　　本来、ワーズワスと同様にコールリッジも抒情詩人であった。両者共に神秘的なビジョンの瞬間を経験として持っていたが、ワーズワスがどれ程神秘的な経験であれ日常的人生の中で捉え、自然物の影響力と結びつけようとしたのに対して、コールリッジは神秘的体験に伴う超越的知覚や異様な無限の感覚を強調して、彼独自の詩的神話世界を構築しようとしたのである。コールリッジは『文学的自叙伝』第14章の中で、『抒情民謡集』における両者の詩風の相違に触れて、自らの努力は詩的信仰を形成する様な超自然詩に向けられ、他方ワーズワスは日常的事物に新奇の美を見出す様な詩を自分の目標としていたと述べている。この様な両者の詩的心象の相違は、情緒的な志向性や知的志向性の相違によるものである。ワーズワスの詩の形象は、それをしのぐ情緒や精神的興奮状態のために用いられており、コールリッジの詩の形象は形而上的心理的経験を現実的なものとするために用いられて、創造的な神話の世界を具象化させる象徴によって詩の統一がはかられている。ワーズワスは自然物によって、霊的真実に対する神秘的直観を表現するのが最善と感じているが、コールリッジは『局面一変』における "Let Nature be your Teacher"（l. 16）というワーズワスの主張を斥けている。『失意の賦』に表現された詩人コールリッジの苦悩は、彼の詩的想像力の特質を示すものに他ならない。

> I may not hope from outward forms to win
> The passion and the life, whose fountains are within.

（Stanza Ⅲ, ll. 45-6）

幼少年期に身につけた受容性を持ち続けていたワーズワスは、ビジョンの瞬間を自然物の影響力による感化作用と考え、自然の霊的恩沢である神秘的経験や高揚した精神が、彼の情緒的均衡を乱すことはなかった。要するに、ワーズワスにとっては、感性的な主観的印象のみが第一義的に存在するのであり、観念的思想は本来第二義的な存在であった。これに対して、知性と感性との相克に苦悩したコールリッジは、神秘的経験とは精神の内奥に根源を持つものだと考えていた。自然物を第一義的に先験的な内的原理の象徴と見なしたコールリッジの態度は、あらゆる知識や感性の基礎的行為として、事物の認識の中心的な位置を占めているのである。

In looking at objects of Nature while I am thinking , as at yonder moon
dim-glimmering through the dewy window pane , I seem rather to be seeking,
as it were asking for , a symbolic language for something within me that
always and for ever exists , than observing anything new . Even when that
latter is the case , yet still I have always an obscure feeling as if that
new phenomenon were the dim awaking of a forgotten or hidden truth of my
inner nature . (7)

コールリッジにとって、内なる自然のみが詩の対象となるのであり、自然物自体は本質的に何ら積
極的な意味を持たぬ死物であったと言える。外的自然は詩人の精神に集約されて内在的存在となる
が、自然物を直接の詩の心象としないコールリッジの詩は、自然物そのものを究極的現実として描
写することがなかった。この事が生来の哲学的探究心と共に、彼の詩作を困難なものにしていたの
である。コールリッジ自身は詩人としての大成を望んでいたが、感性や想像力によって詩作するこ
とと、理性的思弁を積み重ねて理論的な思索に入る形而上学とは本来合入れないものであった。詩
人としてのコールリッジの絶頂は、ワーズワスと最も親しく交際を続けた時期に突然訪れ、その後
急速に詩心を喪失することになる。しかし、詩作において妨げとなった形而上学的思弁は、文芸批
評の面ではコールリッジに確固たる思想的基盤を与えることになったのである。M.H.エイブラム
ズは『鏡とランプ』の中で、コールリッジ生来の思考方式の特質が哲学的思索に深く結びついてい
ることに触れて次の様に言及している。

In criticism as in science , to his way of thinking , empirical investiga-
tion without a prior 'idea' is helpless , and discoveries can only be made
by the prepared spirit . (8)

この様なコールリッジ生来の思考様式が、彼の形而上学の前提となり、独自の哲学体系を模索しな
がら、批評の実践においては、まず根源的な批評原理の確立へと向い、詩の構造と創作過程におけ
る人間精神の機能に関する独自の洞察を記録したのであった。コールリッジにとって、詩も科学と
同様にそれ自身の厳密な論理を持っており、詩の論理はより一層微妙で複雑なものであった。コー
ルリッジの哲学的考察はドイツ観念論と出会うことによって、長年考察を続けて来た事柄やまさに
発表しようとしていた事柄をドイツの思想家達の中に見出し、さらに深まりと確信の度合を増して、
詩と批評に関する新たな思想を模索しつつあった。
　コールリッジがワーズワスの詩によって、詩の本質や詩的想像力を考察していたことは、『文学
的自叙伝』の大半がワーズワス批評で占められていることに明らかである。コールリッジの様な知
的俊敏さに欠けていたワーズワスは、コールリッジの思想によって自らの詩の独自性を自覚し、穏
やかな日常性の中で深い道徳的経験の意味を追究することを自己の使命と考えていたことは、『序
曲』がコールリッジを意識して書かれたものであることに如実に示されているのである。詩人ワーズ

ワスの力強い感情の自発性と思想家コールリッジの精神の有機的内発性は、両者の意識の対象が異っていただけであり、ワーズワスの認識の本質がコールリッジの主義主張と実質的には等質のものであったことを示している。ワーズワスの詩心が常に自然物の具体的外在性による刺激を前提としながら、また直接的体験による原感情の重要性を主張しながら、創作上の根本的源泉を回想する精神の内発的な哲学性においた事は、詩人としての大きな特質となっている。詩は静謐のうちに回想された深くて力強い感情から生れるというワーズワスの主張は、回想する精神の思索が深い哲学性を生み出し、この様な回想的傾向が偉大な思想詩『序曲』の重要な中心的思想に発展したことを考えれば、直接的体験に基づく感情の自発性が、回想する心的態度によって、有機的な感受性を伴った精神の内発性を生み出さねばならないことを示しているのである。ワーズワスは静謐の中で回想の操作によって、直接的体験時の原感情を引き出そうとするが、回想された感情をいくら吟味しても原感情は永遠に失われ、原感情に類似した感情が残るだけである。この様に原体験から永遠の疎外にいることを強烈に意識する時、ワーズワスの詩の哲学性が生まれる。つまり、その時ワーズワスの心に定着する感情とは、回想された感情でも原感情でもない、深い哲学的意識を伴った新たな別の感情である。原感情を基盤としながら、そのためにかえって喪失と消失の感じを抱きつつ、新たな感情の生成の過程に想像力を行使するのがワーズワスの詩の性格である。子供の無垢の状態は、作者の経験や郷愁に色どられて、作者の想像力を仲介として作り出される。この様な幼少年期に垣間見た理想的な、少なくとも現実世界よりも無垢な世界への憧れと喪失感は、人間の本性に深く内在するものである。人間の生活は絶えず複雑さを増して進行していく。その中で、幼少年期の人間の姿に次いで、田園の農夫の生活は人間生活の最も基本的な形式を示している。現実の農夫が田園詩を書くことはしない様に、楽園の喪失感を少しでも意識しない人が郷愁を感じることはない。ワーズワスは純朴な人々の間にあって、ただひとりの複雑な洗練された人物であり、自然への回帰、感情と思考の原始的な形態への回帰を求めながら、新たな単純さを背景として自分の問題を眺めることになり、さらにこの問題を鋭く意識するのである。自然に囲まれた田園生活の単純さを背景に置いて、複雑な人間精神を扱うワーズワスの文学では、幼少年期の無垢の姿や田園に生きる純朴な人々の姿や過去のある時期の自分の姿が、年老いて純朴さを失い、苦難に満ちた現実に押しひしがれていく現在にくらべて、牧歌的黄金時代が象徴する完全な状態の諸相として表現される。ワーズワスの深い感情と哲学的な内発性を伴った想像力によって理想化されると、現実の農夫は質朴な出来事の威厳の中で巨大な姿を帯びる。ワーズワスのすぐれた詩では、この様な農夫の姿が個人的な型としてでなく、普遍化された喜びや悲しみを抱く人類全体の象徴として描写されている。厭わしい現実世界から逃れて、神聖な過去や堕罪以前の楽園における人間の栄光を求める態度は、人類に普遍的な本能であると言える。成人した人間の複雑さから幼少年期の夢への移行は、詩人にとって単なる逃避を意味するものではない。成人した時期の問題を幼年期の無垢や田園生活の素朴さに移すのは、これらの問題を綿密に検討するために、新たな単純さを背景として眺めることができる様な時と場所に移すことを意味するのである。この様な問題を鋭く意識した精神の深い哲学性や内発性が強力な自発的感情を導き出す時、ワーズワスの詩の独創性が発揮される。したがって、回想する行為そのものがワーズワスにとって想像力を意味していたと言える。ワーズワスは回想のうちに

自発的に生じた感情や思想を適切な言葉で表現する詩人の力を想像力と考えていた。詩人が啓示として受けた経験は、通常の経験よりも複雑なものであるが故に、それが想像力によって秩序と統一を伴った簡潔な詩的表現を得た時、読者に深遠な詩的感動を伝達することが可能となるのである。コールリッジは『文学的自叙伝』第4章において、ワーズワスの詩のすぐれた特質から受けた印象を次の様に述べて、その独創性を適確に指摘している。

It was the union of deep feeling with profound thought ; the fine balance of truth in observing, with the imaginative faculty in modifying the objects observed ; and above all the original gift of spreading the tone, the *atmosphere,* and with it the depth and height of the ideal world around forms, incidents, and situations, of which, for the common view, custom had bedimmed all the lustre, had dried up the sparkle and the dew drops. [9]

ワーズワスの詩の回想性が、直接的体験による原感情を精神の哲学的な内発性の下で、新たな統一体に再構成するのを見たコールリッジは、詩中において機能している独創的な才能の存在に気づき、これを想像力の働きと断定したのである。ワーズワスの想像力の受容はコールリッジの思想に負うところが多く、想像力説を哲学的根底から理論づけたのは、少なくとも英国文学史上においてコールリッジが初めてであった。そして、詩的想像力を持った理想的詩人像の特性について、コールリッジは "The poet, described in *ideal* perfection, brings the whole soul of man into activity, with the subordination of its faculties to each other, according to their relative worth and dignity." [10] と説明するのである。ワーズワスの『蛭とる人』（決意と独立）や『ティンターン寺院賦』を単なる回想的描写以上のものにしているのは、この様な独創的な想像力の機能のためであった。ワーズワスの詩の独創的特質がコールリッジの批評的精神に強烈な印象を与えた結果、コールリッジは詩的天才を構成する想像力について独自の考察を深めていったのであった。感情と思想の結合によって、理想的な詩作がなされるのはどの様な機構のためか、詩人の心理状態や詩作の根源とはいかなるものか、この様な問題に対してコールリッジは誰もが納得する論理的な解明と説明を与えたいと望んでいた。感動すると共に、直ちにそれが何であるか理解しようとして、ワーズワスの詩から受けた深い感動を基に詩的天才や詩作の根源的機構を分析解明しようとしたコールリッジの批評主義の精神は、"To admire on principle, is the only way to imitate without loss of originality." [11] という言葉に明確に示されている。普遍的興味を有する真理を日常性という無関心から救い出すこと、古いものと新しいものとの矛盾のない合一、万物すべてを天地創造の時の如く清新な感情で観照すること、童児の様な感情を持ち続けて宇宙の謎をさぐり出すこと、これらがワーズワスの詩の優れた特質としてコールリッジが認めた詩的天才の主宰的特徴であった。ワーズワスの詩中に現われた統一する力としての支配的な特質を、コールリッジは詩的想像力の機能として考えたのである。想像力の機能が見せる包括性、統合性を詩的優秀性の基準とした事は、コールリッジの批評理論の主要な原理であった。従って、コールリッジの理論で

は、想像力による包括的性質が宇宙の創造性と共鳴するのであり、この様な審美意識がワーズワス
の直接的自然の位置を占め、詩的価値基準を内発的な有機的統一性に置くことにもなったのである。
想像力の統合機能は植物の発育作用にもたとえられて、成長する生産的な力と考えられ、内発的な
自己の形態を自律的に生み出し形成する本質的生命を持つものと考えられた。コールリッジの想像
力は第一義的なものと第二義的なものとに分けられ、第一義的な想像力はあらゆる知識と感性の基
礎的行為として、事物の認識において中心的位置を占め、人間にとって最も根本的な創造性を意味
するものである。有限なる人間が神の無限の創造性を繰り返すことであり、認識するものとされる
ものとの完全なる結合を求める有限なる人間の無限なる我有りの自意識の行為として述べられてい
る。第二義的な想像力は具体的な詩的想像力の機能を意味するものである。単なる対象の再生を生
み出すのでなく、詩そのものの存在に新たな統一を生み出すために、詩人の心と観照の対象とを相
互に結びつけようとする力であると述べられている。それは人為的技巧と自発的な自然の言語と熱
情との結合を生み出す。詩人は詩作の実践において、この様な行為の過程を本能的習性によって直
覚的に果たさねばならない。コールリッジの理論では、詩的想像力を持つ理想的詩人は特別の洞察
力を持ち、事物の本質を見抜く予言者となり、深い内発性を伴った詩人の自発的な力は、人間のあ
らゆる能力の中で最も積極的な意味を持つもので、神の似像としての人間の創造力を意味するもの
に他ならなかった。コールリッジの想像力の理論は、詩人の想像力の地位を確立し、「詩人は世界
の未公認の立法者」というシェリーの有名な言明に哲学的背景を与えることにもなり、ロマン派詩
人の観念的な基盤となったのである。

　全体の相において物を見つめるコールリッジは、想像力説の前提となるべき認識論、存在論、言
語論に思索を集中させている。コールリッジの哲学の存在論的探求は、ソクラテスの思想やプラト
ンの人生哲学を原点とするもので、哲学が個人的思想にとどまることなく、人類に精神的指導原理
を与える様な普遍的な学問として、偉大な詩と必然的なかかわりを持つ広義の哲学を求めたことを
示すものである。『老水夫の歌』、『クラブ・カーン』、『クリスタベル』といった偉大な詩作の
短い全盛期の後に、溶解してしまうコールリッジの詩心の姿は、実に不自然なものであるが、『文
学的自叙伝』第5，6，7の各章で述べられたハートレーの哲学への傾倒から、さらにこれを論破
するために、プラトン、プロティノス、スピノザ、ブルーノ、ベーメ、デカルト、シェリング、カ
ント等をきわめて幅広く研究を続けた厖大な知識欲には、ひたすら当時の合理主義的機械論を超克
し、詩的直観の世界を普遍的な論理の下で解明しようとした詩人コールリッジの姿が死滅すること
なく存在しているのである。ワーズワスが提起した詩の言語の問題をコールリッジは形而上的な意
識の燃焼の中でどの様に捉えていたであろうか。コールリッジは『文学的自叙伝』第12章の中で、
プロティノスの『エンネアーデス』の第5巻第5章を引用して、存在の根元としての不可視的な超
感覚的ヌース、すなわち一者を熟視直観する魂としての理性とワーズワスの詩的想像力の本性とし
ての "The vision and the faculty divine"（『逍遥』，I,l.79）とが同質のものである
ことを指摘している。この様な認識に立ちながら、コールリッジは言語の伝達性を精神機能の作用
と発生から説きおこそうとするのである。物から思考への意識の展開における言語の重要性に着目
し、さらに詩における感情と言葉の関係にも考察を加えようとしたコールリッジは、自然の様相す

べてが神の言葉であるとする聖ヨハネの「初めに言葉があった」という発想に神の表象としての言葉という新たな認識を見出していく。自然の中に見られる形象は、神である最高の存在者の知恵の言葉であり、瞬間にのみ生きる人間が自らを把握し得る全能なる神との連帯を意識することは、高度な意識の展開による精神活動をしている人間の知性に具現される神の永遠の言葉によってのみ可能となるのである。この様な人間の知性と言葉の必然的な連繋は、深い内省意識を伴うものである。あらゆる国のどの言語にも、時代を通じて全ての階層の人間に普遍的な言葉とは、神の似像としての人間の共通の意識から生まれるもので、コールリッジはカントから得た理性と悟性の弁別を機として、独自の理性論を構築していくのである。

> Reason is therefore most eminently the Revelation of an immortal soul, and it's best Synonime ——— it is the forma formans, which contains in itself the law of it's own conceptions.[12]

コールリッジにとって、この様な理性の存在こそ不死なる魂の啓示であり、forma formans「形成的形成」の論拠となるべきものであった。コールリッジは万物を創造する神の生産的ロゴスの本質を最高理性と定め、神の似像としての人間の知性の本質を純粋理性と呼び、神の生産的ロゴスと同様に能産的機能を持つものだと考えたのである。そして、この理性が神の生産的ロゴスにならって、人間の知性に発動する時に生じる精神機能をコールリッジは想像力と規定したのであった。コールリッジの第一義的な想像力とは、この様な根源的な人間の精神機能を意味するものであった。第一義的な想像力によって生命を与えられた観念は、激しい自己省察の過程と第二義的な想像力の過程の中で定着する言語としての "a language of spirits (sermo interior)"[13] によって、思想の肉体化へと発展展開することになるのである。不死なる魂としての理性の生成力を見つめながら、神の似像としての人間の言語の伝達性を考えるコールリッジの意識は、少年時代から抱いていた偉大なる無限への畏敬の念とプロティノスの理論やキリスト教との接点を見出したのである。知的存在者たる人間の思考が、楽園喪失による神からの疎外という意識の中で、常に偉大なる無限の絶対者へと志向することを認め、コールリッジは堕落した人間の原罪を贖う機能を神から派生した言葉としての言語観の中から導き出して、"Language is the sacred Fire in the Temple of Humanity."[14] と結論づけたのであった。人間の存在そのものと不可分な知性は、表象としての神の観念を象徴的言語の中で捉えるのであり、しかも、その観念の真実性は言葉そのものよりも、真実性を伝達しようとする内発的な意志の作用の中にあるとコールリッジは主張して、"This becomes intelligible to no man by the ministry of mere words from without."[15] と述べて、単なる概念的な生命力のない言葉の理解と厳しく区別するのである。人間の自由な意識作用の中で、真理の正しい伝達がなされるためには、人間の自意識があらゆるものの接点となり、総ての知識の源泉としての知性との統合体として、人間の高度な存在様式を志向する創造的過程を見せなければならないのである。自然界と人間の相互作用を見つめるべき芸術家の精神機能は、生産的な知性に焦点を持たねばならず、深い内省意識を伴った人間の自意識が、神の

似像としての人間の創造力を発揮するものだと考えたコールリッジは、"Man's mind is the very focus of all the rays of intellect which are scattered throughout the image of nature," [16] と明言するのである。そして、至上の存在たる神の意識の存在を志向し把握しようとする人間の理性が、自意識と知性の相互作用を可能にする。したがって、コールリッジにとって、理性は信仰そのものと不可分であり、理性に対する信頼が彼の詩的信仰を不動のものとしたのであった。この様に、神の存在と人間の存在との交わりや連鎖性の下で、神の意識を表象する象徴としての言葉の伝達性を思索するコールリッジの態度は、創造的で生産的な人間の知性や自意識の活動の過程に注目しながら、言葉に対する独自の哲学的考察を生み出したのであった。

註

論文中、原作品からの引用は Hartley Coleridge(ed.) *Coleridge Poetical Works* (Oxford, 1974) 版, Thomas Hutchinson(ed.) *Wordsworth Poetical Works* (Oxford, 1973) 版、Ernest de Selincourt(ed.) *Wordsworth The Prelude* (Oxford, 1975) 版による。

(1) Edmund D. Jones (ed.) *English Critical Essays Nineteenth Century* (Oxford, 1971), p.3

(2) Ibid.

(3) Jones，前掲書，p.22

(4) George Watson : *The Literary Critics* (Penguin, 1963), p.117

(5) John Shawcross (ed.) *Biographia Literaria* (Oxford, 1907), vol.2, pp.39-40

(6) Graham Hough : *The Romantic Poets* (Hutchinson, 1978), p.57

(7) E.H. Coleridge (ed.) *Anima Poetae* (London, 1895), p.136

(8) M.H. Abrams : *The Mirror and the Lamp* (Oxford, 1976), p.115

(9) Shawcross，前掲書，vol.1，p.59

(10) Ibid, vol.2，p.12

(11) Ibid, vol.1，p.62

(12) E.L. Griggs (ed.) *Collected Letters of Samuel Taylor Coleridge* (Oxford, 1966), vol.2，p.1198

(13) Shawcross，前掲書，vol.1，p.191

(14) Griggs，前掲書，vol.3，p.522

(15) Shawcross，前掲書，vol.1，p.168

(16) Ibid, vol.2，p.258

参考文献

○ Coleridge, E.H. (ed.) *Anima Poetae* (London, 1895)

○ Watson, George : *The Literary Critics* (Penguin, 1963)

○ Shawcross, John (ed.) *Biographia Literaria* (Oxford, 1907)

○ Griggs, E.L. (ed.) *Collected Letters of Samuel Taylor Coleridge* (Oxford, 1966)

○ Hutchinson, Thomas (ed.) *Wordsworth Poetical Works* (Oxford, 1973)

○ Coleridge, Hartley (ed.) *Coleridge Poetical Works* (Oxford, 1974)

○ Selincourt, Ernest de (ed.) *Wordsworth The Prelude* (Oxford, 1975)

○ Jones, Edmund D. (ed.) *English Critical Essays Nineteenth Century* (Oxford, 1971)

○ Abrams, M.H. : *The Mirror and the Lamp* (Oxford, 1976)

○ Hough, Graham : *The Romantic Poets* (Hutchinson, 1978)

PREFACE TO LYRICAL BALLADS

The first volume of these poems has already been submitted to general perusal. It was published as an experiment, which I hoped might be of some use to ascertain how far, by fitting to metrical arrangement a selection of the real language of men in a state of vivid sensation, that sort of pleasure and that quantity of pleasure may be imparted, which a poet may rationally endeavor to impart.   5

I had formed no very inaccurate estimate of the probable effect of those poems: I flattered myself that they who should be pleased with them would read them with more than common pleasure: and, on the other hand, I was well aware that by those who should dislike them they would be read with more than common dislike. The result has differed from my expectation in this only, that a greater num- 10 ber have been pleased than I ventured to hope I should please.

Several of my friends are anxious for the success of these poems, from a belief that, if the views with which they were composed were indeed realized, a class of poetry would be produced, well adapted to interest mankind permanently, and not unimportant in the quality and in the multiplicity of its moral relations: and on 15 this account they have advised me to prefix a systematic defence of the theory upon which the poems were written. But I was unwilling to undertake the task, knowing that on this occasion the reader would look coldly upon my arguments, since I might be suspected of having been principally influenced by the selfish and foolish hope of *reasoning* him into an approbation of these particular poems; and 20 I was still more unwilling to undertake the task, because adequately to display the opinions, and fully to enforce the arguments, would require a space wholly disproportionate to a preface. For to treat the subject with the clearness and coherence of which it is susceptible, it would be necessary to give a full account of the present state of the public taste in this country, and to determine how far this 25 taste is healthy or depraved; which, again, could not be determined, without pointing out in what manner language and the human mind act and re-act on each other, and without retracing the revolutions, not of literature alone, but likewise of society itself. I have therefore altogether declined to enter regularly upon this defence; yet I am sensible that there would be something like impropriety in 30 abruptly obtruding upon the public, without a few words of introduction, poems so materially different from those upon which general approbation is at present bestowed.

It is supposed that by the act of writing in verse an author makes a formal engagement that he will gratify certain known habits of association; that he not only 35 thus apprises the reader that certain classes of ideas and expressions will be found in his book, but that others will be carefully excluded. This exponent or symbol held forth by metrical language must in different eras of literature have excited very different expectations: for example, in the age of Catullus, Terence, and Lucretius, and that of Statius or Claudian; and in our own country, in the age of 40 Shakespeare and Beaumont and Fletcher, and that of Donne and Cowley, or Dryden, or Pope. I will not take upon me to determine the exact import of the promise which, by the act of writing in verse, an author in the present day makes to his reader; but it will undoubtedly appear to many persons that I have not fulfilled the terms of an engagement thus voluntarily contracted. They who have 45

1

been accustomed to the gaudiness and inane phraseology of many modern writers, if they persist in reading this book to its conclusion, will, no doubt, frequently have to struggle with feelings of strangeness and awkwardness: they will look round for poetry, and will be induced to inquire by what species of courtesy these 5 attempts can be permitted to assume that title. I hope, therefore, the reader will not censure me for attempting to state what I have proposed to myself to perform; and also (as far as the limits of a preface will permit) to explain some of the chief reasons which have determined me in the choice of my purpose: that at least he may be spared any unpleasant feeling of disappointment, and that I myself may 10 be protected from one of the most dishonorable accusations which can be brought against an author; namely, that of an indolence which prevents him from endeavoring to ascertain what is his duty, or, when his duty is ascertained, prevents him from performing it.

The principal object, then, proposed in these poems was to choose incidents 15 and situations from common life, and to relate or describe them, throughout, as far as was possible in a selection of language really used by men, and, at the same time, to throw over them a certain coloring of imagination, whereby ordinary things should be presented to the mind in an unusual aspect; and further, and above all, to make these incidents and situations interesting by tracing in them, 20 truly though not ostentatiously, the primary laws of our nature: chiefly, as far as regards the manner in which we associate ideas in a state of excitement. Humble and rustic life was generally chosen, because in that condition the essential passions of the heart find a better soil in which they can attain their maturity, are less under restraint, and speak a plainer and more emphatic language; because 25 in that condition of life our elementary feelings coexist in a state of greater simplicity, and consequently may be more accurately contemplated and more forcibly communicated; because the manners of rural life germinate from those elementary feelings, and, from the necessary character of rural occupations, are more easily comprehended, and are more durable; and, lastly, because in that 30 condition the passions of men are incorporated with the beautiful and permanent forms of nature. The language, too, of these men has been adopted (purified indeed from what appear to be its real defects, from all lasting and rational causes of dislike or disgust) because such men hourly communicate with the best objects from which the best part of language is originally derived; and because, from 35 their rank in society and the sameness and narrow circle of their intercourse, being less under the influence of social vanity, they convey their feelings and notions in simple and unelaborated expressions. Accordingly, such a language, arising out of repeated experience and regular feelings, is a more permanent and a far more philosophical language than that which is frequently substituted for it by 40 poets, who think that they are conferring honor upon themselves and their art, in proportion as they separate themselves from the sympathies of men, and indulge in arbitrary and capricious habits of expression, in order to furnish food for fickle tastes, and fickle appetites, of their own creation.[1]

I cannot, however, be insensible to the present outcry against the triviality and 45 meanness, both of thought and language, which some of my contemporaries have occasionally introduced into their metrical compositions; and I acknowledge that

1. It is worth while here to observe that the affecting parts of Chaucer are almost always expressed in language pure and universally intelligible even to this day.

this defect, where it exists, is more dishonorable to the writer's own character than false refinement or arbitrary innovation, though I should contend at the same time that it is far less pernicious in the sum of its consequences. From such verses the poems in these volumes will be found distinguished at least by one mark of difference, that each of them has a worthy *purpose*. Not that I always began to 5 write with a distinct purpose formally conceived; but habits of meditation have, I trust, so prompted and regulated my feelings, that my descriptions of such objects as strongly excite those feelings will be found to carry along with them a *purpose*. If this opinion be erroneous, I can have little right to the name of a poet. For all good poetry is the spontaneous overflow of powerful feelings: and though 10 this be true, poems to which any value can be attached were never produced on any variety of subjects but by a man who, being possessed of more than usual organic sensibility, had also thought long and deeply. For our continued influxes of feeling are modified and directed by our thoughts, which are indeed the representatives of all our past feelings; and, as by contemplating the relation of these 15 general representatives to each other, we discover what is really important to men, so, by the repetition and continuance of this act, our feelings will be connected with important subjects, till at length, if we be originally possessed of much sensibility, such habits of mind will be produced that, by obeying blindly and mechanically the impulses of those habits, we shall describe objects, and utter 20 sentiments, of such a nature, and in such connection with each other, that the understanding of the reader must necessarily be in some degree enlightened, and his affections strengthened and purified.

It has been said that each of these poems has a purpose. Another circumstance must be mentioned which distinguishes these poems from the popular poetry of 25 the day; it is this, that the feeling therein developed gives importance to the action and situation, and not the action and situation to the feeling.

A sense of false modesty shall not prevent me from asserting that the reader's attention is pointed to this mark of distinction, far less for the sake of these particular poems than from the general importance of the subject. The subject is in- 30 deed important! For the human mind is capable of being excited without the application of gross and violent stimulants: and he must have a very faint perception of its beauty and dignity who does not know this, and who does not further know that one being is elevated above another in proportion as he possesses this capability. It has therefore appeared to me that to endeavor to produce or 35 enlarge this capability is one of the best services in which, at any period, a writer can be engaged; but this service, excellent at all times, is especially so at the present day. For a multitude of causes, unknown to former times, are now acting with a combined force to blunt the discriminating powers of the mind, and, unfitting it for all voluntary exertion, to reduce it to a state of almost savage 40 torpor. The most effective of these causes are the great national events which are daily taking place, and the increasing accumulation of men in cities, where the uniformity of their occupations produces a craving for extraordinary incident, which the rapid communication of intelligence hourly gratifies. To this tendency of life and manners the literature and theatrical exhibitions of the country have 45 conformed themselves. The invaluable works of our elder writers, I had almost said the works of Shakespeare and Milton, are driven into neglect by frantic novels, sickly and stupid German tragedies. and deluges of idle and extravagant stories in verse. When I think upon this degrading thirst after outrageous stimulation, I am almost ashamed to have spoken of the feeble endeavor made in these volumes to counteract it; and, reflecting upon the magnitude of the general evil, I should be oppressed with no dishonorable melancholy, had I not a deep impression of certain inherent and indestructible qualities of the human mind, and likewise of certain powers in the great and permanent objects that act upon it, which are equally inherent and indestructible; and were there not added to this impression a belief that the time is approaching when the evil will be systematically opposed, by men of greater powers, and with far more distinguished success.

Having dwelt thus long on the subjects and aim of these poems, I shall request the reader's permission to apprise him of a few circumstances relating to their *style*, in order, among other reasons, that he may not censure me for not having performed what I never attempted. The reader will find that personifications of abstract ideas rarely occur in these volumes, and are utterly rejected, as an ordinary device to elevate the style, and raise it above prose. My purpose was to imitate, and, as far as possible, to adopt the very language of men; and assuredly such personifications do not make any natural or regular part of that language. They are, indeed, a figure of speech occasionally prompted by passion, and I have made use of them as such; but have endeavored utterly to reject them as a mechanical device of style, or as a family language which writers in meter seem to lay claim to by prescription. I have wished to keep the reader in the company of flesh and blood, persuaded that by so doing I shall interest him. Others who pursue a different track will interest him likewise; I do not interfere with their claim, but wish to prefer a claim of my own. There will also be found in these volumes little of what is usually called poetic diction; as much pains has been taken to avoid it as is ordinarily taken to produce it; this has been done for the reason already alleged, to bring my language near to the language of men; and further, because the pleasure which I have proposed to myself to impart is of a kind very different from that which is supposed by many persons to be the proper object of poetry. Without being culpably particular, I do not know how to give my reader a more exact notion of the style in which it was my wish and intention to write, than by informing him that I have at all times endeavored to look steadily at my subject; consequently there is, I hope, in these poems little falsehood of description, and my ideas are expressed in language fitted to their respective importance. Something must have been gained by this practice, as it is friendly to one property of all good poetry, namely, good sense: but it has necessarily cut me off from a large portion of phrases and figures of speech which from father to son have long been regarded as the common inheritance of poets. I have also thought it expedient to restrict myself still further, having abstained from the use of many expressions, in themselves proper and beautiful, but which have been foolishly repeated by bad poets, till such feelings of disgust are connected with them as it is scarcely possible by any art of association to overpower.

If in a poem there should be found a series of lines, or even a single line, in which the language, though naturally arranged, and according to the strict laws of meter, does not differ from that of prose, there is a numerous class of critics, who, when they stumble upon these prosaisms, as they call them, imagine that they have made a notable discovery, and exult over the poet as over a man ignorant of his own profession. Now these men would establish a canon of criticism which the reader will conclude he must utterly reject, if he wishes to be pleased with these volumes. And it would be a most easy task to prove to him that not only the language of a large portion of every good poem, even of the most elevated character, must necessarily, except with reference to the meter, in no respect differ from that of good prose, but likewise that some of the most interesting parts 5 of the best poems will be found to be strictly the language of prose when prose is well written. The truth of this assertion might be demonstrated by innumerable passages from almost all the poetical writings, even of Milton himself. To illustrate the subject in a general manner, I will here adduce a short composition of Gray, who was at the head of those who, by their reasonings, have attempted to 10 widen the space of separation betwixt prose and metrical composition, and was more than any other man curiously elaborate in the structure of his own poetic diction.

> In vain to me the smiling mornings shine,
> And reddening Phoebus lifts his golden fire: 15
> The birds in vain their amorous descant join,
> Or cheerful fields resume their green attire.
> These ears, alas! for other notes repine;
> *A different object do these eyes require;*
> *My lonely anguish melts no heart but mine;* 20
> *And in my breast the imperfect joys expire;*
> Yet morning smiles the busy race to cheer,
> And new-born pleasure brings to happier men;
> The fields to all their wonted tribute bear;
> To warm their little loves the birds complain. 25
> *I fruitless mourn to him that cannot hear,*
> *And weep the more because I weep in vain.*

It will easily be perceived, that the only part of this sonnet which is of any value is the lines printed in italics; it is equally obvious that, except in the rhyme, and in the use of the single word "fruitless" for fruitlessly, which is so far a defect, 30 the language of these lines does in no respect differ from that of prose.

By the foregoing quotation it has been shown that the language of prose may yet be well adapted to poetry; and it was previously asserted that a large portion of the language of every good poem can in no respect differ from that of good prose. We will go further. It may be safely affirmed that there neither is, nor can 35 be, any *essential* difference between the language of prose and metrical composition. We are fond of tracing the resemblance between poetry and painting, and, accordingly, we call them sisters: but where shall we find bonds of connection sufficiently strict to typify the affinity betwixt metrical and prose composition? They both speak by and to the same organs; the bodies in which both of them 40 are clothed may be said to be of the same substance, their affections are kindred, and almost identical, not necessarily differing even in degree; poetry sheds no tears "such as angels weep," but natural and human tears; she can boast of no celestial ichor that distinguishes her vital juices from those of prose; the same human blood circulates through the veins of them both. 45

If it be affirmed that rhyme and metrical arrangement of themselves constitute

a distinction which overturns what has just been said on the strict affinity of metrical language with that of prose, and paves the way for other artificial distinctions which the mind voluntarily admits, I answer that the language of such poetry as is here recommended is, as far as is possible, a selection of the language
5 really spoken by men; that this selection, wherever it is made with true taste and feeling, will of itself form a distinction far greater than would at first be imagined, and will entirely separate the composition from the vulgarity and meanness of ordinary life; and, if meter be superadded thereto, I believe that a dissimilitude will be produced altogether sufficient for the gratification of a rational mind.
10 What other distinction would we have? Whence is it to come? And where is it to exist? Not, surely, where the poet speaks through the mouths of his characters: it cannot be necessary here, either for elevation of style, or any of its supposed ornaments: for, if the poet's subject be judiciously chosen, it will naturally, and upon fit occasion, lead him to passions the language of which, if selected truly
15 and judiciously, must necessarily be dignified and variegated, and alive with metaphors and figures. I forbear to speak of an incongruity which would shock the intelligent reader, should the poet interweave any foreign splendor of his own with that which the passion naturally suggests: it is sufficient to say that such addition is unnecessary. And surely it is more probable that those passages which
20 with propriety abound with metaphors and figures will have their due effect, if, upon other occasions where the passions are of a milder character, the style also be subdued and temperate.

But as the pleasure which I hope to give by the poems now presented to the reader must depend entirely on just notions upon this subject, and as it is in itself
25 of high importance to our taste and moral feelings, I cannot content myself with these detached remarks. And if, in what I am about to say, it shall appear to some that my labor is unnecessary, and that I am like a man fighting a battle without enemies, such persons may be reminded that, whatever be the language outwardly holden by men, a practical faith in the opinions which I am wishing to establish
30 is almost unknown. If my conclusions are admitted, and carried as far as they must be carried if admitted at all, our judgments concerning the works of the greatest poets both ancient and modern will be far different from what they are at present, both when we praise, and when we censure; and our moral feelings influencing and influenced by these judgments will, I believe, be corrected and
35 purified.

Taking up the subject, then, upon general grounds, let me ask, what is meant by the word Poet? What is a poet? To whom does he address himself? And what language is to be expected from him?—He is a man speaking to men: a man, it is true, endowed with more lively sensibility, more enthusiasm and tenderness,
40 who has a greater knowledge of human nature, and a more comprehensive soul, than are supposed to be common among mankind; a man pleased with his own passions and volitions, and who rejoices more than other men in the spirit of life that is in him; delighting to contemplate similar volitions and passions as manifested in the goings-on of the universe, and habitually impelled to create them
45 where he does not find them. To these qualities he has added a disposition to be affected more than other men by absent things as if they were present; an ability of conjuring up in himself passions which are indeed far from being the same as those produced by real events, yet (especially in those parts of the general sym-

pathy which are pleasing and delightful) do more nearly resemble the passions produced by real events than anything which, from the motions of their own minds merely, other men are accustomed to feel in themselves—whence, and from practice, he has acquired a greater readiness and power in expressing what he thinks and feels, and especially those thoughts and feelings which, by his own 5 choice, or from the structure of his own mind, arise in him without immediate external excitement.

But whatever portion of this faculty we may suppose even the greatest poet to possess, there cannot be a doubt that the language which it will suggest to him must often, in liveliness and truth, fall short of that which is uttered by men 10 in real life under the actual pressure of those passions, certain shadows of which the poet thus produces, or feels to be produced, in himself.

However exalted a notion we would wish to cherish of the character of a poet, it is obvious that while he describes and imitates passions, his employment is in some degree mechanical, compared with the freedom and power of real and sub- 15 stantial action and suffering. So that it will be the wish of the poet to bring his feelings near to those of the persons whose feelings he describes, nay, for short spaces of time, perhaps, to let himself slip into an entire delusion, and even confound and identify his own feelings with theirs; modifying only the language which is thus suggested to him by a consideration that he describes for a par- 20 ticular purpose, that of giving pleasure. Here, then, he will apply the principle of selection which has been already insisted upon. He will depend upon this for removing what would otherwise be painful or disgusting in the passion; he will feel that there is no necessity to trick out or to elevate nature: and, the more industriously he applies this principle, the deeper will be his faith that no words 25 which *his* fancy or imagination can suggest will be to be compared with those which are the emanations of reality and truth.

But it may be said by those who do not object to the general spirit of these remarks, that, as it is impossible for the poet to produce upon all occasions language as exquisitely fitted for the passion as that which the real passion itself 30 suggests, it is proper that he should consider himself as in the situation of a translator, who does not scruple to substitute excellencies of another kind for those which are unattainable by him, and endeavors occasionally to surpass his original, in order to make some amends for the general inferiority to which he feels that he must submit. But this would be to encourage idleness and unmanly 35 despair. Further, it is the language of men who speak of what they do not understand; who talk of poetry as of a matter of amusement and idle pleasure; who will converse with us as gravely about a *taste* for poetry, as they express it, as if it were a thing as indifferent as a taste for rope-dancing, or Frontiniac or Sherry. Aristotle, I have been told, has said that poetry is the most philosophic 40 of all writing: it is so: its object is truth, not individual and local, but general, and operative; not standing upon external testimony, but carried alive into the heart by passion; truth which is its own testimony, which gives competence and confidence to the tribunal to which it appeals, and receives them from the same tribunal. Poetry is the image of man and nature. The obstacles which stand in 45 the way of the fidelity of the biographer and historian, and of their consequent utility, are incalculably greater than those which are to be encountered by the poet who comprehends the dignity of his art. The poet writes under one restric-

tion only, namely, the necessity of giving immediate pleasure to a human being possessed of that information which may be expected from him, not as a lawyer, a physician, a mariner, an astronomer, or a natural philosopher, but as a man. Except this one restriction, there is no object standing between the poet and the
5 image of things; between this, and the biographer and historian, there are a thousand.

Nor let this necessity of producing immediate pleasure be considered as a degradation of the poet's art. It is far otherwise. It is an acknowledgment of the beauty of the universe, an acknowledgment the more sincere, because not formal,
10 but indirect; it is a task light and easy to him who looks at the world in the spirit of love: further, it is a homage paid to the native and naked dignity of man, to the grand elementary principle of pleasure, by which he knows, and feels, and lives, and moves. We have no sympathy but what is propagated by pleasure: I would not be misunderstood; but wherever we sympathize with pain, it will be
15 found that the sympathy is produced and carried on by subtle combinations with pleasure. We have no knowledge, that is, no general principles drawn from the contemplation of particular facts, but what has been built up by pleasure, and exists in us by pleasure alone. The man of science, the chemist and mathematician, whatever difficulties and disgusts they may have had to struggle with, know
20 and feel this. However painful may be the objects with which the anatomist's knowledge is connected, he feels that his knowledge is pleasure; and where he has no pleasure he has no knowledge. What then does the poet? He considers man and the objects that surround him as acting and reacting upon each other, so as to produce an infinite complexity of pain and pleasure; he considers man
25 in his own nature and in his ordinary life as contemplating this with a certain quantity of immediate knowledge, with certain convictions, intuitions, and deductions, which from habit acquire the quality of intuitions; he considers him as looking upon this complex scene of ideas and sensations, and finding everywhere objects that immediately excite in him sympathies which, from the neces-
30 sities of his nature, are accompanied by an overbalance of enjoyment.

To this knowledge which all men carry about with them, and to these sympathies in which, without any other discipline than that of our daily life, we are fitted to take delight, the poet principally directs his attention. He considers man and nature as essentially adapted to each other, and the mind of man as
35 naturally the mirror of the fairest and most interesting properties of nature. And thus the poet, prompted by this feeling of pleasure, which accompanies him through the whole course of his studies, converses with general nature, with affections akin to those which, through labor and length of time, the man of science has raised up in himself, by conversing with those particular parts of
40 nature which are the objects of his studies. The knowledge both of the poet and the man of science is pleasure; but the knowledge of the one cleaves to us as a necessary part of our existence, our natural and unalienable inheritance; the other is a personal and individual acquisition, slow to come to us, and by no habitual and direct sympathy connecting us with our fellow-beings. The man of
45 science seeks truth as a remote and unknown benefactor; he cherishes and loves it in his solitude: the poet, singing a song in which all human beings join with him, rejoices in the presence of truth as our visible friend and hourly companion. Poetry is the breath and finer spirit of all knowledge; it is the impassioned ex-

8

pression which is in the countenance of all science. Emphatically may it be said of the poet, as Shakespeare hath said of man, that "he looks before and after." He is the rock of defence for human nature; an upholder and preserver, carrying everywhere with him relationship and love. In spite of difference of soil and climate, of language and manners, of laws and customs; in spite of things silently 5 gone out of mind, and things violently destroyed; the poet binds together by passion and knowledge the vast empire of human society, as it is spread over the whole earth, and over all time. The objects of the poet's thoughts are everywhere; though the eyes and senses of man are, it is true, his favorite guides, yet he will follow wheresoever he can find an atmosphere of sensation in which to move his 10 wings. Poetry is the first and last of all knowledge—it is as immortal as the heart of man. If the labors of men of science should ever create any material revolution, direct or indirect, in our condition, and in the impressions which we habitually receive, the poet will sleep then no more than at present; he will be ready to follow the steps of the man of science, not only in those general indirect effects, 15 but he will be at his side, carrying sensation into the midst of the objects of the science itself. The remotest discoveries of the chemist, the botanist, or mineralogist, will be as proper objects of the poet's art as any upon which it can be employed, if the time should ever come when these things shall be familiar to us, and the relations under which they are contemplated by the followers of these 20 respective sciences shall be manifestly and palpably material to us as enjoying and suffering beings. If the time should ever come when what is now called science, thus familiarized to men, shall be ready to put on, as it were, a form of flesh and blood, the poet will lend his divine spirit to aid the transfiguration, and will welcome the being thus produced, as a dear and genuine inmate of the 25 household of man.—It is not, then, to be supposed that any one who holds that sublime notion of poetry which I have attempted to convey, will break in upon the sanctity and truth of his pictures by transitory and accidental ornaments, and endeavor to excite admiration of himself by arts the necessity of which must manifestly depend upon the assumed meanness of his subject. 30

What has been thus far said applies to poetry in general, but especially to those parts of composition where the poet speaks through the mouths of his characters; and upon this point it appears to authorize the conclusion that there are few persons of good sense who would not allow that the dramatic parts of composition are defective, in proportion as they deviate from the real language of nature, 35 and are colored by a diction of the poet's own, either peculiar to him as an individual poet or belonging simply to poets in general, to a body of men who, from the circumstance of their compositions being in meter, it is expected will employ a particular language.

It is not, then, in the dramatic parts of composition that we look for this dis- 40 tinction of language; but still it may be proper and necessary where the poet speaks to us in his own person and character. To this I answer by referring the reader to the description before given of a poet. Among the qualities there enumerated as principally conducing to form a poet, is implied nothing differing in kind from other men, but only in degree. The sum of what was said is, that the 45 poet is chiefly distinguished from other men by a greater promptness to think and feel without immediate external excitement, and a greater power in expressing such thoughts and feelings as are produced in him in that manner. But these pas-

sions and thoughts and feelings are the general passions and thoughts and feelings of men. And with what are they connected? Undoubtedly with our moral sentiments and animal sensations, and with the causes which excite these; with the operations of the elements, and the appearances of the visible universe; with
5 storm and sunshine, with the revolutions of the seasons, with cold and heat, with loss of friends and kindred, with injuries and resentments, gratitude and hope, with fear and sorrow. These, and the like, are the sensations and objects which the poet describes, as they are the sensations of other men, and the objects which interest them. The poet thinks and feels in the spirit of human passions. How,
10 then, can his language differ in any material degree from that of all other men who feel vividly and see clearly? It might be *proved* that it is impossible. But supposing that this were not the case, the poet might then be allowed to use a peculiar language when expressing his feelings for his own gratification, or that of men like himself. But poets do not write for poets alone, but for men. Unless,
15 therefore, we are advocates for that admiration which subsists upon ignorance, and that pleasure which arises from hearing what we do not understand, the poet must descend from this supposed height; and, in order to excite rational sympathy, he must express himself as other men express themselves. To this it may be added that while he is only selecting from the real language of men, or,
20 which amounts to the same thing, composing accurately in the spirit of such selection, he is treading upon safe ground, and we know what we are to expect from him. Our feelings are the same with respect to meter; for, as it may be proper to remind the reader, the distinction of meter is regular and uniform, and not, like that which is produced by what is usually called POETIC DICTION, arbi-
25 trary, and subject to infinite caprices upon which no calculation whatever can be made. In the one case, the reader is utterly at the mercy of the poet, respecting what imagery or diction he may choose to connect with the passion; whereas in the other, the meter obeys certain laws, to which the poet and reader both willingly submit because they are certain, and because no interference is made by
30 them with the passion, but such as the concurring testimony of ages has shown to heighten and improve the pleasure which coexists with it.

It will now be proper to answer an obvious question, namely, Why, professing these opinions, have I written in verse? To this, in addition to such answer as is included in what has been already said, I reply, in the first place, Because,
35 however I may have restricted myself, there is still left open to me what confessedly constitutes the most valuable object of all writing, whether in prose or verse—the great and universal passions of men, the most general and interesting of their occupations, and the entire world of nature before me—to supply endless combinations of forms and imagery. Now, supposing for a moment that whatever
40 is interesting in these objects may be as vividly described in prose, why should I be condemned for attempting to superadd to such description the charm which, by the consent of all nations, is acknowledged to exist in metrical language? To this, by such as are yet unconvinced, it may be answered that a very small part of the pleasure given by poetry depends upon the meter, and that it is injudicious
45 to write in meter, unless it be accompanied with the other artificial distinctions of style with which meter is usually accompanied, and that, by such deviation, more will be lost from the shock which will thereby be given to the reader's as-

sociations than will be counterbalanced by any pleasure which he can derive from the general power of numbers. In answer to those who still contend for the necessity of accompanying meter with certain appropriate colors of style in order to the accomplishment of its approriate end, and who also, in my opinion, greatly underrate the power of meter in itself, it might, perhaps, as far as relates 5 to these volumes, have been almost sufficient to observe that poems are extant, written upon more humble subjects, and in a still more naked and simple style, which have continued to give pleasure from generation to generation. Now if nakedness and simplicity be a defect, the fact here mentioned affords a strong presumption that poems somewhat less naked and simple are capable of affording 10 pleasure at the present day; and what I wished *chiefly* to attempt, at present, was to justify myself for having written under the impression of this belief.

But various causes might be pointed out why, when the style is manly, and the subject of some importance, words metrically arranged will long continue to impart such a pleasure to mankind as he who proves the extent of that pleasure 15 will be desirous to impart. The end of poetry is to produce excitement in coexistence with an overbalance of pleasure; but, by the supposition, excitement is an unusual and irregular state of the mind; ideas and feelings do not, in that state, succeed each other in accustomed order. If the words, however, by which this excitement is produced be in themselves powerful, or the images and feelings 20 have an undue proportion of pain connected with them, there is some danger that the excitement may be carried beyond its proper bounds. Now the co-presence of something regular, something to which the mind has been accustomed in various moods and in a less excited state, cannot but have great efficacy in tempering and restraining the passion by an intertexture of ordinary feeling, and 25 of feeling not strictly and necessarily connected with the passion. This is unquestionably true; and hence, though the opinion will at first appear paradoxical, from the tendency of meter to divest language, in a certain degree, of its reality, and thus to throw a sort of half-consciousness of unsubstantial existence over the whole composition, there can be little doubt but that more pathetic situations and 30 sentiments, that is, those which have a greater proportion of pain connected with them, may be endured in metrical composition, especially in rhyme, than in prose. The meter of the old ballads is very artless, yet they contain many passages which would illustrate this opinion; and, I hope, if the following poems be attentively perused, similar instances will be found in them. This opinion may be further 35 illustrated by appealing to the reader's own experience of the reluctance with which he comes to the reperusal of the distressful parts of *Clarissa Harlowe*, or *The Gamester*, while Shakespeare's writings, in the most pathetic scenes, never act upon us, as pathetic, beyond the bounds of pleasure—an effect which, in a much greater degree than might at first be imagined, is to be ascribed to small 40 but continual and regular impulses of pleasurable surprise from the metrical arrangement.—On the other hand (what it must be allowed will much more frequently happen), if the poet's words should be incommensurate with the passion, and inadequate to raise the reader to a height of desirable excitement, then (unless the poet's choice of his meter has been grossly injudicious) in the feelings 45 of pleasure which the reader has been accustomed to connect with meter in general, and in the feeling, whether cheerful or melancholy, which he has been accustomed to connect with that particular movement of meter, there will be found something which will greatly contribute to impart passion to the words, and to effect the complex end which the poet proposes to himself.

If I had undertaken a SYSTEMATIC defence of the theory here maintained, it would have been my duty to develop the various causes upon which the pleasure received from metrical language depends. Among the chief of these causes is to be reckoned a principle which must be well known to those who have made any of the arts the object of accurate reflection; namely, the pleasure which the mind derives from the perception of similitude in dissimilitude. This principle is the great spring of the activity of our minds, and their chief feeder. From this principle the direction of the sexual appetite, and all the passions connected with it, take their origin: it is the life of our ordinary conversation; and upon the accuracy with which similitude in dissimilitude, and dissimilitude in similitude are perceived, depend our taste and our moral feelings. It would not be a useless employment to apply this principle to the consideration of meter, and to show that meter is hence enabled to afford much pleasure, and to point out in what manner that pleasure is produced. But my limits will not permit me to enter upon this subject, and I must content myself with a general summary.

I have said that poetry is the spontaneous overflow of powerful feelings; it takes its origin from emotion recollected in tranquillity: the emotion is contemplated till, by a species of reaction, the tranquillity gradually disappears, and an emotion, kindred to that which was before the subject of contemplation, is gradually produced, and does itself actually exist in the mind. In this mood successful composition generally begins, and in a mood similar to this it is carried on; but the emotion, of whatever kind, and in whatever degree, from various causes, is qualified by various pleasures, so that in describing any passions whatsoever, which are voluntarily described, the mind will, upon the whole, be in a state of enjoyment. If Nature be thus cautious to preserve in a state of enjoyment a being so employed, the poet ought to profit by the lesson held forth to him, and ought especially to take care that, whatever passions he communicates to his reader, those passions, if his reader's mind be sound and vigorous, should always be accompanied with an overbalance of pleasure. Now the music of harmonious metrical language, the sense of difficulty overcome, and the blind association of pleasure which has been previously received from works of rhyme or meter of the same or similar construction, an indistinct perception perpetually renewed of language closely resembling that of real life, and yet, in the circumstance of meter, differing from it so widely—all these imperceptibly make up a complex feeling of delight, which is of the most important use in tempering the painful feeling always found intermingled with powerful descriptions of the deeper passions. This effect is always produced in pathetic and impassioned poetry; while in lighter compositions the ease and gracefulness with which the poet manages his numbers are themselves confessedly a principal source of the gratification of the reader. All that it is *necessary* to say, however, upon this subject, may be effected by affirming, what few persons will deny, that of two descriptions, either of passions, manners, or characters, each of them equally well executed, the one in prose and the other in verse, the verse will be read a hundred times where the prose is read once.

Having thus explained a few of my reasons for writing in verse, and why I have chosen subjects from common life, and endeavored to bring my language near to the real language of men, if I have been too minute in pleading my own cause, I have at the same time been treating a subject of general interest; and for this reason a few words shall be added with reference solely to these particular poems, and to some defects which will probably be found in them. I am sensible that my associations must have sometimes been particular instead of general, and that, consequently, giving to things a false importance, I may have sometimes written upon unworthy subjects; but I am less apprehensive on this account, than that my language may frequently have suffered from those arbitrary connections of feelings and ideas with particular words and phrases, from which no man can altogether protect himself. Hence I have no doubt that, in some instances, feelings, even of the ludicrous, may be given to my readers by expressions which appeared to me tender and pathetic. Such faulty expressions, were I convinced they were faulty at present, and that they must necessarily continue to be so, I would willingly take all reasonable pains to correct. But it is dangerous to make these alterations on the simple authority of a few individuals, or even of certain classes of men; for where the understanding of an author is not convinced, or his feelings altered, this cannot be done without great injury to himself: for his own feelings are his stay and support; and, if he set them aside in one instance, he may be induced to repeat this act till his mind shall lose all confidence in itself, and become utterly debilitated. To this it may be added that the critic ought never to forget that he is himself exposed to the same errors as the poet, and perhaps in a much greater degree: for there can be no presumption in saying of most readers that it is not probable they will be so well acquainted with the various stages of meaning through which words have passed, or with the fickleness or stability of the relations of particular ideas to each other; and, above all, since they are so much less interested in the subject, they may decide lightly and carelessly.

Long as the reader has been detained, I hope he will permit me to caution him against a mode of false criticism which has been applied to poetry, in which the language closely resembles that of life and nature. Such verses have been triumphed over in parodies, of which Dr. Johnson's stanza is a fair specimen:—

> I put my hat upon my head
> And walked into the Strand,
> And there I met another man
> Whose hat was in his hand.

Immediately under these lines let us place one of the most justly admired stanzas of the "Babes in the Woods."

> These pretty babes with hand in hand
> Went wandering up and down;
> But never more they saw the man
> Approaching from the town.

In both these stanzas the words, and the order of the words, in no respect differ from the most unimpassioned conversation. There are words in both, for example,

"the Strand," and "the town," connected with none but the most familiar ideas; yet the one stanza we admit as admirable, and the other as a fair example of the superlatively contemptible. Whence arises this difference? Not from the meter, not from the language, not from the order of the words; but the *matter* expressed
5 in Dr. Johnson's stanza is contemptible. The proper method of treating trivial and simple verses to which Dr. Johnson's stanza would be a fair parallelism, is not to say, This is a bad kind of poetry, or This is not poetry; but, This wants sense; it is neither interesting in itself, nor can *lead* to anything interesting; the images neither originate in that sane state of feeling which arises out of thought,
10 nor can excite thought or feeling in the reader. This is the only sensible manner of dealing with such verses. Why trouble yourself about the species till you have previously decided upon the genus? Why take pains to prove that an ape is not a Newton, when it is self-evident that he is not a man?

One request I must make of my reader, which is, that in judging these poems
15 he would decide by his own feelings genuinely, and not by reflection upon what will probably be the judgment of others. How common is it to hear a person say, I myself do not object to this style of composition, or this or that expression, but to such and such classes of people it will appear mean or ludicrous! This mode of criticism, so destructive of all sound unadulterated judgment, is almost uni-
20 versal: let the reader then abide, independently, by his own feelings, and, if he finds himself affected, let him not suffer such conjectures to interfere with his pleasure.

If an author, by any single composition, has impressed us with respect for his talents, it is useful to consider this as affording a presumption that on other occa-
25 sions, where we have been displeased, he nevertheless may not have written ill or absurdly; and further, to give him so much credit for this one composition as may induce us to review what has displeased us with more care than we should otherwise have bestowed upon it. This is not only an act of justice, but, in our decisions upon poetry especially, may conduce in a high degree to the improve-
30 ment of our own taste; for an *accurate* taste in poetry, and in all the other arts, as Sir Joshua Reynolds has observed, is an *acquired* talent, which can only be produced by thought and a long-continued intercourse with the best models of composition. This is mentioned, not with so ridiculous a purpose as to prevent the most inexperienced reader from judging for himself (I have already said that
35 I wish him to judge for himself), but merely to temper the rashness of decision, and to suggest that, if poetry be a subject on which much time has not been bestowed, the judgment may be erroneous; and that, in many cases, it necessarily will be so.

Nothing would, I know, have so effectually contributed to further the end which
40 I have in view, as to have shown of what kind the pleasure is, and how that pleasure is produced, which is confessedly produced by metrical composition essentially different from that which I have here endeavored to recommend: for the reader will say that he has been pleased by such composition; and what more can be done for him? The power of any art is limited; and he will suspect that,
45 if it be proposed to furnish him with new friends, that can be only upon condition of his abandoning his old friends. Besides, as I have said, the reader is himself conscious of the pleasure which he has received from such composition, composition to which he has peculiarly attached the endearing name of poetry;

14

and all men feel an habitual gratitude, and something of an honorable bigotry, for the objects which have long continued to please them: we not only wish to be pleased, but to be pleased in that particular way in which we have been accustomed to be pleased. There is in these feelings enough to resist a host of arguments; and I should be the less able to combat them successfully, as I am willing to allow that, in order entirely to enjoy the poetry which I am recommending, it would be necessary to give up much of what is ordinarily enjoyed. But, would my limits have permitted me to point out how this pleasure is produced, many obstacles might have been removed, and the reader assisted in perceiving that the powers of language are not so limited as he may suppose; and that it is possible for poetry to give other enjoyments, of a purer, more lasting, and more exquisite nature. This part of the subject has not been altogether neglected, but it has not been so much my present aim to prove that the interest excited by some other kinds of poetry is less vivid, and less worthy of the nobler powers of the mind, as to offer reasons for presuming that, if my purpose were fulfilled, a species of poetry would be produced which is genuine poetry, in its nature well adapted to interest mankind permanently, and likewise important in the multiplicity and quality of its moral relations.

From what has been said, and from a perusal of the poems, the reader will be able clearly to perceive the object which I had in view: he will determine how far it has been attained; and, what is a much more important question, whether it be worth attaining: and upon the decision of these two questions will rest my claim to the approbation of the public.

1800

THE THORN

I

There is a thorn—it looks so old,
In truth you'd find it hard to say
How it could ever have been young,
It looks so old and grey.
5   Not higher than a two years' child
It stands erect, this aged thorn;
No leaves it has, no thorny points;
It is a mass of knotted joints,
A wretched thing forlorn.
10   It stands erect, and like a stone
With lichens it is overgrown.

II

Like rock or stone, it is o'ergrown
With lichens to the very top,
And hung with heavy tufts of moss,
15   A melancholy crop:
Up from the earth these mosses creep,
And this poor thorn they clasp it round
So close, you'd say that they were bent
With plain and manifest intent
20   To drag it to the ground:
And all had joined in one endeavour
To bury this poor thorn for ever.

III

High on a mountain's highest ridge,
Where oft the stormy winter gale
25   Cuts like a scythe, while through the clouds
It sweeps from vale to vale;
Not five yards from the mountain path,
This thorn you on your left espy;
And to the left, three yards beyond,
30   You see a little muddy pond
Of water never dry;
I've measured it from side to side:
'Tis three feet long, and two feet wide.

IV

And close beside this aged thorn
35   There is a fresh and lovely sight,
A beauteous heap, a hill of moss,
Just half a foot in height.
All lovely colours there you see,
All colours that were ever seen;
40   And mossy net-work too is there,
As if by hand of lady fair
The work had woven been;
And cups, the darlings of the eye,
So deep is their vermilion dye.

V

Ah me! what lovely tints are there!   45
Of olive green and scarlet bright,
In spikes, in branches, and in stars,
Green, red, and pearly white.
This heap of earth o'ergrown with moss,
Which close beside the thorn you see,   50
So fresh in all its beauteous dyes,
Is like an infant's grave in size,
As like as like can be:
But never, never anywhere
An infant's grave was half so fair.   55

VI

Now would you see this aged thorn,
This pond, and beauteous hill of moss,
You must take care and choose your time
The mountain when to cross.
For oft there sits, between the heap   60
That's like an infant's grave in size,
And that same pond of which I spoke,
A woman in a scarlet cloak,
And to herself she cries,
'Oh misery! oh misery!   65
Oh woe is me! oh misery!'

VII

At all times of the day and night
This wretched woman thither goes;
And she is known to every star,
And every wind that blows;   70
And there beside the thorn she sits
When the blue daylight's in the skies,
And when the whirlwind's on the hill,
Or frosty air is keen and still,
And to herself she cries,   75
'Oh misery! oh misery!
Oh woe is me! oh misery!'

VIII

'Now wherefore thus, by day and night,
In rain, in tempest and in snow,
Thus to the dreary mountain-top   80
Does this poor woman go?
And why sits she beside the thorn
When the blue daylight's in the sky,
Or when the whirlwind's on the hill,
Or frosty air is keen and still,   85
And wherefore does she cry?
Oh wherefore? wherefore? tell me why
Does she repeat that doleful cry?'

IX

I cannot tell; I wish I could;
For the true reason no one knows: 90
But if you'd gladly view the spot,

The spot to which she goes;
The heap that's like an infant's grave,
The pond—and thorn, so old and grey;
Pass by her door—'tis seldom shut—
And, if you see her in her hut,
Then to the spot away!
I never heard of such as dare
Approach the spot when she is there.

X

'But wherefore to the mountain-top
Can this unhappy woman go,
Whatever star is in the skies,
Whatever wind may blow?'
Nay, rack your brain—'tis all in vain,
I'll tell you everything I know;
But to the thorn, and to the pond
Which is a little step beyond,
I wish that you would go:
Perhaps, when you are at the place,
You something of her tale may trace.

XI

I'll give you the best help I can:
Before you up the mountain go,
Up to the dreary mountain-top,
I'll tell you all I know.
'Tis now some two-and-twenty years
Since she (her name is Martha Ray)
Gave with a maiden's true good will
Her company to Stephen Hill;
And she was blithe and gay,
And she was happy, happy still
Whene'er she thought of Stephen Hill.

XII

And they had fixed the wedding-day,
The morning that must wed them both;
But Stephen to another maid
Had sworn another oath;
And with this other maid to church
Unthinking Stephen went—
Poor Martha! on that woeful day
A cruel, cruel fire, they say,
Into her bones was sent:
It dried her body like a cinder,
And almost turned her brain to tinder.

XIII

They say, full six months after this,
While yet the summer leaves were green,
She to the mountain-top would go,
And there was often seen.
'Tis said, a child was in her womb,
As now to any eye was plain;
She was with child, and she was mad;

Yet often she was sober sad   140
From her exceeding pain.
Oh me! ten thousand times I'd rather
That he had died, that cruel father!
                    XIV
Sad case for such a brain to hold
Communion with a stirring child!   145
Sad case, as you may think, for one
Who had a brain so wild!
Last Christmas when we talked of this,
Old farmer Simpson did maintain
That in her womb the infant wrought   150
About its mother's heart, and brought
Her senses back again:
And when at last her time drew near,
Her looks were calm, her senses clear.
                    XV
No more I know, I wish I did,   155
And I would tell it all to you;
For what became of this poor child
There's none that ever knew:
And if a child was born or no,
There's no one that could ever tell;   160
And if 'twas born alive or dead,
There's no one knows, as I have said;
But some remember well
That Martha Ray about this time
Would up the mountain often climb.   165
                    XVI
And all that winter, when at night
The wind blew from the mountain-peak,
'Twas worth your while, though in the dark,
The churchyard path to seek:
For many a time and oft were heard   170
Cries coming from the mountain-head:
Some plainly living voices were;
And others, I've heard many swear,
Were voices of the dead:
I cannot think, whate'er they say,   175
They had to do with Martha Ray.
                    XVII
But that she goes to this old thorn,
The thorn which I've described to you,
And there sits in a scarlet cloak,
I will be sworn is true.   180
For one day with my telescope,
To view the ocean wide and bright,
When to this country first I came,
Ere I had heard of Martha's name,
I climbed the mountain's height: 185
A storm came on, and I could see
No object higher than my knee.

'Twas mist and rain, and storm and rain,
No screen, no fence could I discover,
190 And then the wind! in faith, it was
A wind full ten times over.
I looked around, I thought I saw
A jutting crag, and off I ran,
Head-foremost, through the driving rain,
195 The shelter of the crag to gain,
And, as I am a man,
Instead of jutting crag, I found
A woman seated on the ground.

XIX

I did not speak—I saw her face,
200 In truth it was enough for me;
I turned about and heard her cry,
'Oh misery! Oh misery!'
And there she sits, until the moon
Through half the clear blue sky will go;
205 And when the little breezes make
The waters of the pond to shake,
As all the country know,
She shudders, and you hear her cry,
'Oh misery! Oh misery!'

XX

210 'But what's the thorn? and what's the pond?
And what's the hill of moss to her?
And what's the creeping breeze that comes
The little pond to stir?'
I cannot tell; but some will say
215 She hanged her baby on the tree;
Some say she drowned it in the pond
Which is a little step beyond:
But all and each agree
The little babe was buried there,
220 Beneath that hill of moss so fair.

XXI

I've heard, the moss is spotted red
With drops of that poor infant's blood:
But kill a new-born infant thus,
I do not think she could.
225 Some say, if to the pond you go,
And fix on it a steady view,
The shadow of a babe you trace,
A baby and a baby's face,
And that it looks at you;
230 Whene'er you look on it, 'tis plain
The baby looks at you again.

XXII

And some had sworn an oath that she
Should be to public justice brought;
And for the little infant's bones

With spades they would have sought.   235
But then the beauteous hill of moss
Before their eyes began to stir;
And for full fifty yards around
The grass it shook upon the ground;
But all do still aver   240
The little babe is buried there,
Beneath that hill of moss so fair.

XXIII

I cannot tell how this may be:
But plain it is, the thorn is bound
With heavy tufts of moss, that strive   245
To drag it to the ground;
And this I know, full many a time,
When she was on the mountain high,
By day, and in the silent night,
When all the stars shone clear and bright,   250
That I have heard her cry,
'Oh misery! Oh misery!
Oh woe is me! Oh misery!'

WE ARE SEVEN

A simple child, dear brother Jim,
That lightly draws its breath,
And feels its life in every limb,
What should it know of death?

I met a little cottage girl: 5
She was eight years old, she said;
Her hair was thick with many a curl
That clustered round her head.

She had a rustic, woodland air,
And she was wildly clad;   10
Her eyes were fair, and very fair;
Her beauty made me glad.

'Sisters and brothers, little maid,
How many may you be?'
'How many? Seven in all,' she said,   15
And wondering looked at me.

'And where are they? I pray you tell.'
She answered, 'Seven are we;
And two of us at Conway dwell,
And two are gone to sea.   20

'Two of us in the churchyard lie,

My sister and my brother;
And in the churchyard cottage I
Dwell near them with my mother.'

25 'You say that two at Conway dwell,
And two are gone to sea,
Yet you are seven; I pray you tell,
Sweet maid, how this may be?'
Then did the little maid reply,
30 'Seven boys and girls are we;
Two of us in the churchyard lie,
Beneath the churchyard tree.'

'You run about, my little maid,
Your limbs they are alive;
35 If two are in the churchyard laid,
Then ye are only five.'

'Their graves are green, they may be seen,'
The little maid replied,
'Twelve steps or more from mother's door,
40 And they are side by side.

'My stockings there I often knit,
My kerchief there I hem;
And there upon the ground I sit—
I sit and sing to them.

45 'And often after sunset, sir,
When it is light and fair,
I take my little porringer,
And eat my supper there.

'The first that died was little Jane;
50 In bed she moaning lay,
Till God released her of her pain;
And then she went away.

'So in the churchyard she was laid;
And all the summer dry
55 Together round her grave we played,
My brother John and I.

'And when the ground was white with snow,
And I could run and slide,
My brother John was forced to go,
60 And he lies by her side.'

'How many are you then,' said I,
'If they two are in Heaven?'
The little maiden did reply,

'O master! we are seven.'

'But they are dead: those two are dead!   65
Their spirits are in Heaven!'
'Twas throwing words away; for still
The little maid would have her will,
And said, 'Nay, we are seven!'

HART–LEAP WELL

*Hart-Leap Well is a small spring of water about five miles
from Richmond in Yorkshire, and near the side of the road
which leads from Richmond to Askrigg. Its name is derived
from a remarkable chase, the memory of which is preserved
by the monuments spoken of in the second part of the following
poem, which monuments do now exist as I have there
described them.*

The knight had ridden down from Wensley moor
With the slow motion of a summer's cloud;
He turned aside towards a vassal's door,
And 'Bring another horse!' he cried aloud.

'Another horse!'—That shout the vassal heard,   5
And saddled his best steed, a comely grey;
Sir Walter mounted him; he was the third
Which he had mounted on that glorious day.

Joy sparkled in the prancing courser's eyes;
The horse and horseman are a happy pair;   10
But, though Sir Walter like a falcon flies,
There is a doleful silence in the air.

A rout this morning left Sir Walter's hall,
That as they galloped made the echoes roar;
But horse and man are vanished, one and all;   15
Such race, I think, was never seen before.

Sir Walter, restless as a veering wind,
Calls to the few tired dogs that yet remain;
Brach, Swift, and Music, noblest of their kind,
Follow, and up the weary mountain strain.   20

The knight hallooed, he chid and cheered them on
With suppliant gestures and upbraidings stern;
But breath and eyesight fail; and one by one
The dogs are stretched among the mountain fern.

25

Where is the throng, the tumult of the race?
The bugles that so joyfully were blown?
This chase it looks not like an earthly chase;
Sir Walter and the hart are left alone.

30

The poor hart toils along the mountain side;
I will not stop to tell how far he fled,
Nor will I mention by what death he died;
But now the knight beholds him lying dead.

35

Dismounting then, he leaned against a thorn;
He had no follower, dog, nor man, nor boy:
He neither smacked his whip, nor blew his horn,
But gazed upon the spoil with silent joy.

40

Close to the thorn on which Sir Walter leaned,
Stood his dumb partner in this glorious act;
Weak as a lamb the hour that it is yeaned,
And foaming like a mountain cataract.

Upon his side the hart was lying stretched:
His nose half-touched a spring beneath a hill,
And with the last deep groan his breath had
  fetched
The waters of the spring were trembling still.

45

And now, too happy for repose or rest
(Was never man in such a joyful case!),
Sir Walter walked all round, north, south, and
    west,
And gazed and gazed upon that darling place.

50

And climbing up the hill (it was at least
Nine roods of sheer ascent) Sir Walter found
Three several hoof-marks which the hunted
    beast
Had left imprinted on the verdant ground.

55

Sir Walter wiped his face and cried, 'Till now
Such sight was never seen by living eyes:
Three leaps have borne him from this lofty
    brow,
Down to the very fountain where he lies.

60

'I'll build a pleasure-house upon this spot,
And a small arbour, made for rural joy;
'Twill be the traveller's shed, the pilgrim's cot,
A place of love for damsels that are coy.

'A cunning artist will I have to frame
A basin for that fountain in the dell;
And they who do make mention of the same
From this day forth, shall call it HART-LEAP WELL.

'And, gallant brute! to make thy praises known,   65
Another monument shall here be raised:
Three several pillars, each a rough-hewn stone,
And planted where thy hoofs the turf have
    grazed.

'And in the summer-time when days are long,
I will come hither with my paramour;   70
And with the dancers, and the minstrel's song,
We will make merry in that pleasant bower.

'Till the foundations of the mountains fail
My mansion with its arbour shall endure:
The joy of them who till the fields of Swale,   75
And them who dwell among the woods of Ure!'

Then home he went, and left the hart, stone-
    dead,
With breathless nostrils stretched above the
    spring.
And soon the knight performed what he had said,
The fame whereof through many a land did ring.   80

Ere thrice the moon into her port had steered,
A cup of stone received the living well;
Three pillars of rude stone Sir Walter reared,
And built a house of pleasure in the dell.

And near the fountain, flowers of stature tall   85
With trailing plants and trees were intertwined,
Which soon composed a little sylvan hall,
A leafy shelter from the sun and wind.

And thither, when the summer-days were long,
Sir Walter journeyed with his paramour;   90
And with the dancers and the minstrel's song
Made merriment within that pleasant bower.

The knight, Sir Walter, died in course of time,
And his bones lie in his paternal vale.—
But there is matter for a second rhyme,   95
And I to this would add another tale.

PART SECOND

The moving accident is not my trade:
To freeze the blood I have no ready arts:
'Tis my delight, alone in summer shade,
To pipe a simple song to thinking hearts.   100

As I from Hawes to Richmond did repair,
It chanced that I saw standing in a dell
Three aspens at three corners of a square,
And one, not four yards distant, near a well.

What this imported I could ill divine:
And, pulling now the rein my horse to stop,
I saw three pillars standing in a line,
The last stone pillar on a dark hill-top.

The trees were grey, with neither arms nor head;
Half-wasted the square mound of tawny green;
So that you just might say, as then I said,
'Here in old time the hand of man has been.'

I looked upon the hills both far and near,
More doleful place did never eye survey;
It seemed as if the spring-time came not here,
And Nature here were willing to decay.

I stood in various thoughts and fancies lost,
When one, who was in shepherd's garb attired,
Came up the hollow. Him did I accost,
And what this place might be I then enquired.

The shepherd stopped, and that same story told
Which in my former rhyme I have rehearsed.
'A jolly place,' said he, 'in times of old!
But something ails it now; the spot is cursed.

'You see these lifeless stumps of aspen wood—
Some say that they are beeches, others elms—
These were the bower; and here a mansion stood;
The finest palace of a hundred realms!

'The arbour does its own condition tell;
You see the stones, the fountain, and the
        stream,
But as to the great lodge! you might as well
Hunt half a day for a forgotten dream.

'There's neither dog nor heifer, horse nor sheep
Will wet his lips within that cup of stone;
And oftentimes, when all are fast asleep,
This water doth send forth a dolorous groan.

'Some say that here a murder has been done,
And blood cries out for blood; but for my part,
I've guessed, when I've been sitting in the sun,
That it was all for that unhappy hart.

'What thoughts must through the creature's brain
        have passed!
From the stone upon the summit of the steep
Are but three bounds—and look, sir, at this last—
O master! it has been a cruel leap.

'For thirteen hours he ran a desperate race;   145
And in my simple mind we cannot tell
What cause the hart might have to love this place,
And come and make his death-bed near the well.

'Here on the grass perhaps asleep he sank,
Lulled by this fountain in the summer-tide;   150
This water was perhaps the first he drank
When he had wandered from his mother's side.

'In April here beneath the scented thorn
He heard the birds their morning carols sing;
And he, perhaps, for aught we know was born   155
Not half a furlong from that self-same spring.

'But now here's neither grass nor pleasant shade;
The sun on drearier hollow never shone:
So will it be, as I have often said,
Till trees, and stones, and fountain all are gone.'   160

'Grey-headed shepherd, thou hast spoken well;
Small difference lies between thy creed and mine:
This beast not unobserved by Nature fell;
His death was mourned by sympathy divine.

'The Being that is in the clouds and air,   165
That is in the green leaves among the groves,
Maintains a deep and reverential care
For them the quiet creatures whom he loves.

'The pleasure-house is dust; behind, before,
This is no common waste, no common gloom;   170
But Nature, in due course of time, once more
Shall here put on her beauty and her bloom.

'She leaves these objects to a slow decay,
That what we are, and have been, may be
        known;
But at the coming of the milder day,   175
These monuments shall all be overgrown.

'One lesson, shepherd, let us two divide,
Taught both by what she shows, and what
        conceals,
Never to blend our pleasure or our pride
With sorrow of the meanest thing that feels.'   180

'THERE WAS A BOY'

There was a boy, ye knew him well, ye cliffs
And islands of Winander! Many a time,
At evening, when the stars had just begun
To move along the edges of the hills,
Rising or setting, would he stand alone,
Beneath the trees, or by the glimmering lake;
And there, with fingers interwoven, both hands
Pressed closely palm to palm and to his mouth
Uplifted, he, as through an instrument,
Blew mimic hootings to the silent owls
That they might answer him. And they would shout
Across the watery vale, and shout again
Responsive to his call, with quivering peals,
And long halloos, and screams, and echoes loud
Redoubled and redoubled; concourse wild
Of mirth and jocund din! And, when it chanced
That pauses of deep silence mocked his skill,
Then, sometimes, in that silence, while he hung
Listening, a gentle shock of mild surprise
Has carried far into his heart the voice
Of mountain torrents; or the visible scene
Would enter unawares into his mind
With all its solemn imagery, its rocks,
Its woods, and that uncertain heaven, received
Into the bosom of the steady lake.

This boy was taken from his mates, and died
In childhood, ere he was full ten years old.
Fair are the woods, and beauteous is the spot,
The vale where he was born; the churchyard hangs
Upon a slope above the village school,
And there, along that bank, when I have passed
At evening, I believe that oftentimes
A full half-hour together I have stood
Mute—looking at the grave in which he lies.

THE BROTHERS

A PASTORAL POEM

'These tourists, Heaven preserve us! needs must live
A profitable life: some glance along,
Rapid and gay, as if the earth were air
And they were butterflies, to wheel about
Long as their summer lasted; some, as wise,
Upon the forehead of a jutting crag
Sit perched, with book and pencil on their knee,
And look and scribble, and scribble on and look,

Until a man might travel twelve stout miles,
Or reap an acre of his neighbour's corn.   10
But, for that moping son of idleness,
Why can he tarry *yonder*?—In our churchyard
Is neither epitaph nor monument,
Tombstone nor name—only the turf we tread,
And a few natural graves.' To Jane, his wife,   15
Thus spake the homely priest of Ennerdale.
It was a July evening; and he sat
Upon the long stone-seat beneath the eaves
Of his old cottage, as it chanced, that day
Employed in winter's work. Upon the stone   20
His wife sat near him, teasing matted wool,
While from the twin cards toothed with glittering wire
He fed the spindle of his youngest child,
Who turned her large round wheel in the open air
With back and forward steps. Towards the field   25
In which the parish chapel stood alone,
Girt round with a bare ring of mossy wall,
While half an hour went by, the priest had sent
Many a long look of wonder, and at last,
Risen from his seat, beside the snow-white ridge   30
Of carded wool which the old man had piled
He laid his implements with gentle care,
Each in the other locked; and down the path
Which from his cottage to the churchyard led
He took his way, impatient to accost   35
The stranger, whom he saw still lingering there.

'Twas one well-known to him in former days,
A shepherd lad; who ere his thirteenth year
Had changed his calling, with the mariners
A fellow-mariner, and so had fared   40
Through twenty seasons; but he had been reared
Among the mountains, and he in his heart
Was half a shepherd on the stormy seas.
Oft in the piping shrouds had Leonard heard
The tones of waterfalls, and inland sounds   45
Of caves and trees; and when the regular wind
Between the tropics filled the steady sail,
And blew with the same breath through days and
        weeks,
Lengthening invisibly its weary line
Along the cloudless main, he in those hours   50
Of tiresome indolence would often hang
Over the vessel's side, and gaze and gaze,
And while the broad green wave and sparkling foam
Flashed round him images and hues that wrought
In union with the employment of his heart,   55
He, thus by feverish passion overcome,
Even with the organs of his bodily eye
Below him in the bosom of the deep

Saw mountains, saw the forms of sheep that grazed
60 On verdant hills, with dwellings among trees,
And shepherds clad in the same country grey
Which he himself had worn.

                                        And now at length
From perils manifold, with some small wealth
Acquired by traffic in the Indian isles,
65 To his paternal home he is returned,
With a determined purpose to resume
The life which he lived there; both for the sake
Of many darling pleasures, and the love
Which to an only brother he has borne
70 In all his hardships, since that happy time
When, whether it blew foul or fair, they two
Were brother shepherds on their native hills.
—They were the last of all their race: and now
When Leonard had approached his home, his heart
75 Failed in him; and, not venturing to enquire
Tidings of one whom he so dearly loved,
Towards the churchyard he had turned aside,
That as he knew in what particular spot
His family were laid, he thence might learn
80 If still his brother lived, or to the file
Another grave was added.—He had found
Another grave, near which a full half-hour
He had remained; but as he gazed, there grew
Such a confusion in his memory
85 That he began to doubt, and he had hopes
That he had seen this heap of turf before;
That it was not another grave, but one
He had forgotten. He had lost his path,
As up the vale he came that afternoon,
90 Through fields which once had been well known
          to him.
And oh! what joy the recollection now
Sent to his heart! He lifted up his eyes,
And looking round, he thought that he perceived
Strange alteration wrought on every side
95 Among the woods and fields, and that the rocks
And the eternal hills themselves were changed.

By this the priest, who down the field had come
Unseen by Leonard, at the churchyard gate
Stopped short, and thence, at leisure, limb by limb
100 He scanned him with a gay complacency.
Ay, thought the vicar, smiling to himself,
'Tis one of those who needs must leave the path
Of the world's business to go wild alone:
His arms have a perpetual holiday;
105 The happy man will creep about the fields
Following his fancies by the hour, to bring

Tears down his cheeks, or solitary smiles
Into his face, until the setting sun
Write *Fool* upon his forehead. Planted thus
Beneath a shed that over-arched the gate   110
Of this rude churchyard, till the stars appeared
The good man might have communed with himself,
But that the stranger, who had left the grave,
Approached; he recognised the priest at once,
And after greetings interchanged, and given   115
By Leonard to the vicar as to one
Unknown to him, this dialogue ensued.

LEONARD
You live, sir, in these dales a quiet life:
Your years make up one peaceful family;
And who would grieve and fret if, welcome come   120
And welcome gone, they are so like each other
They cannot be remembered? Scarce a funeral
Comes to this churchyard once in eighteen months;
And yet, some changes must take place among you:
And you, who dwell here, even among these rocks   125
Can trace the finger of mortality,
And see that with our threescore years and ten
We are not all that perish.—I remember,
For many years ago I passed this road,
There was a foot-way all along the fields   130
By the brook-side—'tis gone; and that dark cleft!
To me it does not seem to wear the face
Which then it had.

PRIEST
      Why, sir, for aught I know,
The chasm is much the same—
LEONARD
        But, surely, yonder—
PRIEST
Ay, there, indeed, your memory is a friend   135
That does not play you false. On that tall pike
(It is the loneliest place of all these hills)
There were two springs which bubbled side by side,
As if they had been made that they might be
Companions for each other; ten years back,   140
Close to those brother fountains, the huge crag
Was rent with lightning: one is dead and gone,
The other, left behind, is flowing still.
For accidents and changes such as these,
Why, we have store of them! a water-spout   145
Will bring down half a mountain; what a feast
For folks that wander up and down like you
To see an acre's breadth of that wide cliff
One roaring cataract! A sharp May storm
Will come with loads of January snow,   150

31

And in one night send twenty score of sheep
To feed the ravens; or a shepherd dies
By some untoward death among the rocks;
The ice breaks up and sweeps away a bridge;
155 A wood is felled—and then, for our own homes!
A child is born or christened, a field ploughed,
A daughter sent to service, a web spun,
The old house-clock is decked with a new face;
And hence, so far from wanting facts or dates
160 To chronicle the time, we all have here
A pair of diaries, one serving, sir,
For the whole dale, and one for each fire-side.
Yours was a stranger's judgment: for historians,
Commend me to these valleys.

LEONARD

                        Yet your churchyard
165 Seems, if such freedom may be used with you,
To say that you are heedless of the past.
An orphan could not find his mother's grave:
Here's neither head- nor foot-stone, plate of brass,
Cross-bones or skull, type of our earthly state
170 Or emblem of our hopes: the dead man's home
Is but a fellow to that pasture-field.

PRIEST

Why, there, sir, is a thought that's new to me.
The stone-cutters, 'tis true, might beg their bread
If every English churchyard were like ours:
175 Yet your conclusion wanders from the truth.
We have no need of names and epitaphs;
We talk about the dead by our fire-sides,
And then, for our immortal part—*we* want
No symbols, sir, to tell us that plain tale:
180 The thought of death sits easy on the man
Who has been born and dies among the mountains.

LEONARD

Your dalesmen, then, do in each other's thoughts
Possess a kind of second life: no doubt
You, sir, could help me to the history
Of half these graves?

PRIEST

                For eight-score winters past,
185 With what I've witnessed, and with what I've heard,
Perhaps I might; and on a winter's evening,
If you were seated at my chimney's nook,
By turning o'er these hillocks one by one
190 We two could travel, sir, through a strange round,
Yet all in the broad highway of the world.
Now there's a grave—your foot is half upon it,
It looks just like the rest; and yet that man
Died broken-hearted.

LEONARD
'Tis a common case.
We'll take another: who is he that lies   195
Beneath yon ridge, the last of those three graves?
It touches on that piece of native rock
Left in the churchyard wall.

PRIEST
That's Walter Ewbank.
He had as white a head and fresh a cheek
As ever were produced by youth and age   200
Engendering in the blood of hale fourscore.
For five long generations had the heart
Of Walter's forefathers o'erflowed the bounds
Of their inheritance, that single cottage—
You see it yonder!—and those few green fields.   205
They toiled and wrought, and still, from sire to son,
Each struggled, and each yielded as before
A little—yet a little—and old Walter,
They left to him the family heart, and land
With other burthens than the crop it bore.   210
Year after year the old man still kept up
A cheerful mind, and buffeted with bond,
Interest and mortgages; at last he sank,
And went into his grave before his time.
Poor Walter! whether it was care that spurred him   215
God only knows, but to the very last
He had the lightest foot in Ennerdale:
His pace was never that of an old man:
I almost see him tripping down the path
With his two grandsons after him—but you,   220
Unless our landlord be your host tonight,
Have far to travel, and in these rough paths
Even in the longest days of midsummer—

LEONARD
But these two orphans!

PRIEST
Orphans! Such they were—
Yet not while Walter lived: for though their parents   225
Lay buried side by side as now they lie,
The old man was a father to the boys,
Two fathers in one father; and if tears,
Shed when he talked of them where they were not,
And hauntings from the infirmity of love,   230
Are aught of what makes up a mother's heart,
This old man in the day of his old age
Was half a mother to them.—If you weep, sir,
To hear a stranger talking about strangers,
Heaven bless you when you are among your kindred!   235
Ay. You may turn that way: it is a grave
Which will bear looking at.

LEONARD
These boys—I hope

They loved this good old man?

                        They did—and truly:
But that was what we almost overlooked,
240   They were such darlings of each other. For
Though from their cradles they had lived with Walter,
The only kinsman near them in the house,
Yet he being old, they had much love to spare,
And it all went into each other's hearts.
245   Leonard, the elder by just eighteen months,
Was two years taller: 'twas a joy to see,
To hear, to meet them! from their house the school
Was distant three short miles; and in the time
Of storm and thaw, when every water-course
250   And unbridged stream, such as you may have
        noticed
Crossing our roads at every hundred steps,
Was swollen into a noisy rivulet,
Would Leonard then, when elder boys perhaps
Remained at home, go staggering through the fords
255   Bearing his brother on his back. I've seen him
On windy days, in one of those stray brooks,
Ay, more than once I've seen him mid-leg deep,
Their two books lying both on a dry stone
Upon the hither side; and once I said,
260   As I remember, looking round these rocks
And hills on which we all of us were born,
That God who made the great book of the world
Would bless such piety—

LEONARD
                It may be then—

PRIEST
Never did worthier lads break English bread!
265   The finest Sunday that the autumn saw,
With all its mealy clusters of ripe nuts,
Could never keep these boys away from church,
Or tempt them to an hour of sabbath breach.
Leonard and James! I warrant, every corner
270   Among these rocks, and every hollow place
Where foot could come, to one or both of them
Was known as well as to the flowers that grow there.
Like roebucks they went bounding o'er the hills;
They played like two young ravens on the crags;
275   Then they could write, ay and speak too, as well
As many of their betters; and for Leonard!
The very night before he went away,
In my own house I put into his hand
A Bible, and I'd wager twenty pounds
280   That if he is alive, he has it yet.

LEONARD
It seems these brothers have not lived to be
A comfort to each other.
PRIEST
That they might
Live to that end, is what both old and young
In this our valley all of us have wished,
And what, for my part, I have often prayed: 285
But Leonard—

LEONARD
Then James still is left among you?

PRIEST
'Tis of the elder brother I am speaking:
They had an uncle, he was at that time
A thriving man, and trafficked on the seas;
And but for this same uncle, to this hour   290
Leonard had never handled rope or shroud.
For the boy loved the life which we lead here;
And though a very stripling, twelve years old,
His soul was knit to this his native soil.
But as I said, old Walter was too weak   295
To strive with such a torrent: when he died
The estate and house were sold, and all their sheep,
A pretty flock, and which for aught I know
Had clothed the Ewbanks for a thousand years.
Well—all was gone, and they were destitute.   300
And Leonard, chiefly for his brother's sake,
Resolved to try his fortune on the seas.
'Tis now twelve years since we had tidings from him.
If there was one among us who had heard
That Leonard Ewbank was come home again,   305
From the Great Gavel down by Leeza's banks,
And down the Enna far as Egremont
The day would be a very festival,
And those two bells of ours, which there you see
Hanging in the open air—but, O good sir!   310
This is sad talk—they'll never sound for him
Living or dead. When last we heard of him
He was in slavery among the Moors
Upon the Barbary coast. 'Twas not a little
That would bring down his spirit, and no doubt   315
Before it ended in his death the lad
Was sadly crossed. Poor Leonard! When we parted,
He took me by the hand and said to me,
If ever the day came when he was rich,
He would return, and on his father's land   320
He would grow old among us.

LEONARD
If that day
Should come, 'twould needs be a glad day for him;
He would himself, no doubt, be happy then

As any that should meet him—

PRIEST
                                    Happy! Sir,—

LEONARD
325   You said his kindred all were in their graves,
And that he had one brother—

PRIEST
                                    That is but
A fellow tale of sorrow. From his youth
James, though not sickly, yet was delicate;
And Leonard being always by his side
330   Had done so many offices about him
That, though he was not of a timid nature,
Yet still the spirit of a mountain boy
In him was somewhat checked; and when his brother
Was gone to sea and he was left alone,
335   The little colour that he had was soon
Stolen from his cheek, he drooped, and pined and
        pined—

LEONARD
But these are all the graves of full-grown men!

PRIEST
Ay, sir, that passed away: we took him to us.
He was the child of all the dale—he lived
340   Three months with one, and six months with
        another;
And wanted neither food, nor clothes, nor love:
And many, many happy days were his.
But whether blithe or sad, 'tis my belief
His absent brother still was at his heart.
345   And when he lived beneath our roof, we found
(A practice till this time unknown to him)
That often, rising from his bed at night,
He in his sleep would walk about, and sleeping
He sought his brother Leonard.—You are moved!
350   Forgive me, sir: before I spoke to you
I judged you most unkindly.

LEONARD
                                    But this youth,
How did he die at last?

PRIEST
                                    One sweet May morning,
It will be twelve years since when spring returns,
He had gone forth among the new-dropped lambs,
355   With two or three companions whom it chanced
Some further business summoned to a house
Which stands at the dale-head. James, tired perhaps,
Or from some other cause, remained behind.
You see yon precipice—it almost looks

Like some vast building made of many crags;   360
And in the midst is one particular rock
That rises like a column from the vale,
Whence by our shepherds it is called the Pillar.
James pointed to its summit, over which
They all had purposed to return together,   365
And told them that he there would wait for them:
They parted, and his comrades passed that way
Some two hours after, but they did not find him
Upon the Pillar at the appointed place.
Of this they took no heed: but one of them,   370
Going by chance at night into the house
Which at that time was James's home, there learned
That nobody had seen him all that day:
The morning came, and still he was unheard of:
The neighbours were alarmed, and to the brook   375
Some went, and some towards the lake: ere noon
They found him at the foot of that same rock—
Dead, and with mangled limbs. The third day after
I buried him, poor lad, and there he lies.

LEONARD

And that then *is* his grave?—Before his death   380
You said that he saw many happy years?

PRIEST

Ay, that he did—

LEONARD

         And all went well with him—

PRIEST

If he had one, the lad had twenty homes.

LEONARD

And you believe, then, that his mind was easy—

PRIEST

Yes, long before he died, he found that time   385
Is a true friend to sorrow; and unless
His thoughts were turned on Leonard's luckless
    fortune,
He talked about him with a cheerful love.

LEONARD

He could not come to an unhallowed end?

PRIEST

Nay, God forbid! You recollect I mentioned   390
A habit which disquietude and grief
Had brought upon him; and we all conjectured
That as the day was warm, he had lain down
Upon the grass and, waiting for his comrades,
He there had fallen asleep; that in his sleep   395
He to the margin of the precipice
Had walked, and from the summit had fallen

headlong,
And so no doubt he perished; at the time
We guess that in his hands he must have had
His shepherd's staff: for midway in the cliff
It had been caught; and there for many years
It hung, and mouldered there.

————————

The priest here ended;
The stranger would have thanked him, but he felt
Tears rushing in. Both left the spot in silence;
And Leonard, when they reached the churchyard
gate,
As the priest lifted up the latch, turned round,
And, looking at the grave, he said, 'My brother.'
The vicar did not hear the words; and now,
Pointing towards the cottage, he entreated
That Leonard would partake his homely fare;
The other thanked him with a fervent voice,
But added that, the evening being calm,
He would pursue his journey. So they parted.

It was not long ere Leonard reached a grove
That overhung the road; he there stopped short,
And, sitting down beneath the trees, reviewed
All that the priest had said: his early years
Were with him in his heart; his cherished hopes
And thoughts which had been his an hour before
All pressed on him with such a weight, that now
This vale, where he had been so happy, seemed
A place in which he could not bear to live:
So he relinquished all his purposes.
He travelled on to Egremont; and thence,
That night, he wrote a letter to the priest
Reminding him of what had passed between them;
And adding, with a hope to be forgiven,
That it was from the weakness of his heart
He had not dared to tell him who he was.

This done, he went on shipboard, and is now
A seaman, a grey-headed mariner.

EXPOSTULATION AND REPLY

'Why, William, on that old grey stone,
Thus for the length of half a day,
Why, William, sit you thus alone,
And dream your time away?

'Where are your books?—that light   5
        bequeathed
To beings else forlorn and blind!
Up! up! and drink the spirit breathed
From dead men to their kind.

'You look round on your mother earth,
As if she for no purpose bore you;   10
As if you were her first-born birth,
And none had lived before you!'

One morning thus, by Esthwaite lake,
When life was sweet, I knew not why,
To me my good friend Matthew spake,   15
And thus I made reply:

'The eye it cannot choose but see;
We cannot bid the ear be still;
Our bodies feel, where'er they be,
Against, or with our will.   20

'Nor less I deem that there are powers
Which of themselves our minds impress;
That we can feed this mind of ours
In a wise passiveness.

'Think you, 'mid all this mighty sum   25
Of things for ever speaking,
That nothing of itself will come,
But we must still be seeking?

'—Then ask not wherefore, here, alone,
Conversing as I may,   30
I sit upon this old grey stone,
And dream my time away.'

THE TABLES TURNED

AN EVENING SCENE, ON THE SAME SUBJECT

Up! up! my friend, and clear your looks;
Why all this toil and trouble?
Up! up! my friend, and quit your books,
Or surely you'll grow double.

5 The sun, above the mountain's head,
A freshening lustre mellow
Through all the long green fields has spread,
His first sweet evening yellow.

Books! 'tis a dull and endless strife:
10 Come, hear the woodland linnet,
How sweet his music! on my life
There's more of wisdom in it.

And hark! how blithe the throstle sings!
And he is no mean preacher:
15 Come forth into the light of things,
Let Nature be your teacher.

She has a world of ready wealth,
Our minds and hearts to bless—
Spontaneous wisdom breathed by health,
20 Truth breathed by cheerfulness.

One impulse from a vernal wood
May teach you more of man,
Of moral evil and of good,
Than all the sages can.

25 Sweet is the lore which Nature brings;
Our meddling intellect
Misshapes the beauteous forms of things—
We murder to dissect.

Enough of science and of art;
30 Close up these barren leaves;
Come forth, and bring with you a heart
That watches and receives.

LUCY GRAY

Oft I had heard of Lucy Gray:
And, when I crossed the wild,
I chanced to see at break of day
The solitary child.

5 No mate, no comrade Lucy knew;

40

She dwelt on a wide moor—
The sweetest thing that ever grew
Beside a human door!

You yet may spy the fawn at play,
The hare upon the green;   10
But the sweet face of Lucy Gray
Will never more be seen.

'Tonight will be a stormy night;
You to the town must go,
And take a lantern, child, to light   15
Your mother through the snow.'

'That, father, will I gladly do;
'Tis scarcely afternoon:
The Minster clock has just struck two,
And yonder is the moon.'   20

At this the father raised his hook
And snapped a faggot-band;
He plied his work, and Lucy took
The lantern in her hand.

Not blither is the mountain roe: 25
With many a wanton stroke
Her feet disperse the powdery snow,
That rises up like smoke.

The storm came on before its time:
She wandered up and down;   30
And many a hill did Lucy climb,
But never reached the town.

The wretched parents all that night
Went shouting far and wide;
But there was neither sound nor sight   35
To serve them for a guide.

At daybreak on a hill they stood
That overlooked the moor;
And thence they saw the bridge of wood,
A furlong from their door.   40

And now they homeward turned, and cried
'In Heaven we all shall meet!'
—When in the snow the mother spied
The print of Lucy's feet.

Then downward from the steep hill's edge   45
They tracked the footmarks small;

And through the broken hawthorn-hedge,
And by the long stone-wall:

And then an open field they crossed:
50 The marks were still the same;
They tracked them on, nor ever lost;
And to the bridge they came.

They followed from the snowy bank
The footmarks, one by one,
55 Into the middle of the plank;
And further there was none.

—Yet some maintain that to this day
She is a living child;
That you may see sweet Lucy Gray
60 Upon the lonesome wild.

O'er rough and smooth she trips along,
And never looks behind;
And sings a solitary song
That whistles in the wind.

POOR SUSAN

At the corner of Wood Street, when daylight appears,
There's a thrush that sings loud, it has sung for three
years:
Poor Susan has passed by the spot, and has heard
In the silence of morning the song of the bird.

5 'Tis a note of enchantment; what ails her? She sees
A mountain ascending, a vision of trees;
Bright volumes of vapour through Lothbury glide,
And a river flows on through the vale of Cheapside.

Green pastures she views in the midst of the dale,
10 Down which she so often has tripped with her pail;
And a single small cottage, a nest like a dove's,
The one only dwelling on earth that she loves.

She looks, and her heart is in heaven: but they fade,
The mist and the river, the hill and the shade;
15 The stream will not flow, and the hill will not rise,
And the colours have all passed away from her eyes.

RUTH

When Ruth was left half-desolate
Her father took another mate;
And Ruth, not seven years old,
A slighted child, at her own will
Went wandering over dale and hill,   5
In thoughtless freedom bold.

And she had made a pipe of straw,
And from that oaten pipe could draw
All sounds of winds and floods;
Had built a bower upon the green,   10
As if she from her birth had been
An infant of the woods.

Beneath her father's roof, alone
She seemed to live; her thoughts her own;
Herself her own delight: 15
Pleased with herself, nor sad nor gay,
She passed her time; and in this way
Grew up to woman's height.

There came a youth from Georgia's shore:
A military casque he wore   20
With splendid feathers dressed;
He brought them from the Cherokees;
The feathers nodded in the breeze,
And made a gallant crest.

From Indian blood you deem him sprung: 25
Ah, no! he spake the English tongue,
And bore a soldier's name;
And when America was free
From battle and from jeopardy,
He 'cross the ocean came.   30

With hues of genius on his cheek
In finest tones the youth could speak;
While he was yet a boy,
The moon, the glory of the sun,
And streams that murmur as they run,   35
Had been his dearest joy.

He was a lovely youth! I guess
The panther in the wilderness
Was not so fair as he;
And when he chose to sport and play,   40
No dolphin ever was so gay
Upon the tropic sea.

Among the Indians he had fought;
And with him many tales he brought
Of pleasure and of fear;
Such tales as, told to any maid
By such a youth in the green shade,
Were perilous to hear.

He told of girls, a happy rout!
Who quit their fold with dance and shout,
Their pleasant Indian town,
To gather strawberries all day long,
Returning with a choral song
When daylight is gone down.

He spake of plants divine and strange
That every hour their blossoms change,
Ten thousand lovely hues!
With budding, fading, faded flowers
They stand the wonder of the bowers
From morn to evening dews.

Of march and ambush, siege and fight,
Then did he tell; and with delight
The heart of Ruth would ache;
Wild histories they were, and dear:
But 'twas a thing of heaven to hear
When of himself he spake!

Sometimes most earnestly he said:
'Oh Ruth! I have been worse than dead;
False thoughts, thoughts bold and vain,
Encompassed me on every side
When I, in confidence and pride,
Had crossed the Atlantic main.

'It was a fresh and glorious world,
A banner bright that was unfurled
Before me suddenly:
I looked upon those hills and plains,
And seemed as if let loose from chains
To live at liberty.

'But wherefore speak of this? for now,
Sweet Ruth! with thee, I know not how,
I feel my spirit burn;
Even as the east when day comes forth,
And to the west, and south, and north,
The morning doth return.

'It is a purer, better mind: 85
O maiden innocent and kind,
What sights I might have seen!
Even now upon my eyes they break!'
—And he again began to speak
Of lands where he had been.   90

He told of the magnolia, spread
High as a cloud, high overhead!
The cypress and her spire;
Of flowers that with one scarlet gleam
Cover a hundred leagues, and seem   95
To set the hills on fire.

The youth of green savannahs spake,
And many an endless, endless lake,
With all its fairy crowds
Of islands, that together lie   100
As quietly as spots of sky
Among the evening clouds.

And then he said, 'How sweet it were
A fisher or a hunter there,
A gardener in the shade,   105
Still wandering with an easy mind
To build a household fire, and find
A home in every glade!

'What days and what sweet years! Ah me!
Our life were life indeed, with thee   110
So passed in quiet bliss,
And all the while,' said he, 'to know
That we were in a world of woe,
On such an earth as this!'

And then he sometimes interwove   115
Dear thoughts about a father's love;
'For there,' said he, 'are spun
Around the heart such tender ties,
That our own children to our eyes
Are dearer than the sun.   120

'Sweet Ruth! and could you go with me
My helpmate in the woods to be,
Our shed at night to rear;
Or run, my own adopted bride,
A sylvan huntress at my side,   125
And drive the flying deer!

'Beloved Ruth!'—No more he said.
Sweet Ruth alone at midnight shed
A solitary tear.
130 She thought again—and did agree
With him to sail across the sea,
And drive the flying deer.

'And now, as fitting is and right,
We in the church our faith will plight,
135 A husband and a wife.'
Even so they did; and I may say
That to sweet Ruth that happy day
Was more than human life.

Through dream and vision did she sink,
140 Delighted all the while to think
That on those lonesome floods
And green savannahs, she should share
His board with lawful joy, and bear
His name in the wild woods.

145 But, as you have before been told,
This stripling, sportive, gay and bold,
And with his dancing crest
So beautiful, through savage lands
Had roamed about with vagrant bands
150 Of Indians in the west.

The wind, the tempest roaring high,
The tumult of a tropic sky,
Might well be dangerous food
For him, a youth to whom was given
155 So much of earth, so much of Heaven,
And such impetuous blood.

Whatever in those climes he found
Irregular in sight or sound
Did to his mind impart
160 A kindred impulse, seemed allied
To his own powers, and justified
The workings of his heart.

Nor less to feed voluptuous thought
The beauteous forms of nature wrought,
165 Fair trees and lovely flowers;
The breezes their own languor lent;
The stars had feelings, which they sent
Into those magic bowers.

Yet, in his worst pursuits, I ween
That sometimes there did intervene 170
Pure hopes of high intent;
For passions linked to forms so fair
And stately, needs must have their share
Of noble sentiment.

But ill he lived, much evil saw 175
With men to whom no better law
Nor better life was known;
Deliberately and undeceived
Those wild men's vices he received,
And gave them back his own. 180

His genius and his moral frame
Were thus impaired, and he became
The slave of low desires:
A man who without self-control
Would seek what the degraded soul 185
Unworthily admires.

And yet he with no feigned delight
Had wooed the maiden, day and night
Had loved her, night and morn:
What could he less than love a maid 190
Whose heart with so much nature played?
So kind and so forlorn?

But now the pleasant dream was gone;
No hope, no wish remained, not one,
They stirred him now no more; 195
New objects did new pleasure give,
And once again he wished to live
As lawless as before.

Meanwhile, as thus with him it fared,
They for the voyage were prepared, 200
And went to the sea-shore;
But when they thither came, the youth
Deserted his poor bride, and Ruth
Could never find him more.

'God help thee, Ruth!'—Such pains she had 205
That she in half a year was mad,
And in a prison housed;
And there, exulting in her wrongs,
Among the music of her songs
She fearfully caroused. 210

Yet sometimes milder hours she knew,
Nor wanted sun, nor rain, nor dew,
Nor pastimes of the May—
They all were with her in her cell;
215 And a wild brook with cheerful knell
Did o'er the pebbles play.

When Ruth three seasons thus had lain
There came a respite to her pain,
She from her prison fled;
220 But of the vagrant none took thought;
And where it liked her best she sought
Her shelter and her bread.

Among the fields she breathed again:
The master-current of her brain
225 Ran permanent and free;
And coming to the banks of Tone,
There did she rest; and dwell alone
Under the greenwood tree.

The engines of her pain, the tools
230 That shaped her sorrow, rocks and pools,
And airs that gently stir
The vernal leaves, she loved them still,
Nor ever taxed them with the ill
Which had been done to her.

235 A barn her *winter* bed supplies;
But till the warmth of summer skies
And summer days is gone
(And all do in this tale agree),
She sleeps beneath the greenwood tree,
240 And other home hath none.

An innocent life, yet far astray!
And Ruth will long before her day
Be broken down and old.
Sore aches she needs must have! but less
245 Of mind, than body's wretchedness,
From damp and rain and cold.

If she is pressed by want of food,
She from her dwelling in the wood
Repairs to a road-side;
250 And there she begs at one steep place,
Where up and down with easy pace
The horsemen-travellers ride.

That oaten pipe of hers is mute,
Or thrown away; but with a flute
Her loneliness she cheers: 255
This flute, made of a hemlock stalk,
At evening in his homeward walk
The Quantock woodman hears.

I, too, have passed her on the hills
Setting her little water-mills   260
By spouts and fountains wild;
Such small machinery as she turned
Ere she had wept, ere she had mourned,
A young and happy child!

Farewell! and when thy days are told,   265
Ill-fated Ruth! in hallowed mould
Thy corpse shall buried be;
For thee a funeral bell shall ring,
And all the congregation sing
A Christian psalm for thee.   270

NUTTING

                    It seems a day
(I speak of one from many singled out),
One of those heavenly days which cannot die,
When forth I sallied from our cottage-door,
And with a wallet o'er my shoulder slung,   5
A nutting crook in hand, I turned my steps
Towards the distant woods, a figure quaint,
Tricked out in proud disguise of beggar's weeds
Put on for the occasion, by advice
And exhortation of my frugal dame.   10
Motley accoutrement! of power to smile
At thorns, and brakes, and brambles, and in truth
More ragged than need was. Among the woods
And o'er the pathless rocks I forced my way,
Until at length I came to one dear nook   15
Unvisited, where not a broken bough
Drooped with its withered leaves, ungracious sign
Of devastation, but the hazels rose
Tall and erect, with milk-white clusters hung,
A virgin scene!—A little while I stood,   20
Breathing with such suppression of the heart
As joy delights in; and with wise restraint
Voluptuous, fearless of a rival, eyed
The banquet, or beneath the trees I sate
Among the flowers, and with the flowers I played;   25

49

A temper known to those who, after long
And weary expectation, have been blessed
With sudden happiness beyond all hope.
Perhaps it was a bower beneath whose leaves
30 The violets of five seasons reappear
And fade, unseen by any human eye;
Where fairy water-breaks do murmur on
For ever, and I saw the sparkling foam,
And with my cheek on one of those green stones
35 That, fleeced with moss, beneath the shady trees
Lay round me scattered like a flock of sheep,
I heard the murmur and the murmuring sound,
In that sweet mood when pleasure loves to pay
Tribute to ease; and, of its joy secure,
40 The heart luxuriates with indifferent things,
Wasting its kindliness on stocks and stones,
And on the vacant air. Then up I rose,
And dragged to earth both branch and bough, with
    crash
And merciless ravage; and the shady nook
45 Of hazels, and the green and mossy bower,
Deformed and sullied, patiently gave up
Their quiet being: and, unless I now
Confound my present feelings with the past,
Even then, when from the bower I turned away
50 Exulting, rich beyond the wealth of kings,
I felt a sense of pain when I beheld
The silent trees and the intruding sky.

    Then, dearest maiden! move along these shades
In gentleness of heart; with gentle hand
55 Touch,—for there is a spirit in the woods.

THE ANCIENT MARINER

I

[An ancient Mariner meeteth three Gallants bidden to a wedding feast, and detaineth one.]

It is an ancient Mariner,
  And he stoppeth one of three:
'By thy long gray beard and thy glittering eye,
  Now wherefore stoppest me?

5 'The Bridegroom's doors are opened wide,
  And I am next of kin;
The Guests are met, the Feast is set—
  May'st hear the merry din.'

But still he holds the wedding-guest—

'There was a Ship,' quoth he—   10
  'Nay, if thou'st got a laughsome tale,
    Mariner! come with me.'

He holds him with his skinny hand,
  Quoth he, 'There was a Ship—'
'Now get thee hence, thou gray-beard   15
    Loon!
  Or my Staff shall make thee skip.'

[The Wed-
ding-Guest
is spell-
bound by
the eye of
the old sea-
faring man,
and con-
strained to
hear his
tale.]
He holds him with his glittering eye—
  The wedding-guest stood still
And listens like a three years' child;
  The Mariner hath his will.   20

The wedding-guest sate on a stone,
  He cannot choose but hear;
And thus spake on that ancient man,
  The bright-eyed Mariner.

'The Ship was cheered, the Harbour   25
      cleared—
  Merrily did we drop
Below the Kirk, below the Hill,
  Below the Light-house top.

[The Mari-
ner tells
how the
ship sailed
southward
with a good
wind and
fair
weather,
till it
reached
the line.]
The Sun came up upon the left,
  Out of the Sea came he: 30
And he shone bright, and on the right
  Went down into the sea.

Higher and higher every day,
  Till over the mast at noon—'
The wedding-guest here beat his breast, 35
  For he heard the loud bassoon.

[The Wed-
ding-Guest
heareth
the bridal
music; but
the Mari-
ner con-
tinueth his
tale.]
The Bride hath paced into the Hall,
  Red as a rose is she;
Nodding their heads before her go
  The merry Minstrelsy.   40

The wedding-guest he beat his breast,
  Yet he cannot choose but hear:
And thus spake on that ancient Man,
  The bright-eyed Mariner:

[The ship
driven by
a storm
towards
the south
pole.]
'But now the North wind came more   45
      fierce,
  There came a Tempest strong!
And southward still for days and weeks

Like Chaff we drove along.

And now there came both Mist and Snow,
    And it grew wondrous cold;
And Ice mast-high came floating by
    As green as Emerald.

And through the drifts the snowy clifts
    Did send a dismal sheen;
Nor shapes of men nor beasts we ken—
    The Ice was all between.

The Ice was here, the Ice was there,
    The Ice was all around:
It cracked and growled, and roared and
      howled,
    A wild and ceaseless sound.

At length did cross an Albatross,
    Thorough the Fog it came;
As if it had been a Christian Soul,
    We hailed it in God's name.

The Mariners gave it biscuit-worms,
    And round and round it flew.
The Ice did split with a Thunder-fit;
    The Helmsman steered us through.

And a good South wind sprung up behind,
    The Albatross did follow;
And every day for food or play
    Came to the Mariner's hollo!

In mist or cloud on mast or shroud
    It perched for vespers nine,
Whiles all the night through fog-smoke
      white
    Glimmered the white moon-shine.'

'God save thee, antient Mariner,
    From the fiends that plague thee thus!
Why look'st thou so?'—'With my crossbow
    I shot the Albatross.'

II

'The Sun now rose upon the right,
    Out of the Sea came he;
Still hid in mist; and on the left
    Went down into the Sea.

And the good South wind still blew
      behind,

[The land of ice, and of fearful sounds where no living thing was to be seen.]

[Till a great sea-bird, called the Albatross, came through the snow-fog, and was received with great joy and hospitality.]

[And lo! the Albatross proveth a bird of good omen, and followeth the ship as it returned northward through fog and floating ice.]

[The ancient Mariner inhospitably killeth the pious bird of good omen.]

But no sweet Bird did follow,
  Nor any day for food or play
    Came to the Mariner's hollo!

[His ship-
mates cry
out against
the
ancient
Mariner,
for killing
the bird of
good luck.]
And I had done an hellish thing,
  And it would work 'em woe: 90
For all averred, I had killed the Bird
  That made the Breeze to blow.

[But when
the fog
cleared off,
they justify
the same,
and thus
make
themselves
accomplices
in the
crime.]
Nor dim nor red, like an Angel's head,
  The glorious Sun uprist:
Then all averred, I had killed the Bird   95
  That brought the fog and mist.
'Twas right, said they, such birds to slay
  That bring the fog and mist.

[The fair
breeze con-
tinues; the
ship enters
the Pacific
Ocean, and
sails north-
ward, even
till it
reaches
the Line.]
The breezes blew, the white foam flew,
  The furrow followed free: 100
We were the first that ever burst
  Into that silent Sea.

Down dropt the breeze, the Sails dropt down,
  'Twas sad as sad could be;
[The ship
hath been
suddenly
becalmed.]
And we did speak only to break   105
  The silence of the Sea.

All in a hot and copper sky
  The bloody Sun, at noon,
Right up above the mast did stand,
  No bigger than the moon.   110

Day after day, day after day,
  We stuck, nor breath nor motion,
As idle as a painted Ship
  Upon a painted Ocean.

[And the
Albatross
begins to be
avenged.]
Water, water, every where,   115
  And all the boards did shrink;
Water, water, every where,
  Nor any drop to drink.

The very deeps did rot: O Christ!
  That ever this should be!   120
Yea, slimy things did crawl with legs
  Upon the slimy Sea.

About, about, in reel and rout
  The Death-fires danced at night;
The water, like a witch's oils,   125
  Burnt green and blue and white.

[A Spirit
had fol-
lowed
them; one
of the in-
visible in-
habitants
of this
planet.
And some in dreams assuréd were
  Of the Spirit that plagued us so:
Nine fathom deep he had followed us
  From the Land of Mist and Snow.   130

neither departed souls nor angels; concerning whom the learned Jew Josephus, and the Platonic Constantinopolitan, Michael Psellus, may be consulted. They are very numerous, and there is no climate or element without one or more.]

And every tongue through utter drouth
　　Was withered at the root;
We could not speak, no more than if
　　We had been choked with soot.

135

[The ship-
mates, in
their sore
distress,
would fain
throw the
whole guilt
on the
ancient
Mariner: in sign whereof they hang the dead sea-bird round his neck.]

Ah well-a-day! what evil looks
　　Had I from old and young!
Instead of the Cross the Albatross
　　About my neck was hung.'

III

'So passed a weary time; each throat
　　Was parched, and glazed each eye.

140

[The
ancient
Mariner
beholdeth
a sign in
the element
afar off.]

When, looking westward, I beheld
　　A something in the sky.

At first it seemed a little speck,
　　And then it seemed a mist;
It moved and moved, and took at last
　　A certain shape, I wist.

145

A speck, a mist, a shape, I wist!
　　And still it ner'd and ner'd;
And as if it dodged a water-sprite
　　It plunged and tacked and veered.

150

[At its
nearer
approach,
it seemeth
him to be
a ship; and
at a dear
ransom he
freeth his
speech
from the
bonds of
thirst.]

With throat unslaked, with black lips
　　baked,
　　We could nor laugh nor wail;
Through utter drouth all dumb we stood
Till I bit my arm and sucked the blood,
　　And cried, A sail! a sail!

155

With throat unslaked, with black lips
　　baked,
　　Agape they heard me call:
[A flash of
joy;

Gramercy! they for joy did grin,
And all at once their breath drew in
　　As they were drinking all.

160

And horror
follows.
For can it
be a ship
that comes
onward
without
wind or
tide?]

See! See! (I cried) she tacks no more!
　　Hither to work us weal
Without a breeze, without a tide,
　　She steddies with upright keel!

The western wave was all a flame. 165
   The day was well-nigh done!
Almost upon the western wave
   Rested the broad bright Sun;
When that strange shape drove suddenly
   Betwixt us and the Sun. 170

And straight the Sun was flecked with
     bars
   (Heaven's Mother send us grace!)
As if through a dungeon grate he peered
   With broad and burning face.

Alas! (thought I, and my heart beat 175
     loud)
   How fast she neres and neres!
Are those *her* Sails that glance in the
     Sun
   Like restless gossameres?

Are those *her* Ribs, through which the Sun
   Did peer, as through a grate? 180
And are those two all, all her crew,
   That Woman, and her Mate?

His bones were black with many a crack,
   All black and bare, I ween;
Jet-black and bare, save where with rust 185
Of mouldy damps and charnel crust
   They were patched with purple and green.

Her lips were red, *her* looks were free,
   Her locks were yellow as gold:
Her skin was as white as leprosy, 190
And she was far liker Death than he;
   Her flesh made the still air cold.

The naked Hulk alongside came
   And the Twain were playing dice;
'The Game is done! I've won, I've 195
     won!'
   Quoth she, and whistled thrice.

A gust of wind sterte up behind
   And whistled through his bones;
Thro' the holes of his eyes and the hole
    of his mouth
   Half-whistles and half-groans. 200

With never a whisper in the Sea

Off darts the Spectre-ship;

[At the rising of the Moon.
While clombe above the Eastern bar
The hornéd Moon, with one bright Star
205   Almost between the tips.

One after another.
One after one by the hornéd Moon
    (Listen, O Stranger, to me!)
Each turned his face with a ghastly pang
    And cursed me with his ee.

210   His ship-mates drop down dead.]
Four times fifty living men,
    With never a sigh or groan,
With heavy thump, a lifeless lump,
    They dropped down one by one.

[But Life-in-Death begins her work on the ancient Mariner.]
215
Their souls did from their bodies fly—
    They fled to bliss or woe!
And every soul it passed me by,
    Like the whiz of my cross-bow.'

IV

[The Wedding-Guest feareth that a Spirit is talking to him;
'I fear thee, ancient Mariner!
    I fear thy skinny hand;
220   And thou art long and lank and brown
    As is the ribbed Sea-sand.

'I fear thee and thy glittering eye
    And thy skinny hand so brown.'
But the ancient Mariner assureth him of his bodily life, and proceedeth to relate his horrible penance.]
'Fear not, fear not, thou wedding-guest!
225   This body dropt not down.

Alone, alone, all all alone,
    Alone on the wide wide Sea;
And Christ would take no pity on
    My soul in agony.

230   [He despiseth the creatures of the calm.]
The many men so beautiful,
    And they all dead did lie!
And a million million slimy things
    Lived on—and so did I.

[And envieth that they should live, and so many lie dead.]
235
I looked upon the rotting Sea,
    And drew my eyes away;
I looked upon the ghastly deck,
    And there the dead men lay.

I looked to Heaven, and tried to pray;
    But or ever a prayer had gusht,
240   A wicked whisper came and made
    My heart as dry as dust.

I closed my lids and kept them close,
   Till the balls like pulses beat;
For the sky and the sea, and the sea
    and the sky
Lay like a load on my weary eye,   245
   And the dead were at my feet.

[But the curse liveth for him in the eye of the dead men.]
The cold sweat melted from their limbs,
   Nor rot nor reek did they;
The look with which they looked on me
   Had never passed away.   250

An orphan's curse would drag to Hell
   A spirit from on high:
But oh! more horrible than that
   Is the curse in a dead man's eye!
Seven days, seven nights I saw that   255
    curse,
   And yet I could not die.

[In his loneliness and fixedness he yearneth towards the journeying Moon, and the stars that still sojourn, yet still move onward; and everywhere the blue sky belongs to them, and is their appointed rest, and their native country and their own natural homes, which they enter unannounced, as lords that are certainly expected and yet there is a silent joy at their arrival.]
The moving Moon went up the sky
   And no where did abide;
Softly she was going up
   And a star or two beside—   260

Her beams bemocked the sultry main
   Like April hoar-frost spread;
But where the Ship's huge shadow lay,
The charméd water burnt alway
   A still and awful red.   265

[By the light of the Moon he beholdeth God's creatures of the great calm.]
Beyond the shadow of the ship
   I watched the water-snakes:
They moved in tracks of shining white;
And when they reared, the elfish light
   Fell off in hoary flakes.   270

Within the shadow of the ship
   I watched their rich attire:
Blue, glossy green, and velvet black
They coiled and swam; and every track
   Was a flash of golden fire.   275

[Their beauty and their happiness.]
O happy living things! no tongue
   Their beauty might declare:
A spring of love gusht from my heart,
[He blesseth them in his heart.]
   And I blessed them unaware!
Sure my kind saint took pity on me,   280
   And I blessed them unaware.

[The spell
begins to
break.]
The self-same moment I could pray;
    And from my neck so free
The Albatross fell off, and sank
    Like lead into the sea.'

285

V

'Oh sleep, it is a gentle thing
    Beloved from pole to pole!
To Mary-queen the praise be given,
She sent the gentle sleep from heaven
    That slid into my soul.

290

[By grace
of the holy
Mother,
the ancient
Mariner is
refreshed
with rain.]
The silly buckets on the deck
    That had so long remained,
I dreamt that they were filled with dew,
    And when I awoke it rained.

295

My lips were wet, my throat was cold,
    My garments all were dank;
Sure I had drunken in my dreams,
    And still my body drank.

300

I moved and could not feel my limbs,
    I was so light, almost
I thought that I had died in sleep,
    And was a blessed Ghost.

[He heareth
sounds and
seeth
strange
sights and
commotions
in the sky
and the
element.]
And soon I heard a roaring wind,
    It did not come anear;
305 But with its sound it shook the sails
    That were so thin and sere.

The upper air burst into life,
    And a hundred fire-flags sheen
To and fro they were hurried about;
310 And to and fro, and in and out,
    The wan stars danced between.

And the coming wind did roar more loud;
    And the sails did sigh like sedge;
And the rain poured down from one
        black cloud;
315   The moon was at its edge.

The thick black cloud was cleft, and still
    The Moon was at its side;
Like waters shot from some high crag,

The lightning fell with never a jag
  A river steep and wide. 320

[The bodies
of the ship's
crew are
inspired
and the
ship moves
on;] The loud wind never reached the Ship,
  Yet now the Ship moved on!
Beneath the lightning and the moon
  The dead men gave a groan.

They groaned, they stirred, they all
    uprose, 325
  Nor spake, nor moved their eyes:
It had been strange even in a dream
  To have seen those dead men rise.

The helmsman steered, the ship moved
    on;
  Yet never a breeze up-blew; 330
The Mariners all 'gan work the ropes,
  Where they were wont to do:
They raised their limbs like lifeless
    tools—
  We were a ghastly crew.

The body of my brother's son 335
  Stood by me knee to knee:
The body and I pulled at one rope,
  But he said nought to me.'

'I fear thee, ancient Mariner!'
  'Be calm, thou wedding-guest! 340
[But not by
the souls of
the men,
nor by
dæmons of
earth or
middle air,
but by a
blessed
troop of
angelic
spirits, sent
down by
the invoca-
tion of the
guardian
saint.] 'Twas not those souls, that fled in pain,
Which to their corses came again,
  But a troop of Spirits blest:

For when it dawned—they dropped their
    arms,
  And clustered round the mast: 345
Sweet sounds rose slowly through their
    mouths,
  And from their bodies passed.

Around, around, flew each sweet sound,
  Then darted to the sun;
Slowly the sounds came back again, 350
  Now mixed, now one by one.

Sometimes a-dropping from the sky
  I heard the Sky-lark sing;
Sometimes all little birds that are,
How they seemed to fill the sea and air 355
  With their sweet jargoning!

And now 'twas like all instruments,
    Now like a lonely flute;
And now it is an angel's song
360   That makes the heavens be mute.

It ceased: yet still the sails made on
    A pleasant noise till noon,
A noise like of a hidden brook
    In the leafy month of June,
365   That to the sleeping woods all night
      Singeth a quiet tune.

Till noon we silently sailed on,
    Yet never a breeze did breathe:
Slowly and smoothly went the Ship
370   Moved onward from beneath.

[The lone-
some spirit
from the
south-pole
carries on
the ship as
far as the
Line, in
obedience
to the
angelic
troop, but
still
requireth
vengeance.]

Under the keel nine fathom deep
    From the land of mist and snow
The Spirit slid: and it was He
    That made the ship to go.
375 The sails at noon left off their tune,
    And the Ship stood still also.

The Sun right up above the mast
    Had fixed her to the ocean:
But in a minute she 'gan stir
380   With a short uneasy motion—
Backwards and forwards half her length,
    With a short uneasy motion.

Then, like a pawing horse let go,
    She made a sudden bound:
385 It flung the blood into my head,
    And I fell into a swound.

[The Polar
Spirit's
fellow-
dæmons,
the
invisible
inhabitants
of the
element,
take part
in his
wrong;
and two of
them relate,
one to the
other, that
penance
long and
heavy for
the ancient
Mariner
hath been
accorded to
the Polar
Spirit, who
returneth
southward.]

How long in that same fit I lay,
    I have not to declare;
But ere my living life returned,
390 I heard and in my soul discerned
    Two voices in the air.

"Is it he?" quoth one, "Is this the man?
    By him who died on cross,
With his cruel bow he laid full low
395   The harmless Albatross.

"The Spirit who bideth by himself
    In the land of mist and snow,
He loved the bird that loved the man
    Who shot him with his bow."

The other was a softer voice,
    As soft as honey-dew;
Quoth he, "The man hath penance done,
    And penance more will do." '
400

VI

FIRST VOICE

' "But tell me, tell me! speak again,
    Thy soft response renewing—
What makes that ship drive on so fast?
    What is the Ocean doing?"
405

SECOND VOICE

"Still as a Slave before his Lord,
    The Ocean hath no blast:
His great bright eye most silently
    Up to the moon is cast—
410

"If he may know which way to go,
    For she guides him smooth or grim.
See, brother, see! how graciously
    She looketh down on him."
415

FIRST VOICE

[The Mariner hath been cast into a trance; for the angelic power causeth the vessel to drive northward faster than human life could endure.]

"But why drives on that ship so fast
    Without or wave or wind?"

SECOND VOICE

"The air is cut away before,
    And closes from behind.

"Fly, brother, fly! more high, more high,
    Or we shall be belated:
For slow and slow that ship will go,
    When the Mariner's trance is abated."
420

[The supernatural motion is retarded; the Mariner awakes, and his penance begins anew.]

I woke, and we were sailing on
    As in a gentle weather;
'Twas night, calm night, the moon was
      high;
    The dead men stood together.
425

All stood together on the deck,
    For a charnel-dungeon fitter;
All fixed on me their stony eyes
    That in the moon did glitter.
430

The pang, the curse, with which they died
  Had never passed away;
I could not draw my eyes from theirs,
  Nor turn them up to pray.

435

And now this spell was snapt: once more
  I viewed the ocean green,
And looked far forth, yet little saw
  Of what had else been seen—

440

Like one, that on a lonesome road
  Doth walk in fear and dread,
And having once turned round, walks on
  And turns no more his head;
Because he knows a frightful fiend
  Doth close behind him tread.

445

But soon there breathed a wind on me,
  Nor sound nor motion made:
Its path was not upon the sea
  In ripple or in shade.

450

It raised my hair, it fanned my cheek,
  Like a meadow-gale of spring—
It mingled strangely with my fears,
  Yet it felt like a welcoming.

Swiftly, swiftly flew the ship,
  Yet she sailed softly too;
Sweetly, sweetly blew the breeze—
  On me alone it blew.

455

O dream of joy! is this indeed
  The light-house top I see?
Is this the Hill? Is this the Kirk?
  Is this mine own countrée?

460

We drifted o'er the Harbour-bar,
  And I with sobs did pray—
'O let me be awake, my God!
  Or let me sleep alway.'

465

The harbour-bay was clear as glass,
  So smoothly it was strewn!
And on the bay the moonlight lay,
  And the shadow of the moon.

470

The rock shone bright, the kirk no less
  That stands above the rock:
The moonlight steeped in silentness
  The steady weathercock.

And the bay was white with silent light,
　　Till rising from the same　　　　　　　　　　475
[The
angelic
spirits leave
the dead
bodies,
Full many shapes, that shadows were,
　　In crimson colours came.

And appear
in their
own forms
of light.]
A little distance from the prow
　　Those crimson shadows were:
I turned my eyes upon the deck—
　　O Christ! what saw I there?　　　　　　　　480

Each corse lay flat, lifeless and flat,
　　And, by the Holy rood,
A man all light, a seraph-man,
　　On every corse there stood.　　　　　　　　485

This seraph-band, each waved his hand,
　　It was a heavenly sight!
They stood as signals to the land,
　　Each one a lovely light:

This seraph-band, each waved his hand,　　　490
　　No voice did they impart—
No voice; but oh! the silence sank
　　Like music on my heart.

But soon I heard the dash of oars,
　　I heard the pilot's cheer:　　　　　　　　　495
My head was turned perforce away,
　　And I saw a boat appear.

The pilot and the pilot's boy,
　　I heard them coming fast:
Dear Lord in Heaven! it was a joy　　　　　　500
　　The dead men could not blast.

I saw a third—I heard his voice:
　　It is the Hermit good!
He singeth loud his godly hymns
　　That he makes in the wood.　　　　　　　　505
He'll shrieve my soul, he'll wash away
　　The Albatross's blood.'

VII

[The
Hermit of
the wood.
'This Hermit good lives in that wood
　　Which slopes down to the Sea.
How loudly his sweet voice he rears!　　　　.510
He loves to talk with Mariners
　　That come from a far countrée.

He kneels at morn and noon and eve—
    He hath a cushion plump:
It is the moss that wholly hides
    The rotted old Oak-stump.

515

The Skiff-boat ner'd: I heard them talk,
    "Why, this is strange, I trow!
Where are those lights so many and fair
    That signal made but now?"

520

Approach-
eth the
ship with
wonder.]

"Strange, by my faith!" the Hermit said,
    "And they answered not our cheer.
The planks look warped, and see those
        sails
How thin they are and sere!
I never saw aught like to them
    Unless perchance it were

525

"The skeletons of leaves that lag
    My forest brook along;
When the Ivy-tod is heavy with snow,
And the Owlet whoops to the wolf below
    That eats the she-wolf's young."

530

"Dear Lord! it has a fiendish look,"
    The pilot made reply,
"I am a-feared."—"Push on, push on!"
    Said the Hermit cheerily.

535

The Boat came closer to the Ship,
    But I nor spake nor stirred;
The Boat came close beneath the Ship,
    And straight a sound was heard.

540

[The ship
suddenly
sinketh.]

Under the water it rumbled on,
    Still louder and more dread;
It reached the ship, it split the bay:
    The ship went down like lead.

545

[The
ancient
Mariner is
saved in
the Pilot's
boat.]

Stunned by that loud and dreadful sound,
    Which sky and ocean smote,
Like one that hath been seven days
        drowned
    My body lay afloat;
But, swift as dreams, myself I found
    Within the Pilot's boat.

550

Upon the whirl, where sank the Ship,
    The boat spun round and round,
And all was still, save that the hill
    Was telling of the sound.

I moved my lips: the Pilot shrieked
  And fell down in a fit.   555
The Holy Hermit raised his eyes
  And prayed where he did sit.

I took the oars: the Pilot's boy,
  Who now doth crazy go,
Laughed loud and long, and all the while   560
  His eyes went to and fro,
"Ha! ha!" quoth he, "full plain I see
  The devil knows how to row."

And now all in mine own countrée
  I stood on the firm land!   565
The Hermit stepped forth from the boat,
  And scarcely he could stand.

[The
ancient
Mariner
earnestly
entreateth
the Hermit
to shrieve
him;
and the
penance of
life falls
on him.]
"O shrieve me, shrieve me, holy Man!"
  The Hermit crossed his brow.
"Say quick," quoth he, "I bid thee say   570
  What manner of man art thou?"

Forthwith this frame of mine was wrenched
  With a woeful agony,
Which forced me to begin my tale,
  And then it left me free.   575

[And ever
and anon
throughout
his future
life an
agony con-
straineth
him to
travel from
land to
land;]
Since then, at an uncertain hour,
  That agony returns;
And till my ghastly tale is told
  This heart within me burns.

I pass, like night, from land to land;   580
  I have strange power of speech;
The moment that his face I see
I know the man that must hear me;
  To him my tale I teach.

What loud uproar bursts from that door!   585
  The wedding-guests are there;
But in the garden-bower the bride
  And bride-maids singing are;
And hark the little vesper-bell,
  Which biddeth me to prayer.   590

O wedding-guest! this soul hath been
  Alone on a wide wide sea:
So lonely 'twas, that God himself
  Scarce seeméd there to be.

595   O sweeter than the marriage-feast,
                               'Tis sweeter far to me
                            To walk together to the Kirk
                               With a goodly company:

                            To walk together to the Kirk
600   And all together pray,
                            While each to his great Father bends,
                            Old men, and babes, and loving friends,
                              And youths, and maidens gay.

[And to teach by his own example, love and reverence to all things that God made and loveth.]

605   Farewell, farewell! But this I tell
                            To thee, thou wedding-guest!
                            He prayeth well who loveth well
                            Both man and bird and beast.

                            He prayeth best who loveth best
                            All things both great and small:
610   For the dear God, who loveth us,
                            He made and loveth all.'

                            The Mariner, whose eye is bright,
                            Whose beard with age is hoar,
                            Is gone; and now the wedding-guest
615   Turned from the bride-groom's door.

                            He went, like one that hath been stunned
                            And is of sense forlorn:
                            A sadder and a wiser man
                            He rose the morrow morn.

THE TWO APRIL MORNINGS

                            We walked along, while bright and red
                            Uprose the morning sun;
                            And Matthew stopped, he looked, and said
                            'The will of God be done!'

5   A village schoolmaster was he,
                            With hair of glittering grey;
                            As blithe a man as you could see
                            On a spring holiday.

                            And on that morning, through the grass
10   And by the steaming rills,
                            We travelled merrily, to pass
                            A day among the hills.

'Our work,' said I, 'was well begun;
Then from thy breast what thought,
Beneath so beautiful a sun,
So sad a sigh has brought?'   15

A second time did Matthew stop;
And fixing still his eye
Upon the eastern mountain-top,
To me he made reply: 20

'Yon cloud with that long purple cleft
Brings fresh into my mind
A day like this, which I have left
Full thirty years behind.

'And just above yon slope of corn   25
Such colours and no other
Were in the sky that April morn,
Of this the very brother.

'With rod and line my silent sport
I plied by Derwent's wave;   30
And coming to the church, stopped short
Beside my daughter's grave.

'Nine summers had she scarcely seen,
The pride of all the vale;
And then she sung; she would have been   35
A very nightingale.

'Six feet in earth my Emma lay;
And yet I loved her more,
For so it seemed, than till that day
I e'er had loved before.   40

'And turning from her grave, I met
Beside the churchyard yew
A blooming girl, whose hair was wet
With points of morning dew.

'A basket on her head she bare;   45
Her brow was smooth and white:
To see a child so very fair,
It was a pure delight!

'No fountain from its rocky cave
E'er tripped with foot so free;   50
She seemed as happy as a wave
That dances on the sea.

'There came from me a sigh of pain
Which I could ill confine;
I looked at her and looked again: 55
—And did not wish her mine.'

Matthew is in his grave, yet now
Methinks I see him stand,
As at that moment, with his bough
60   Of wilding in his hand.

THE FOUNTAIN

A CONVERSATION

We talked with open heart, and tongue
Affectionate and true;
A pair of friends, though I was young,
And Matthew seventy-two.

5   We lay beneath a spreading oak,
Beside a mossy seat;
And from the turf a fountain broke,
And gurgled at our feet.

'Now, Matthew! let us try to match
10   This water's pleasant tune
With some old Border song, or catch
That suits a summer's noon.

'Or of the church-clock and the chimes
Sing here beneath the shade,
15   That half-mad thing of witty rhymes
Which you last April made!'

In silence Matthew lay, and eyed
The spring beneath the tree;
And thus the dear old man replied,
20   The grey-haired man of glee:

'Down to the vale this water steers,
How merrily it goes!
'Twill murmur on a thousand years,
And flow as now it flows.

25   'And here, on this delightful day,
I cannot choose but think
How oft, a vigorous man, I lay
Beside this fountain's brink.

'My eyes are dim with childish tears,
30   My heart is idly stirred,
For the same sound is in my ears
Which in those days I heard.

'Thus fares it still in our decay:

And yet the wiser mind
Mourns less for what age takes away   35
Than what it leaves behind.

'The blackbird in the summer trees,
The lark upon the hill,
Let loose their carols when they please,
Are quiet when they will.   40

'With Nature never do *they* wage
A foolish strife; they see
A happy youth, and their old age
Is beautiful and free:

'But we are pressed by heavy laws;   45
And often, glad no more,
We wear a face of joy, because
We have been glad of yore.

'If there is one who need bemoan
His kindred laid in earth,   50
The household hearts that were his own,
It is the man of mirth.

'My days, my friend, are almost gone,
My life has been approved,
And many love me; but by none   55
Am I enough beloved.'

'Now both himself and me he wrongs,
The man who thus complains!
I live and sing my idle songs
Upon these happy plains,   60

'And, Matthew, for thy children dead
I'll be a son to thee!'
At this he grasped his hands, and said
'Alas! that cannot be.'

We rose up from the fountain-side;   65
And down the smooth descent
Of the green sheep-track did we glide;
And through the wood we went;

And, ere we came to Leonard's Rock,
He sang those witty rhymes   70
About the crazy old church clock
And the bewildered chimes.

MICHAEL

A PASTORAL POEM

If from the public way you turn your steps
Up the tumultuous brook of Green-head Gill,
You will suppose that with an upright path
Your feet must struggle; in such bold ascent
The pastoral mountains front you, face to face.
But courage! for beside that boisterous brook
The mountains have all opened out themselves,
And made a hidden valley of their own.
No habitation there is seen; but such
As journey thither find themselves alone
With a few sheep, with rocks and stones, and kites
That overhead are sailing in the sky.
It is in truth an utter solitude;
Nor should I have made mention of this dell
But for one object which you might pass by,
Might see and notice not. Beside the brook
There is a straggling heap of unhewn stones:
And to that place a story appertains
Which, though it be ungarnished with events,
Is not unfit, I deem, for the fireside,
Or for the summer shade. It was the first,
The earliest of those tales that spake to me
Of shepherds, dwellers in the valleys, men
Whom I already loved, not verily
For their own sakes, but for the fields and hills
Where was their occupation and abode.
And hence this tale, while I was yet a boy
Careless of books, yet having felt the power
Of nature, by the gentle agency
Of natural objects led me on to feel
For passions that were not my own, and think
(At random and imperfectly indeed)
On man, the heart of man, and human life.
Therefore, although it be a history
Homely and rude, I will relate the same
For the delight of a few natural hearts,
And, with yet fonder feeling, for the sake
Of youthful poets who among these hills
Will be my second self when I am gone.

Upon the forest-side in Grasmere Vale
There dwelt a shepherd, Michael was his name,
An old man, stout of heart, and strong of limb.
His bodily frame had been from youth to age
Of an unusual strength; his mind was keen,
Intense and frugal, apt for all affairs,
And in his shepherd's calling he was prompt
And watchful more than ordinary men.
Hence he had learned the meanings of all winds,

Of blasts of every tone; and oftentimes
When others heeded not, he heard the South   50
Make subterraneous music, like the noise
Of bagpipers on distant Highland hills;
The shepherd, at such warning, of his flock
Bethought him, and he to himself would say,
'The winds are now devising work for me!'   55
And truly, at all times the storm, that drives
The traveller to a shelter, summoned him
Up to the mountains: he had been alone
Amid the heart of many thousand mists,
That came to him and left him on the heights.   60
So lived he till his eightieth year was past.

And grossly that man errs, who should suppose
That the green valleys and the streams and rocks
Were things indifferent to the shepherd's thoughts.
Fields, where with cheerful spirits he had breathed   65
The common air; the hills, which he so oft
Had climbed with vigorous steps; which had impressed
So many incidents upon his mind
Of hardship, skill or courage, joy or fear;
Which like a book preserved the memory   70
Of the dumb animals whom he had saved,
Had fed or sheltered, linking to such acts,
So grateful in themselves, the certainty
Of honourable gain; these fields, these hills,
Which were his living being, even more   75
Than his own blood—what could they less?—had laid
Strong hold on his affections, were to him
A pleasurable feeling of blind love,
The pleasure which there is in life itself.

He had not passed his days in singleness.   80
He had a wife, a comely matron, old—
Though younger than himself full twenty years.
She was a woman of a stirring life,
Whose heart was in her house; two wheels she had
Of antique form, this large for spinning wool,   85
That small for flax; and if one wheel had rest,
It was because the other was at work.
The pair had but one inmate in their house,
An only child, who had been born to them
When Michael telling o'er his years began   90
To deem that he was old—in shepherd's phrase,
With one foot in the grave. This only son,
With two brave sheep-dogs tried in many a storm,
The one of an inestimable worth,
Made all their household. I may truly say,   95
That they were as a proverb in the vale
For endless industry. When day was gone,
And from their occupations out of doors

The son and father were come home, even then
100 Their labour did not cease; unless when all
Turned to their cleanly supper-board, and there,
Each with a mess of pottage and skimmed milk,
Sat round their basket piled with oaten cakes,
And their plain home-made cheese. Yet when their meal
105 Was ended, Luke (for so the son was named)
And his old father both betook themselves
To such convenient work as might employ
Their hands by the fireside; perhaps to card
Wool for the housewife's spindle, or repair
110 Some injury done to sickle, flail or scythe,
Or other implement of house or field.

Down from the ceiling by the chimney's edge,
Which in our ancient uncouth country style
Did with a huge projection overbrow
115 Large space beneath, as duly as the light
Of day grew dim the housewife hung a lamp;
An aged utensil, which had performed
Service beyond all others of its kind.
Early at evening did it burn and late,
120 Surviving comrade of uncounted hours,
Which going by from year to year had found
And left the couple neither gay perhaps
Nor cheerful, yet with objects and with hopes,
Living a life of eager industry.
125 And now, when Luke was in his eighteenth year,
There by the light of this old lamp they sat,
Father and son, while late into the night
The housewife plied her own peculiar work,
Making the cottage through the silent hours
130 Murmur as with the sound of summer flies.
The light was famous in its neighbourhood,
And was a public symbol of the life
The thrifty pair had lived. For, as it chanced,
Their cottage on a plot of rising ground
135 Stood single, with large prospect, north and south,
High into Easedale, up to Dunmal Raise,
And westward to the village near the lake;
And from this constant light, so regular
And so far seen, the house itself, by all
140 Who dwelt within the limits of the vale,
Both old and young, was named THE EVENING STAR.

Thus living on through such a length of years,
The shepherd, if he loved himself, must needs
Have loved his help-mate; but to Michael's heart
145 The son of his old age was yet more dear—
Effect which might perhaps have been produced
By that instinctive tenderness, the same
Blind spirit, which is in the blood of all;

Or that a child, more than all other gifts,
Brings hope with it, and forward-looking thoughts,   150
And stirrings of inquietude when they
By tendency of nature needs must fail.
From such and other causes, to the thoughts
Of the old man his only son was now
The dearest object that he knew on earth.   155
Exceeding was the love he bare to him,
His heart and his heart's joy! For oftentimes
Old Michael, while he was a babe in arms,
Had done him female service, not alone
For dalliance and delight, as is the use   160
Of fathers, but with patient mind enforced
To acts of tenderness; and he had rocked
His cradle with a woman's gentle hand.

And in a later time, ere yet the boy
Had put on boy's attire, did Michael love,   165
Albeit of a stern unbending mind,
To have the young one in his sight when he
Had work by his own door, or when he sat
With sheep before him on his shepherd's stool
Beneath that large old oak, which near their door   170
Stood, and from its enormous breadth of shade
Chosen for the shearer's covert from the sun,
Thence in our rustic dialect was called
The CLIPPING TREE, a name which yet it bears.
There, while they two were sitting in the shade   175
With others round them, earnest all and blithe,
Would Michael exercise his heart with looks
Of fond correction and reproof bestowed
Upon the child, if he disturbed the sheep
By catching at their legs, or with his shouts   180
Scared them, while they lay still beneath the shears.

And when by Heaven's good grace the boy grew up
A healthy lad, and carried in his cheek
Two steady roses that were five years old,
Then Michael from a winter coppice cut   185
With his own hand a sapling, which he hooped
With iron, making it throughout in all
Due requisites a perfect shepherd's staff,
And gave it to the boy; wherewith equipped
He as a watchman oftentimes was placed   190
At gate or gap, to stem or turn the flock;
And to his office prematurely called
There stood the urchin, as you will divine,
Something between a hindrance and a help;
And for this cause not always, I believe,   195
Receiving from his father hire of praise,
Though nought was left undone which staff or voice,
Or looks, or threatening gestures could perform.
But soon as Luke, full ten years old, could stand

200	Against the mountain blasts, and to the heights,
	Not fearing toil, nor length of weary ways,
	He with his father daily went, and they
	Were as companions—why should I relate
	That objects which the shepherd loved before
205	Were dearer now? that from the boy there came
	Feelings and emanations, things which were
	Light to the sun and music to the wind;
	And that the old man's heart seemed born again.

Thus in his father's sight the boy grew up;
And now when he had reached his eighteenth year,
He was his comfort and his daily hope.

While in the fashion which I have described
This simple household thus were living on
From day to day, to Michael's ear there came
Distressful tidings. Long before the time
Of which I speak, the shepherd had been bound
In surety for his brother's son, a man
Of an industrious life and ample means;
But unforeseen misfortunes suddenly
Had pressed upon him; and old Michael now
Was summoned to discharge the forfeiture,
A grievous penalty, but little less
Than half his substance. This unlooked-for claim,
At the first hearing, for a moment took
More hope out of his life than he supposed
That any old man ever could have lost.
As soon as he had gathered so much strength
That he could look his trouble in the face,
It seemed that his sole refuge was to sell
A portion of his patrimonial fields.
Such was his first resolve: he thought again,
And his heart failed him. 'Isabel,' said he,
Two evenings after he had heard the news,
'I have been toiling more than seventy years,
And in the open sunshine of God's love
Have we all lived; yet if these fields of ours
Should pass into a stranger's hand, I think
That I could not lie quiet in my grave.
Our lot is a hard lot: the sun itself
Has scarcely been more diligent than I,
And I have lived to be a fool at last
To my own family. An evil man
That was, and made an evil choice, if he
Were false to us; and if he were not false,
There are ten thousand to whom loss like this
Had been no sorrow. I forgive him—but
'Twere better to be dumb than to talk thus.
When I began, my purpose was to speak
Of remedies and of a cheerful hope.

Our Luke shall leave us, Isabel; the land   250
Shall not go from us, and it shall be free;
He shall possess it, free as is the wind
That passes over it. We have, thou knowest,
Another kinsman: he will be our friend
In this distress. He is a prosperous man,   255
Thriving in trade; and Luke to him shall go,
And with his kinsman's help and his own thrift
He quickly will repair this loss, and then
May come again to us. If here he stay,
What can be done? Where every one is poor   260
What can be gained?' At this the old man paused,
And Isabel sat silent, for her mind
Was busy, looking back into past times.
There's Richard Bateman, thought she to herself,
He was a parish-boy: at the church-door   265
They made a gathering for him, shillings, pence,
And halfpennies, wherewith the neighbours bought
A basket, which they filled with pedlar's wares;
And with this basket on his arm the lad
Went up to London, found a master there,   270
Who out of many chose the trusty boy
To go and overlook his merchandise
Beyond the seas; where he grew wondrous rich,
And left estates and moneys to the poor,
And at his birth-place built a chapel floored   275
With marble, which he sent from foreign lands.
These thoughts, and many others of like sort,
Passed quickly through the mind of Isabel,
And her face brightened. The old man was glad,
And thus resumed: 'Well, Isabel! this scheme   280
These two days has been meat and drink to me.
Far more than we have lost is left us yet.
We have enough—I wish indeed that I
Were younger—but this hope is a good hope.
Make ready Luke's best garments, of the best   285
Buy for him more, and let us send him forth
Tomorrow, or the next day, or tonight—
If he could go, the boy should go tonight.'
Here Michael ceased, and to the fields went forth
With a light heart. The housewife for five days   290
Was restless morn and night, and all day long
Wrought on with her best fingers to prepare
Things needful for the journey of her son.
But Isabel was glad when Sunday came
To stop her in her work: for when she lay   295
By Michael's side, she for the two last nights
Heard him, how he was troubled in his sleep;
And when they rose at morning she could see
That all his hopes were gone. That day at noon
She said to Luke, while they two by themselves   300
Were sitting at the door, 'Thou must not go:

We have no other child but thee to lose,
None to remember—do not go away,
For if thou leave thy father he will die.'
305 The lad made answer with a jocund voice;
And Isabel, when she had told her fears,
Recovered heart. That evening her best fare
Did she bring forth, and all together sat
Like happy people round a Christmas fire.

310 Next morning Isabel resumed her work;
And all the ensuing week the house appeared
As cheerful as a grove in spring; at length
The expected letter from their kinsman came,
With kind assurances that he would do
315 His utmost for the welfare of the boy;
To which requests were added that forthwith
He might be sent to him. Ten times or more
The letter was read over; Isabel
Went forth to show it to the neighbours round;
320 Nor was there at that time on English land
A prouder heart than Luke's. When Isabel
Had to her house returned, the old man said,
'He shall depart tomorrow.' To this word
The housewife answered, talking much of things
325 Which if at such short notice he should go
Would surely be forgotten. But at length
She gave consent, and Michael was at ease.

Near the tumultuous brook of Green-head Gill,
In that deep valley, Michael had designed
330 To build a sheep-fold; and, before he heard
The tidings of his melancholy loss,
For this same purpose he had gathered up
A heap of stones, which close to the brook side
Lay thrown together, ready for the work.
335 With Luke that evening thitherward he walked;
And soon as they had reached the place he stopped,
And thus the old man spake to him: 'My son,
Tomorrow thou wilt leave me: with full heart
I look upon thee, for thou art the same
340 That wert a promise to me ere thy birth,
And all thy life hast been my daily joy.
I will relate to thee some little part
Of our two histories; 'twill do thee good
When thou art from me, even if I should speak
345 Of things thou canst not know of. After thou
First cam'st into the world, as it befalls
To new-born infants, thou didst sleep away
Two days, and blessings from thy father's tongue
Then fell upon thee. Day by day passed on,
350 And still I loved thee with increasing love.
Never to living ear came sweeter sounds

76

Than when I heard thee by our own fireside
First uttering, without words, a natural tune:
When thou, a feeding babe, didst in thy joy
Sing at thy mother's breast. Month followed month,   355
And in the open fields my life was passed
And in the mountains, else I think that thou
Hadst been brought up upon thy father's knees.
But we were playmates, Luke: among these hills,
As well thou know'st, in us the old and young   360
Have played together, nor with me didst thou
Lack any pleasure which a boy can know.'
Luke had a manly heart; but at these words
He sobbed aloud. The old man grasped his hand,
And said, 'Nay, do not take it so—I see   365
That these are things of which I need not speak.
Even to the utmost I have been to thee
A kind and a good father: and herein
I but repay a gift which I myself
Received at others' hands; for, though now old   370
Beyond the common life of man, I still
Remember them who loved me in my youth.
Both of them sleep together: here they lived,
As all their forefathers had done; and when
At length their time was come, they were not loth   375
To give their bodies to the family mould.
I wished that thou shouldst live the life they lived.
But 'tis a long time to look back, my son,
And see so little gain from sixty years.
These fields were burthened when they came to me;   380
Till I was forty years of age, not more
Than half of my inheritance was mine.
I toiled and toiled; God blessed me in my work,
And till these three weeks past the land was free.
—It looks as if it never could endure   385
Another master. Heaven forgive me, Luke,
If I judge ill for thee, but it seems good
That thou shouldst go.' At this the old man paused;
Then, pointing to the stones near which they stood,
Thus, after a short silence, he resumed: 390
'This was a work for us; and now, my son,
It is a work for me. But, lay one stone—
Here, lay it for me, Luke, with thine own hands.
Nay, boy, be of good hope—we both may live
To see a better day. At eighty-four   395
I still am strong and stout; do thou thy part,
I will do mine. I will begin again
With many tasks that were resigned to thee;
Up to the heights, and in among the storms,
Will I without thee go again, and do   400
All works which I was wont to do alone
Before I knew thy face. Heaven bless thee, boy!
Thy heart these two weeks has been beating fast

With many hopes—it should be so—yes—yes—
405   I knew that thou couldst never have a wish
To leave me, Luke: thou hast been bound to me
Only by links of love: when thou art gone,
What will be left to us!—But I forget
My purposes. Lay now the corner-stone,
410   As I requested; and hereafter, Luke,
When thou art gone away, should evil men
Be thy companions, think of me, my son,
And of this moment; hither turn thy thoughts,
And God will strengthen thee; amid all fear
415   And all temptation, Luke, I pray that thou
May'st bear in mind the life thy fathers lived,
Who, being innocent, did for that cause
Bestir them in good deeds. Now, fare thee well—
When thou return'st, thou in this place will see
420   A work which is not here; a covenant
'Twill be between us. But whatever fate
Befall thee, I shall love thee to the last,
And bear thy memory with me to the grave.'

The shepherd ended here; and Luke stooped down,
425   And, as his father had requested, laid
The first stone of the sheep-fold. At the sight
The old man's grief broke from him, to his heart
He pressed his son, he kisséd him and wept;
And to the house together they returned.

430   Next morning, as had been resolved, the boy
Began his journey, and when he had reached
The public way, he put on a bold face;
And all the neighbours as he passed their doors
Came forth with wishes and with farewell prayers,
435   That followed him till he was out of sight.

A good report did from their kinsman come
Of Luke and his well-doing; and the boy
Wrote loving letters, full of wondrous news,
Which, as the housewife phrased it, were throughout
440   The prettiest letters that were ever seen.
Both parents read them with rejoicing hearts.
So, many months passed on: and once again
The shepherd went about his daily work
With confident and cheerful thoughts; and now
445   Sometimes when he could find a leisure hour
He to that valley took his way, and there
Wrought at the sheep-fold. Meantime Luke began
To slacken in his duty; and at length
He in the dissolute city gave himself
450   To evil courses: ignominy and shame
Fell on him, so that he was driven at last
To seek a hiding-place beyond the seas.

There is a comfort in the strength of love;
'Twill make a thing endurable, which else
Would break the heart: old Michael found it so.   455
I have conversed with more than one who well
Remember the old man, and what he was
Years after he had heard this heavy news.
His bodily frame had been from youth to age
Of an unusual strength. Among the rocks   460
He went, and still looked up upon the sun,
And listened to the wind; and as before
Performed all kinds of labour for his sheep,
And for the land his small inheritance.
And to that hollow dell from time to time   465
Did he repair, to build the fold of which
His flock had need. 'Tis not forgotten yet
The pity which was then in every heart
For the old man—and 'tis believed by all
That many and many a day he thither went,   470
And never lifted up a single stone.

There, by the sheep-fold, sometimes was he seen
Sitting alone, with that his faithful dog,
Then old, beside him, lying at his feet.
The length of full seven years from time to time   475
He at the building of this sheep-fold wrought,
And left the work unfinished when he died.
Three years, or little more, did Isabel
Survive her husband; at her death the estate
Was sold, and went into a stranger's hand.   480
The cottage which was named THE EVENING STAR
Is gone—the ploughshare has been through the
     ground
On which it stood; great changes have been wrought
In all the neighbourhood: yet the oak is left
That grew beside their door; and the remains   485
Of the unfinished sheep-fold may be seen
Beside the boisterous brook of Green-head Gill.

LOVE

All thoughts, all passions, all delights,
Whatever stirs this mortal frame,
All are but ministers of Love,
     And feed his sacred flame.

Oft in my waking dreams do I
Live o'er again that happy hour,
When midway on the mount I lay
    Beside the ruined tower.

The moonshine stealing o'er the scene
Had blended with the lights of eve;
And she was there, my hope, my joy,
    My own dear Genevieve!

She leaned against the arméd man,
The statue of the arméd knight;
She stood and listened to my harp
    Amid the lingering light.

Few sorrows hath she of her own,
My hope, my joy, my Genevieve!
She loves me best whene'er I sing
    The songs that make her grieve.

I played a soft and doleful air,
I sang an old and moving story—
An old rude song that fitted well
    The ruin wild and hoary.

She listened with a flitting blush,
With downcast eyes and modest grace;
For well she knew, I could not choose
    But gaze upon her face.

I told her of the knight that wore
Upon his shield a burning brand;
And that for ten long years he wooed
    The lady of the land.

I told her how he pined: and ah!
The low, the deep, the pleading tone
With which I sang another's love
    Interpreted my own.

She listened with a flitting blush,
With downcast eyes and modest grace;
And she forgave me, that I gazed
    Too fondly on her face!

But when I told the cruel scorn
Which crazed this bold and lovely knight,
And that he crossed the mountain woods
    Nor rested day nor night;

That sometimes from the savage den,
And sometimes from the darksome shade,
And sometimes starting up at once
    In green and sunny glade,

There came, and looked him in the face,
An angel beautiful and bright;
And that he knew it was a fiend,
    This miserable knight!

And how, unknowing what he did,
He leapt amid a murderous band,
And saved from outrage worse than death
    The lady of the land;

And how she wept and clasped his knees,
And how she tended him in vain;
And ever strove to expiate
    The scorn that crazed his brain;

And that she nursed him in a cave;
And how his madness went away
When on the yellow forest leaves
    A dying man he lay;

His dying words—but when I reached
That tenderest strain of all the ditty,
My faltering voice and pausing harp
    Disturbed her soul with pity!

All impulses of soul and sense
Had thrilled my guileless Genevieve,
The music, and the doleful tale,
    The rich and balmy eve;

And hopes, and fears that kindle hope,
An undistinguishable throng!
And gentle wishes long subdued,
    Subdued and cherished long!

She wept with pity and delight,
She blushed with love and maiden shame;
And, like the murmur of a dream,
    I heard her breathe my name.

Her bosom heaved—she stepped aside;
As conscious of my look, she stepped—
Then suddenly with timorous eye
    She fled to me and wept.

She half enclosed me with her arms,
She pressed me with a meek embrace;
And bending back her head looked up,
    And gazed upon my face.

45

50

55

60

65

70

75

80

85

'Twas partly love, and partly fear,
And partly 'twas a bashful art
That I might rather feel than see
    The swelling of her heart.

I calmed her fears; and she was calm,
And told her love with virgin pride.
And so I won my Genevieve,
    My bright and beauteous bride!

90 (line 90)
95 (line 95)

'STRANGE FITS OF PASSION
I HAVE KNOWN'

Strange fits of passion I have known:
And I will dare to tell,
But in the lover's ear alone,
What once to me befell.

When she I loved was strong and gay
And like a rose in June,
I to her cottage bent my way,
Beneath the evening moon.

Upon the moon I fixed my eye,
All over the wide lea;
My horse trudged on—and we drew nigh
Those paths so dear to me.

And now we reached the orchard plot;
And, as we climbed the hill,
Towards the roof of Lucy's cot
The moon descended still.

In one of those sweet dreams I slept,
Kind Nature's gentlest boon!
And, all the while, my eyes I kept
On the descending moon.

My horse moved on; hoof after hoof
He raised, and never stopped:
When down behind the cottage roof
At once the planet dropped.

What fond and wayward thoughts will slide
Into a lover's head—
'O mercy!' to myself I cried,
'If Lucy should be dead!'

'SHE DWELT AMONG
TH' UNTRODDEN WAYS'

She dwelt among th' untrodden ways
    Beside the springs of Dove,
A maid whom there were none to praise,
    And very few to love.

A violet by a mossy stone   5
    Half-hidden from the eye!
—Fair as a star, when only one
    Is shining in the sky.

She lived unknown, and few could know
    When Lucy ceased to be;   10
But she is in her grave, and oh!
    The difference to me.

'A SLUMBER DID MY SPIRIT SEAL'

A slumber did my spirit seal;
    I had no human fears:
She seemed a thing that could not feel
    The touch of earthly years.

No motion has she now, no force;   5
    She neither hears nor sees,
Rolled round in earth's diurnal course
    With rocks and stones and trees.

'THREE YEARS SHE GREW IN SUN
AND SHOWER'

Three years she grew in sun and shower,
Then Nature said, 'A lovelier flower
On earth was never sown;
This child I to myself will take;
She shall be mine, and I will make   5
A lady of my own.

'Myself will to my darling be
Both law and impulse; and with me
The girl, in rock and plain,
In earth and heaven, in glade and bower,   10
Shall feel an overseeing power
To kindle or restrain.

'She shall be sportive as the fawn
That wild with glee across the lawn

15   Or up the mountain springs;
And hers shall be the breathing balm,
And hers the silence and the calm
Of mute insensate things.

'The floating clouds their state shall lend
20   To her; for her the willow bend;
Nor shall she fail to see
Even in the motions of the storm
Grace that shall mould the maiden's form
By silent sympathy.

25   'The stars of midnight shall be dear
To her; and she shall lean her ear
In many a secret place
Where rivulets dance their wayward round,
And beauty born of murmuring sound
30   Shall pass into her face.

'And vital feelings of delight
Shall rear her form to stately height,
Her virgin bosom swell;
Such thoughts to Lucy I will give
35   While she and I together live
Here in this happy dell.'

Thus Nature spake. The work was done—
How soon my Lucy's race was run!
She died, and left to me
40   This heath, this calm and quiet scene;
The memory of what has been,
And never more will be.

LINES

WRITTEN A FEW MILES ABOVE TINTERN ABBEY, ON
REVISITING THE BANKS OF THE WYE DURING A TOUR.
JULY 13, 1798.

Five years have passed; five summers, with the length
Of five long winters! and again I hear
These waters, rolling from their mountain-springs
With a sweet inland murmur. Once again
5   Do I behold these steep and lofty cliffs,
Which on a wild secluded scene impress
Thoughts of more deep seclusion ; and connect
The landscape with the quiet of the sky.
The day is come when I again repose
10   Here, under this dark sycamore, and view
These plots of cottage-ground, these orchard-tufts,

Which, at this season, with their unripe fruits,
Are clad in one green hue, and lose themselves
Among the woods and copses, nor disturb
The wild green landscape. Once again I see   15
These hedge-rows—hardly hedge-rows, little lines
Of sportive wood run wild; these pastoral farms
Green to the very door; and wreaths of smoke
Sent up, in silence, from among the trees,
With some uncertain notice, as might seem,   20
Of vagrant dwellers in the houseless woods,
Or of some hermit's cave, where by his fire
The hermit sits alone.

                              Though absent long,
These forms of beauty have not been to me
As is a landscape to a blind man's eye;   25
But oft, in lonely rooms, and 'mid the din
Of towns and cities, I have owed to them,
In hours of weariness, sensations sweet,
Felt in the blood, and felt along the heart,
And passing even into my purer mind   30
With tranquil restoration:—feelings too
Of unremembered pleasure: such, perhaps,
As may have had no trivial influence
On that best portion of a good man's life,
His little, nameless, unremembered acts   35
Of kindness and of love. Nor less, I trust,
To them I may have owed another gift,
Of aspect more sublime: that blessed mood
In which the burthen of the mystery,
In which the heavy and the weary weight   40
Of all this unintelligible world
Is lightened; that serene and blessed mood
In which the affections gently lead us on
Until, the breath of this corporeal frame
And even the motion of our human blood   45
Almost suspended, we are laid asleep
In body, and become a living soul;
While with an eye made quiet by the power
Of harmony, and the deep power of joy,
We see into the life of things.   50

                              If this
Be but a vain belief, yet, oh! how oft,
In darkness, and amid the many shapes
Of joyless daylight; when the fretful stir
Unprofitable, and the fever of the world,
Have hung upon the beatings of my heart,   55
How oft, in spirit, have I turned to thee,
O sylvan Wye! Thou wanderer through the woods,
How often has my spirit turned to thee!

And now, with gleams of half-extinguished thought,
With many recognitions dim and faint,
And somewhat of a sad perplexity,
The picture of the mind revives again:
While here I stand, not only with the sense
Of present pleasure, but with pleasing thoughts
That in this moment there is life and food
For future years. And so I dare to hope,
Though changed, no doubt, from what I was when first
I came among these hills: when like a roe
I bounded o'er the mountains, by the sides
Of the deep rivers, and the lonely streams,
Wherever nature led; more like a man
Flying from something that he dreads, than one
Who sought the thing he loved. For nature then
(The coarser pleasures of my boyish days
And their glad animal movements all gone by)
To me was all in all.—I cannot paint
What then I was. The sounding cataract
Haunted me like a passion; the tall rock,
The mountain, and the deep and gloomy wood,
Their colours and their forms, were then to me
An appetite: a feeling and a love,
That had no need of a remoter charm
By thought supplied, or any interest
Unborrowed from the eye.—That time is past,
And all its aching joys are now no more,
And all its dizzy raptures. Not for this
Faint I, nor mourn nor murmur; other gifts
Have followed, for such loss, I would believe,
Abundant recompense. For I have learned
To look on nature, not as in the hour
Of thoughtless youth, but hearing oftentimes
The still, sad music of humanity,
Nor harsh nor grating, though of ample power
To chasten and subdue. And I have felt
A presence that disturbs me with the joy
Of elevated thoughts: a sense sublime
Of something far more deeply interfused,
Whose dwelling is the light of setting suns,
And the round ocean and the living air,
And the blue sky, and in the mind of man;
A motion and a spirit, that impels
All thinking things, all objects of all thought,
And rolls through all things.—Therefore am I still
A lover of the meadows and the woods
And mountains; and of all that we behold
From this green earth; of all the mighty world
Of eye and ear, both what they half create
And what perceive; well pleased to recognise
In nature and the language of the sense
The anchor of my purest thoughts, the nurse,

The guide, the guardian of my heart, and soul
Of all my moral being.

          Nor, perchance,
If I were not thus taught, should I the more
Suffer my genial spirits to decay:
For thou art with me, here, upon the banks   115
Of this fair river; thou, my dearest friend,
My dear, dear friend, and in thy voice I catch
The language of my former heart, and read
My former pleasures in the shooting lights
Of thy wild eyes. Oh! yet a little while   120
May I behold in thee what I was once,
My dear, dear sister! And this prayer I make,
Knowing that Nature never did betray
The heart that loved her; 'tis her privilege,
Through all the years of this our life, to lead   125
From joy to joy: for she can so inform
The mind that is within us, so impress
With quietness and beauty, and so feed
With lofty thoughts, that neither evil tongues,
Rash judgments, nor the sneers of selfish men,   130
Nor greetings where no kindness is, nor all
The dreary intercourse of daily life,
Shall e'er prevail against us, or disturb
Our cheerful faith that all which we behold
Is full of blessings. Therefore let the moon   135
Shine on thee in thy solitary walk;
And let the misty mountain winds be free
To blow against thee: and, in after years,
When these wild ecstasies shall be matured
Into a sober pleasure, when thy mind   140
Shall be a mansion for all lovely forms,
Thy memory be as a dwelling-place
For all sweet sounds and harmonies; oh! then,
If solitude, or fear, or pain, or grief
Should be thy portion, with what healing thoughts   145
Of tender joy wilt thou remember me,
And these my exhortations! Nor, perchance,
If I should be where I no more can hear
Thy voice, nor catch from thy wild eyes these gleams
Of past existence, wilt thou then forget   150
That on the banks of this delightful stream
We stood together; and that I, so long
A worshipper of Nature, hither came
Unwearied in that service: rather say
With warmer love, oh! with far deeper zeal   155
Of holier love. Nor wilt thou then forget
That after many wanderings, many years
Of absence, these steep woods and lofty cliffs,
And this green pastoral landscape, were to me
More dear, both for themselves and for thy sake.   160

GOODY BLAKE AND HARRY GILL

A TRUE STORY

Oh! what's the matter? what's the matter?
What is't that ails young Harry Gill?
That evermore his teeth they chatter,
Chatter, chatter, chatter still.
5   Of waistcoats Harry has no lack,
Good duffle grey, and flannel fine;
He has a blanket on his back,
And coats enough to smother nine.

In March, December, and in July,
10   'Tis all the same with Harry Gill;
The neighbours tell, and tell you truly,
His teeth they chatter, chatter still.
At night, at morning, and at noon,
'Tis all the same with Harry Gill;
15   Beneath the sun, beneath the moon,
His teeth they chatter, chatter still.

Young Harry was a lusty drover,
And who so stout of limb as he?
His cheeks were red as ruddy clover;
20   His voice was like the voice of three.
Old Goody Blake was old and poor;
Ill fed she was, and thinly clad;
And any man who passed her door
Might see how poor a hut she had.

25   All day she spun in her poor dwelling;
And then her three hours' work at night!
Alas! 'twas hardly worth the telling,
It would not pay for candle-light.
This woman dwelt in Dorsetshire,
30   Her hut was on a cold hill-side,
And in that country coals are dear,
For they come far by wind and tide.

By the same fire to boil their pottage,
Two poor old dames, as I have known,
35   Will often live in one small cottage;
But she, poor woman! dwelt alone.
'Twas well enough when summer came,
The long, warm, lightsome summer-day,
Then at her door the canty dame
40   Would sit, as any linnet gay.

But when the ice our streams did fetter,
Oh! then how her old bones would shake!
You would have said if you had met her
'Twas a hard time for Goody Blake.
45   Her evenings then were dull and dead;
Sad case it was, as you may think,
For very cold to go to bed;
And then for cold not sleep a wink.

Oh joy for her! whene'er in winter
The winds at night had made a rout,   50
And scattered many a lusty splinter
And many a rotten bough about.
Yet never had she, well or sick,
As every man who knew her says,
A pile beforehand, wood or stick,   55
Enough to warm her for three days.

Now, when the frost was past enduring,
And made her poor old bones to ache,
Could any thing be more alluring
Than an old hedge to Goody Blake?   60
And now and then, it must be said,
When her old bones were cold and chill,
She left her fire, or left her bed,
To seek the hedge of Harry Gill.

Now Harry he had long suspected   65
This trespass of old Goody Blake;
And vowed that she should be detected,
And he on her would vengeance take.
And oft from his warm fire he'd go,
And to the fields his road would take;   70
And there, at night, in frost and snow,
He watched to seize old Goody Blake.

And once, behind a rick of barley,
Thus looking out did Harry stand:
The moon was full and shining clearly,   75
And crisp with frost the stubble land.
He hears a noise—he's all awake—
Again?—on tip-toe down the hill
He softly creeps—'tis Goody Blake,
She's at the hedge of Harry Gill.   80

Right glad was he when he beheld her:
Stick after stick did Goody pull:
He stood behind a bush of elder,
Till she had filled her apron full.
When with her load she turned about,   85
The bye-road back again to take,
He started forward with a shout,
And sprang upon poor Goody Blake.

And fiercely by the arm he took her,
And by the arm he held her fast,   90
And fiercely by the arm he shook her,
And cried, 'I've caught you then at last!'
Then Goody, who had nothing said,
Her bundle from her lap let fall;
And, kneeling on the sticks, she prayed   95
To God that is the judge of all.

She prayed, her withered hand uprearing,
While Harry held her by the arm—
'God! who art never out of hearing,
O may he never more be warm!'
The cold, cold moon above her head,
Thus on her knees did Goody pray.
Young Harry heard what she had said,
And icy cold he turned away.

He went complaining all the morrow
That he was cold and very chill:
His face was gloom, his heart was sorrow,
Alas! that day for Harry Gill!
That day he wore a riding-coat,
But not a whit the warmer he:
Another was on Thursday brought,
And ere the Sabbath he had three.

'Twas all in vain, a useless matter,
And blankets were about him pinned;
Yet still his jaws and teeth they clatter,
Like a loose casement in the wind.
And Harry's flesh it fell away;
And all who see him say, 'tis plain
That live as long as live he may,
He never will be warm again.

No word to any man he utters,
Abed or up, to young or old;
But ever to himself he mutters,
'Poor Harry Gill is very cold.'
Abed or up, by night or day;
His teeth they chatter, chatter still.
Now think, ye farmers all, I pray,
Of Goody Blake and Harry Gill.

100

105

110

115

120

125

SIMON LEE, THE OLD HUNTSMAN,

WITH AN INCIDENT IN WHICH
HE WAS CONCERNED.

In the sweet shire of Cardigan,
Not far from pleasant Ivor Hall,
An old man dwells, a little man,
I've heard he once was tall.
Of years he has upon his back,
No doubt, a burthen weighty;

5

He says he is threescore and ten,
But others say he's eighty.

A long blue livery-coat has he,
That's fair behind, and fair before;   10
Yet meet him where you will, you see
At once that he is poor.
Full five-and-twenty years he lived
A running huntsman merry;
And though he has but one eye left,   15
His cheek is like a cherry.

No man like him the horn could sound,
And no man was so full of glee;
To say the least, four counties round
Had heard of Simon Lee: 20
His master's dead, and no one now
Dwells in the Hall of Ivor;
Men, dogs, and horses, all are dead;
He is the sole survivor.

And he is lean and he is sick,   25
His dwindled body's half awry;
His ankles they are swollen and thick;
His legs are thin and dry.
When he was young he little knew
Of husbandry or tillage;   30
And now he's forced to work, though weak,
—The weakest in the village.

He all the country could outrun,
Could leave both man and horse behind;
And often, ere the race was done,   35
He reeled and was stone-blind.
And still there's something in the world
At which his heart rejoices;
For when the chiming hounds are out,
He dearly loves their voices!   40

His hunting feats have him bereft
Of his right eye, as you may see:
And then, what limbs those feats have left
To poor old Simon Lee!
He has no son, he has no child,   45
His wife, an aged woman,
Lives with him near the waterfall,
Upon the village common.

Old Ruth works out of doors with him,
And does what Simon cannot do;   50
For she, not over-stout of limb,

Is stouter of the two.
And though you with your utmost skill
From labour could not wean them,
55   Alas! 'tis very little, all
Which they can do between them.

Beside their moss-grown hut of clay,
Not twenty paces from the door,
A scrap of land they have, but they
60   Are poorest of the poor.
This scrap of land he from the heath
Enclosed when he was stronger;
But what avails the land to them,
Which they can till no longer?

65   Few months of life has he in store,
As he to you will tell,
For still, the more he works, the more
His poor old ankles swell.
My gentle reader, I perceive
70   How patiently you've waited,
And I'm afraid that you expect
Some tale will be related.

O reader! had you in your mind
Such stores as silent thought can bring,
75   O gentle reader! you would find
A tale in everything.
What more I have to say is short,
I hope you'll kindly take it:
It is no tale; but, should you think,
80   Perhaps a tale you'll make it.

One summer day I chanced to see
This old man doing all he could
About the root of an old tree,
A stump of rotten wood.
85   The mattock tottered in his hand;
So vain was his endeavour
That at the root of the old tree
He might have worked for ever.

'You're overtasked, good Simon Lee,
90   Give me your tool,' to him I said;
And at the word right gladly he
Received my proffered aid.
I struck, and with a single blow
The tangled root I severed,
95   At which the poor old man so long
And vainly had endeavoured.

The tears into his eyes were brought,
And thanks and praises seemed to run
So fast out of his heart, I thought
They never would have done. 100
—I've heard of hearts unkind, kind deeds
With coldness still returning.
Alas! the gratitude of men
Has oftener left me mourning.

LINES

LEFT UPON A SEAT IN A YEW-TREE, WHICH STANDS NEAR
THE LAKE OF ESTHWAITE, ON A DESOLATE PART OF THE
SHORE, YET COMMANDING A BEAUTIFUL PROSPECT.

Nay, traveller! rest. This lonely yew-tree stands
Far from all human dwelling: what if here
No sparkling rivulet spread the verdant herb?
What if these barren boughs the bee not loves?
Yet, if the wind breathe soft, the curling waves, 5
That break against the shore, shall lull thy mind
By one soft impulse saved from vacancy.

                              Who he was
That piled these stones, and with the mossy sod
First covered o'er, and taught this aged tree 10
With its dark arms to form a circling bower,
I well remember. He was one who owned
No common soul. In youth by science nursed,
And led by nature into a wild scene
Of lofty hopes, he to the world went forth 15
A favoured being, knowing no desire
Which genius did not hallow, 'gainst the taint
Of dissolute tongues, and jealousy, and hate,
And scorn, against all enemies prepared,
All but neglect. The world, for so it thought, 20
Owed him no service: wherefore he at once
With indignation turned himself away,
And with the food of pride sustained his soul
In solitude. — Stranger! these gloomy boughs
Had charms for him; and here he loved to sit, 25
His only visitants a straggling sheep,
The stone-chat, or the glancing sand-piper;
And on these barren rocks, with juniper
And heath and thistle thinly sprinkled o'er,
Fixing his down-cast eye, he many an hour 30
A morbid pleasure nourished, tracing here
An emblem of his own unfruitful life;
And lifting up his head, he then would gaze
On the more distant scene—how lovely 'tis
Thou seest—and he would gaze till it became 35

Far lovelier, and his heart could not sustain
The beauty still more beauteous. Nor, that time,
When Nature had subdued him to herself,
Would he forget those beings to whose minds,
40 Warm from the labours of benevolence,
The world, and man himself, appeared a scene
Of kindred loveliness: then he would sigh
With mournful joy, to think that others felt
What he must never feel: and so, lost man!
45 On visionary views would fancy feed,
Till his eye streamed with tears. In this deep vale
He died,—this seat his only monument.

If thou be one whose heart the holy forms
Of young imagination have kept pure,
50 Stranger! henceforth be warned; and know that pride,
Howe'er disguised in its own majesty,
Is littleness; that he who feels contempt
For any living thing, hath faculties
Which he has never used; that thought with him
55 Is in its infancy. The man whose eye
Is ever on himself doth look on one,
The least of nature's works, one who might move
The wise man to that scorn which wisdom holds
Unlawful, ever. O be wiser, thou!
60 Instructed that true knowledge leads to love,
True dignity abides with him alone
Who, in the silent hour of inward thought,
Can still suspect, and still revere himself,
In lowliness of heart.

THE FEMALE VAGRANT

My father was a good and pious man,
An honest man by honest parents bred;
And I believe that soon as I began
To lisp, he made me kneel beside my bed,
5 And in his hearing there my prayers I said:
And afterwards, by my good father taught,
I read, and loved the books in which I read;
For books in every neighbouring house I sought,
And nothing to my mind a sweeter pleasure brought.

10 The suns of twenty summers danced along,—
Ah! little marked how fast they rolled away:
Then rose a stately hall our woods among,
And cottage after cottage owned its sway.
No joy to see a neighbouring house, or stray

Through pastures not his own, the master took;   15
My father dared his greedy wish gainsay:
He loved his old hereditary nook,
And ill could I the thought of such sad parting brook.

But when he had refused the proffered gold,
To cruel injuries he became a prey,   20
Sore traversed in whate'er he bought and sold:
His troubles grew upon him day by day,
And all his substance fell into decay.
They dealt most hardly with him, and he tried
To move their hearts—but it was vain—for they   25
Seized all he had; and, weeping side by side,
We sought a home where we uninjured might abide.

It was in truth a lamentable hour,
When from the last hill-top my sire surveyed,
Peering above the trees, the steeple tower   30
That on his marriage-day sweet music made.
Till then he hoped his bones might there be laid,
Close by my mother, in their native bowers;
Bidding me trust in God, he stood and prayed,—
I could not pray: through tears that fell in showers   35
I saw our own dear home, that was no longer ours.

There was a youth, whom I had loved so long
That when I loved him not I cannot say.
'Mid the green mountains many and many a song
We two had sung, like gladsome birds in May.   40
When we began to tire of childish play
We seemed still more and more to prize each other;
We talked of marriage and our marriage-day;
And I in truth did love him like a brother;
For never could I hope to meet with such another.   45

Two years were passed, since to a distant town
He had repaired to ply the artist's trade.
What tears of bitter grief till then unknown!
What tender vows our last sad kiss delayed!
To him we turned: we had no other aid.   50
Like one revived, upon his neck I wept;
And her whom he had loved in joy, he said
He well could love in grief: his faith he kept;
And in a quiet home once more my father slept.

We lived in peace and comfort; and were blest   55
With daily bread, by constant toil supplied.
Three lovely infants lay upon my breast;
And often, viewing their sweet smiles, I sighed,
And knew not why. My happy father died
When sad distress reduced the children's meal: 60
Thrice happy! that from him the grave did hide

The empty loom, cold hearth, and silent wheel,
And tears that flowed for ills which patience could
      not heal.
'Twas a hard change, an evil time was come;
65   We had no hope, and no relief could gain.
But soon, day after day, the noisy drum
Beat round, to sweep the streets of want and pain.
My husband's arms now only served to strain
Me and his children hungering in his view;
70   In such dismay my prayers and tears were vain:
To join those miserable men he flew;
And now to the sea-coast, with numbers more, we drew.

There, long were we neglected, and we bore
Much sorrow ere the fleet its anchor weighed;
75   Green fields before us and our native shore,
We breathed a pestilential air that made
Ravage for which no knell was heard. We prayed
For our departure; wished and wished—nor knew
'Mid that long sickness, and those hopes delayed,
80   That happier days we never more must view;
The parting signal streamed, at last the land withdrew.

But the calm summer season now was past.
On as we drove, the equinoctial deep
Ran mountains-high before the howling blast;
85   And many perished in the whirlwind's sweep.
We gazed with terror on their gloomy sleep,
Untaught that soon such anguish must ensue,
Our hopes such harvest of affliction reap,
That we the mercy of the waves should rue.
90   We reached the western world, a poor, devoted crew.

The pains and plagues that on our heads came down,
Disease and famine, agony and fear,
In wood or wilderness, in camp or town,
It would thy brain unsettle, even to hear.
95   All perished: all, in one remorseless year,
Husband and children! one by one, by sword
And ravenous plague, all perished: every tear
Dried up, despairing, desolate, on board
A British ship I waked, as from a trance restored.

100   Peaceful as some immeasurable plain
By the first beams of dawning light impressed,
In the calm sunshine slept the glittering main.
The very ocean has its hour of rest.
I too was calm, though heavily distressed;
105   Oh me, how quiet sky and ocean were!
My heart was healed within me, I was blest
And looked, and looked along the silent air,

Until it seemed to bring a joy to my despair.

Ah! how unlike those late terrific sleeps!
And groans, that rage of racking famine spoke;   110
The unburied dead that lay in festering heaps;
The breathing pestilence that rose like smoke;
The shriek that from the distant battle broke;
The mine's dire earthquake, and the pallid host
Driven by the bomb's incessant thunder-stroke   115
To loathsome vaults, where heart-sick anguish tossed,
Hope died, and fear itself in agony was lost!

At midnight once the storming army came;
Yet do I see the miserable sight,
The bayonet, the soldier, and the flame   120
That followed us and faced us in our flight;
When Rape and Murder by the ghastly light
Seized their joint prey, the mother and the child!
But I must leave these thoughts. From night to night,
From day to day, the air breathed soft and mild;   125
And on the gliding vessel Heaven and Ocean smiled.

Some mighty gulf of separation past,
I seemed transported to another world:—
A thought resigned with pain, when from the mast
The impatient mariner the sail unfurled,   130
And, whistling, called the wind that hardly curled
The silent sea. From the sweet thoughts of home
And from all hope I was for ever hurled.
For me—farthest from earthly port to roam
Was best, could I but shun the spot where man might
    come.   135

And oft I thought (my fancy was so strong)
That I at last a resting-place had found;
'Here will I dwell,' said I, 'my whole life long,
Roaming the illimitable waters round;
Here will I live—of every friend disowned,   140
Here will I roam about the ocean flood.'
To break my dream the vessel reached its bound:
And homeless near a thousand homes I stood,
And near a thousand tables pined, and wanted food.

By grief enfeebled was I turned adrift,   145
Helpless as sailor cast on desert rock;
Nor morsel to my mouth that day did lift,
Nor dared my hand at any door to knock.
I lay where, with his drowsy mates, the cock
From the cross-timber of an out-house hung;   150
Dismally tolled, that night, the city clock!

At morn my sick heart hunger scarcely stung,
Nor to the beggar's language could I frame my tongue.

So passed another day, and so the third;
155   Then did I try in vain the crowd's resort.
—In deep despair by frightful wishes stirred,
Near the sea-side I reached a ruined fort:
There, pains which nature could no more support,
With blindness linked, did on my vitals fall,
160   And I had many interruptions short
Of hideous sense; I sank, nor step could crawl,
And thence was carried to a neighbouring hospital.

Recovery came with food; but still my brain
Was weak, nor of the past had memory.
165   I heard my neighbours in their beds complain
Of many things which never troubled me:
Of feet still bustling round with busy glee;
Of looks where common kindness had no part;
Of service done with careless cruelty,
170   Fretting the fever round the languid heart;
And groans which, as they said, would make a dead man
          start.

These things just served to stir the torpid sense,
Nor pain nor pity in my bosom raised.
My memory and my strength returned; and thence
175   Dismissed, again on open day I gazed,
At houses, men, and common light amazed.
The lanes I sought, and, as the sun retired,
Came where beneath the trees a faggot blazed;
The travellers saw me weep, my fate enquired,
And gave me food—and rest, more welcome, more
180   desired.

My heart is touched to think that men like these,
Wild houseless wanderers, were my first relief:
How kindly did they paint their vagrant ease,
And their long holiday that feared not grief!
185   For all belonged to all, and each was chief.
No plough their sinews strained; on grating road
No wain they drove; and yet the yellow sheaf
In every vale for their delight was stowed;
In every field with milk their dairy overflowed.

They with their panniered asses semblance made
190   Of potters wandering on from door to door:
But life of happier sort to me portrayed,
And other joys my fancy to allure;
The bagpipe dinning on the midnight moor
195   In barn uplighted, and companions boon

Well met from far with revelry secure
Among the forest glades, when jocund June
Rolled fast along the sky his warm and genial moon.

But ill they suited me: those journeys dark
O'er moor and mountain, midnight theft to hatch!   200
To charm the surly house-dog's faithful bark,
Or hang on tip-toe at the lifted latch;
The gloomy lantern and the dim blue match,
The black disguise, the warning whistle shrill,
And ear still busy on its nightly watch   205
Were not for me, brought up in nothing ill:
Besides, on griefs so fresh my thoughts were brooding
        still.

What could I do, unaided and unblest?
My father! gone was every friend of thine;
And kindred of dead husband are at best   210
Small help; and after marriage such as mine
With little kindness would to me incline.
Ill was I then for toil or service fit:
With tears whose course no effort could confine,
By the road-side forgetful would I sit   215
Whole hours, my idle arms in moping sorrow knit.

I led a wandering life among the fields;
Contentedly, yet sometimes self-accused,
I lived upon what casual bounty yields,
Now coldly given, now utterly refused.   220
The ground I for my bed have often used:
But what afflicts my peace with keenest ruth
Is that I have my inner self abused,
Forgone the home delight of constant truth,
And clear and open soul, so prized in fearless youth.   225

Three years thus wandering, often have I viewed,
In tears, the sun towards that country tend
Where my poor heart lost all its fortitude:
And now across this moor my steps I bend—
Oh! tell me whither; for no earthly friend   230
Have I.—She ceased, and weeping turned away,
As if because her tale was at an end
She wept; because she had no more to say
Of that perpetual weight which on her spirit lay.

LINES

WRITTEN AT A SMALL DISTANCE FROM MY HOUSE,
AND SENT BY MY LITTLE BOY TO THE PERSON TO
WHOM THEY ARE ADDRESSED.

It is the first mild day of March:
Each minute sweeter than before,
The redbreast sings from the tall larch
That stands beside our door.

5   There is a blessing in the air,
Which seems a sense of joy to yield
To the bare trees, and mountains bare,
And grass in the green field.

My sister! ('tis a wish of mine)
10   Now that our morning meal is done,
Make haste, your morning task resign;
Come forth and feel the sun.

Edward will come with you; and pray,
Put on with speed your woodland dress,
15   And bring no book: for this one day
We'll give to idleness.

No joyless forms shall regulate
Our living calendar:
We from today, my friend, will date
20   The opening of the year.

Love, now an universal birth,
From heart to heart is stealing,
From earth to man, from man to earth:
It is the hour of feeling.

25   One moment now may give us more
Than fifty years of reason:
Our minds shall drink at every pore
The spirit of the season.

Some silent laws our hearts may make,
30   Which they shall long obey:
We for the year to come may take
Our temper from today.

And from the blessed power that rolls
About, below, above,
35   We'll frame the measure of our souls:
They shall be tuned to love.

Then come, my sister! come, I pray,
With speed put on your woodland dress;
And bring no book: for this one day
40   We'll give to idleness.

THE FOSTER-MOTHER'S TALE

A NARRATION IN DRAMATIC BLANK VERSE

MARIA

But that entrance, mother!

FOSTER-MOTHER

Can no one hear? It is a perilous tale!

MARIA

No one.

FOSTER-MOTHER

My husband's father told it me,
Poor old Leoni! Angels rest his soul!
He was a woodman, and could fell and saw   5
With lusty arm. You know that huge round beam
Which props the hanging wall of the old chapel;
Beneath that tree, while yet it was a tree,
He found a baby wrapped in mosses lined
With thistle-beards, and such small locks of wool   10
As hang on brambles. Well, he brought him home,
And reared him at the then Lord Velez's cost.
And so the babe grew up a pretty boy,
A pretty boy, but most unteachable;
And never learnt a prayer, nor told a bead,   15
But knew the names of birds, and mocked their notes,
And whistled, as he were a bird himself:
And all the autumn 'twas his only play
To gather seeds of wild flowers, and to plant them
With earth and water on the stumps of trees.   20
A friar, who sought for simples in the wood,
A grey-haired man, he loved this little boy,
The boy loved him; and when the friar taught him
He soon could write with the pen; and from that time
Lived chiefly at the convent or the castle.   25
So he became a very learned youth.
But, oh! poor wretch, he read, and read, and read,
Till his brain turned; and ere his twentieth year
He had unlawful thoughts of many things:
And though he prayed, he never loved to pray   30
With holy men, nor in a holy place;
But yet his speech, it was so soft and sweet,
The late Lord Velez ne'er was wearied with him.
And once, as by the north side of the chapel
They stood together, chained in deep discourse,   35
The earth heaved under them with such a groan
That the wall tottered, and had well-nigh fallen
Right on their heads. My lord was sorely frightened;
A fever seized him, and he made confession
Of all the heretical and lawless talk   40
Which brought this judgment: so the youth was
    seized
And cast into that cell. My husband's father

Sobbed like a child—it almost broke his heart;
And once as he was working near the cell
45 He heard a voice distinctly: 'twas the youth's,
Who sang a doleful song about green fields,
How sweet it were on lake or wild savannah
To hunt for food, and be a naked man,
And wander up and down at liberty.
50 Leoni doted on the youth, and now
His love grew desperate; and defying death,
He made that cunning entrance I described:
And the young man escaped.

MARIA
'Tis a sweet tale.
And what became of him?

FOSTER-MOTHER
He went on ship-board,
55 With those bold voyagers who made discovery
Of golden lands. Leoni's younger brother
Went likewise; and when he returned to Spain,
He told Leoni that the poor mad youth,
Soon after they arrived in that new world,
60 In spite of his dissuasion, seized a boat,
And, all alone, set sail by silent moonlight
Up a great river, great as any sea,
And ne'er was heard of more: but 'tis supposed
He lived and died among the savage men.

LINES WRITTEN IN EARLY SPRING

I heard a thousand blended notes,
While in a grove I sate reclined,
In that sweet mood when pleasant thoughts
Bring sad thoughts to the mind.

5 To her fair works did Nature link
The human soul that through me ran;
And much it grieved my heart to think
What man has made of man.

Through primrose tufts, in that sweet bower,
10 The periwinkle trailed its wreaths;
And 'tis my faith that every flower
Enjoys the air it breathes.

The birds around me hopped and played;
Their thoughts I cannot measure:
15 But the least motion which they made,

It seemed a thrill of pleasure.

The budding twigs spread out their fan,
To catch the breezy air;
And I must think, do all I can,
That there was pleasure there.   20

If I these thoughts may not prevent,
If such be of my creed the plan,
Have I not reason to lament
What man has made of man?

THE NIGHTINGALE

WRITTEN IN APRIL, 1798.

No cloud, no relic of the sunken day
Distinguishes the west, no long thin slip
Of sullen light, no obscure trembling hues.
Come, we will rest on this old mossy bridge!
You see the glimmer of the stream beneath,   5
But hear no murmuring: it flows silently
O'er its soft bed of verdure. All is still,
A balmy night! and though the stars be dim,
Yet let us think upon the vernal showers
That gladden the green earth, and we shall find   10
A pleasure in the dimness of the stars.
And hark! the nightingale begins its song,
'Most musical, most melancholy' bird!
A melancholy bird? O idle thought!
In nature there is nothing melancholy.   15
But some night-wandering man, whose heart was
        pierced
With the remembrance of a grievous wrong,
Or slow distemper, or neglected love,
(And so, poor wretch! filled all things with himself,
And made all gentle sounds tell back the tale   20
Of his own sorrows) he and such as he
First named these notes a melancholy strain;
And many a poet echoes the conceit:
Poet, who hath been building up the rhyme
When he had better far have stretched his limbs   25
Beside a brook in mossy forest-dell
By sun- or moon-light, to the influxes
Of shapes and sounds and shifting elements
Surrendering his whole spirit, of his song
And of his fame forgetful! so his fame   30
Should share in nature's immortality,
A venerable thing! and so his song
Should make all nature lovelier, and itself

Be loved, like nature!—But 'twill not be so;
35 And youths and maidens most poetical
Who lose the deep'ning twilights of the spring
In ballrooms and hot theatres, they still
Full of meek sympathy must heave their sighs
O'er Philomela's pity-pleading strains.

40 My friend, and my friend's sister! we have learnt
A different lore: we may not thus profane
Nature's sweet voices always full of love
And joyance! 'Tis the merry nightingale
That crowds, and hurries, and precipitates
45 With fast thick warble his delicious notes,
As he were fearful that an April night
Would be too short for him to utter forth
His love-chant, and disburthen his full soul
Of all its music! And I know a grove
50 Of large extent, hard by a castle huge
Which the great lord inhabits not: and so
This grove is wild with tangling underwood,
And the trim walks are broken up, and grass,
Thin grass and king-cups grow within the paths.
55 But never elsewhere in one place I knew
So many nightingales: and far and near
In wood and thicket over the wide grove
They answer and provoke each other's songs—
With skirmish and capricious passagings,
60 And murmurs musical and swift jug jug
And one low piping sound more sweet than all—
Stirring the air with such an harmony,
That should you close your eyes, you might almost
Forget it was not day.
                                    A most gentle maid
65 Who dwelleth in her hospitable home
Hard by the castle, and at latest eve
(Even like a lady vowed and dedicate
To something more than nature in the grove)
Glides through the pathways; she knows all their
        notes,
70 That gentle maid! and oft, a moment's space,
What time the moon was lost behind a cloud,
Hath heard a pause of silence: till the moon
Emerging, hath awakened earth and sky
With one sensation, and those wakeful birds
75 Have all burst forth with choral minstrelsy,
As if one quick and sudden gale had swept
An hundred airy harps! And she hath watched
Many a nightingale perch giddily
On blosmy twig still swinging from the breeze,
80 And to that motion tune his wanton song,
Like tipsy Joy that reels with tossing head.

Farewell, O warbler! till tomorrow eve,
And you, my friends! farewell, a short farewell!
We have been loitering long and pleasantly,
And now for our dear homes.—That strain again!   85
Full fain it would delay me! My dear babe,
Who, capable of no articulate sound,
Mars all things with his imitative lisp,
How he would place his hand beside his ear,
His little hand, the small forefinger up,   90
And bid us listen! And I deem it wise
To make him Nature's playmate. He knows well
The evening star; and once when he awoke
In most distressful mood (some inward pain
Had made up that strange thing, an infant's dream)   95
I hurried with him to our orchard plot,
And he beholds the moon, and hushed at once
Suspends his sobs, and laughs most silently,
While his fair eyes that swam with undropped tears
Did glitter in the yellow moonbeam! Well—   100
It is a father's tale. But if that Heaven
Should give me life, his childhood shall grow up
Familiar with these songs, that with the night
He may associate joy! Once more farewell,
Sweet nightingale! once more, my friends! farewell.   105

THE LAST OF THE FLOCK

In distant countries I have been,
And yet I have not often seen
A healthy man, a man full-grown,
Weep in the public roads alone.
But such a one, on English ground,   5
And in the broad high-way, I met;
Along the broad high-way he came,
His cheeks with tears were wet.
Sturdy he seemed, though he was sad;
And in his arms a lamb he had.   10

He saw me, and he turned aside,
As if he wished himself to hide;
Then with his coat he made essay
To wipe those briny tears away.
I followed him, and said, 'My friend,   15
What ails you? wherefore weep you so?'
'Shame on me, sir! this lusty lamb,
He makes my tears to flow.
Today I fetched him from the rock;
He is the last of all my flock.   20

'When I was young, a single man,
And after youthful follies ran,
Though little given to care and thought,
Yet so it was, a ewe I bought;
25   And other sheep from her I raised,
As healthy sheep as you might see;
And then I married, and was rich
As I could wish to be;
Of sheep I numbered a full score,
30   And every year increased my store.

'Year after year my stock it grew,
And from this one, this single ewe,
Full fifty comely sheep I raised,
As sweet a flock as ever grazed!
35   Upon the mountain did they feed,
They throve, and we at home did thrive.
—This lusty lamb of all my store
Is all that is alive;
And now I care not if we die,
40   And perish all of poverty.

'Six children, sir! had I to feed,
Hard labour in a time of need!
My pride was tamed, and in our grief
I of the parish asked relief.
45   They said I was a wealthy man;
My sheep upon the mountain fed,
And it was fit that thence I took
Whereof to buy us bread.
"Do this: how can we give to you,"
50   They cried, "what to the poor is due?"

'I sold a sheep, as they had said,
And bought my little children bread,
And they were healthy with their food;
For me—it never did me good.
55   A woeful time it was for me,
To see the end of all my gains,
The pretty flock which I had reared
With all my care and pains,
To see it melt like snow away!
60   For me it was a woeful day.

'Another still; and still another;
A little lamb, and then its mother.
It was a vein that never stopped:
Like blood-drops from my heart they dropped.
65   Till thirty were not left alive
They dwindled, dwindled, one by one,
And I may say that many a time
I wished they all were gone:
They dwindled one by one away;
70   For me it was a woeful day.

'To wicked deeds I was inclined,
And wicked fancies crossed my mind;
And every man I chanced to see
I thought he knew some ill of me.
No peace, no comfort could I find,   75
No ease, within doors or without,
And crazily, and wearily,
I went my work about.
Oft-times I thought to run away;
For me it was a woeful day.   80

'Sir! 'twas a precious flock to me,
As dear as my own children be;
For daily with my growing store
I loved my children more and more.
Alas! it was an evil time;   85
God cursed me in my sore distress;
I prayed, yet every day I thought
I loved my children less;
And every week, and every day,
My flock, it seemed to melt away.   90

'They dwindled, sir, sad sight to see!
From ten to five, from five to three,
A lamb, a wether, and a ewe;
And then, at last, from three to two;
And of my fifty, yesterday   95
I had but only one:
And here it lies upon my arm,
Alas! and I have none;
Today I fetched it from the rock;
It is the last of all my flock.'   100

NOTES

PREFACE TO LYRICAL BALLADS

1- 1 **The first volume of these poems** 1798年に初版として出された時は1巻物であった。その後1800年に再版された時に新たに第2巻が加えられた。

1 **submitted**＝presented.

5 **impart**＝bestow, give.

7 **I flattered myself** 「心ひそかに信じていた」

10 **The result** 1798年の初版の後、2巻本となった増補新版として1800年の再版（実際は1801年1月に出版されている）が出され、さらに1802年、1805年と再版を重ねていることは、当時の読者に与えたこの詩集に対する関心の深さを示すものである。

20 **approbation**＝approval.

22 **enforce**＝press home. 「（議論を）十分納得されるように説く」

30 **impropriety**＝unsuitableness.

36 **apprises**＝informs.

37 **exponent**＝indication, suggestion.

38 **held forth**＜hold forth＝offer.

39 **Catullus** ガーユス・ワレリウス・カトゥルス（Gaius Valerius）紀元前84-54年頃のローマの抒情詩人。

39 **Terence** プブリウス・テレンティウス・アーフェル（Publius Terentius Afer）紀元前195-159年頃のローマの喜劇作家。

40 **Lucretius** ティトゥス・ルクレーティウス・カールス（Titus Lucretius Carus）紀元前94-55年頃のローマの哲学者。彼の唯一の長編哲学詩『物の本質について』は6巻より成る大作で英文学にも大いに影響を与えた。

40 **Statius** ププリウス・パーピニウス・スターティウス（Publius Papinius Statius）紀元後45-96年頃のローマの詩人。

40 **Claudian** クラウディウス・クラウディアーヌス（Claudius Claudianus）4世紀から5世紀頃のローマの詩人。

41 **Shakespeare** ウィリアム・シェイクスピア（William Shakespeare）1564-1616年。イギリスの詩人、劇作家。

41 **Beaumont** フランシス・ボーモント（Francis Beaumont）1584-1616年。イギリスの劇作家。フレッチャーとの合作が多い。

41 **Fletcher** ジョン・フレッチャー（John Fletcher）1579-1625年。イギリスの劇作家。

41 **Donne** ジョン・ダン（John Donne）1572-1631年。イギリスの詩人。神学者。17世紀イギリスの形而上詩人の代表的存在。T.S.エリオットをはじめとする現代詩人達に影響を与えた。

41 **Cowley** エイブラハム・カウリー（Abraham Cowley）1618-1667年。イギリスの詩人。形而上派詩人の一人。

42 **Dryden** ジョン・ドライデン（John Dryden）1631-1700年。イギリスの詩人、劇作家、批評家。当時のイギリス文壇の大御所であった。

42 **Pope** アレグサンダー・ポープ（Alexander Pope）1688-1744年。イギリスの詩人。風刺詩に特にすぐれていた。ドライデンが礎石をきずいたイギリス古典主義文学を開花させ完成させて、後のS.ジョンソン博士へとその成果をひきわたす役割を果たした。

42 **take upon me**＝take upon myself.「思い切って～する」

42 **import**＝meaning, significance.

2- 1 **inane phraseology**＝empty wording.

4 **courtesy**＝indulgence, favour.

11 **indolence**＝idleness.

14 **The principal object** コールリッジは1817年出版した『文学的自叙伝』第14章の中で、『抒情民謡詩集』製作のいきさつについて同様のことを語っている。ワーズワスと自分との役割分担について次の様に述べている。

" …my endeavours should be directed to persons and characters supernatural, or at least romantic; yet so as to transfer from our inward nature a human interest and a semblance of truth sufficient to procure for these shadows of imagination that willing suspension of disbelief for the moment, which constitutes poetic faith. Mr.Wordsworth, on the other hand, was to propose to himself as his object, to give the charm of novelty to things of every day, and to excite a feeling analogous to the supernatural, by awakening the mind's attention from the lethargy of custom, and directing it to the loveliness and the wonders of the world before us; an inehaustible treasure, but for which, in consequence of the film of familiarity and selfish solicitude we have eyes, yet see not, ears that hear not, and hearts that neither feel nor understand. "

なお、両者の詩風や題材の相違は、詩論における根本的相違となってコールリッジの論争をひき起こすことになった。この序文をめぐるコールリッジの議論については本書のINTRODUCTIONを参照すること。

20 **ostentatiously**＝boastfully, gaudily.

24 **emphatic**＝forcibly expressive.

27 **germinate**＝develop.

38 **regular**＝harmonious, constant.

40 **conferring**＝bestowing

42 **arbitrary**＝capricious, despotic.

43 **fickle**＝changeable, inconstant.

44 **outcry**＝accusation.

3- 3 **pernicious**＝highly injurious.

7 **prompted**＝incited, instigated.

12-3 **being possessed of more than usual organic sensibility** ＝ being originally possessed of much innate sensibility.

17-8 our feelings will be connected with important subject. このあたりの議論はワーズワスの詩論の中心的部分となっており、彼が単に自発的な感情の流出を素朴に詩と考えていたのではないことがわかる。ここに述べられているような行為や感情の持続的繰り返しと一般的代表物の重要性との相互関係、あらゆる過去一切の代表たる思想と詩の題材との関係、豊かな感受性と感情を浄化するような心理的習慣、情緒と思考などの問題は、現代詩人のT. S. エリオットの標榜する「客観的相関物」の考え方なども参考にすると非常に興味あるものを含んでいる。

32 **application**＝use.

41 **torpor**＝apathy, numbness.

42 **the great national events** 18世紀末から19世紀にかけてイギリスでは国家的大事件が相次いで起こった。まず第一に、1765年のジェイムズ・ワットの蒸気機関の発明に端を発する産業革命が、イギリスを中心として当時の社会組織の大変革をひき起こした。さらに1775年にアメリカ独立戦争が勃発、1778年にフランスから、また翌年にはスペインから宣戦布告を受けた。1780年から4年間オランダとも戦争状態に入った。1783年にはイギリスは正式にアメリカの独立を承認せざるを得なくなった。そして、1789年に勃発したフランス革命がヨーロッパ社会に動乱をもたらすことになった。その余波を受けたイギリスは1793年ふたたびフランスとの間に宣戦布告を交わすことになり、さらにナポレオンの抬頭によってヨーロッパ大陸から孤立することになった。一連の歴史的大変動の直接の原因となったフランス革命の影響によって、当時の世相は物情騒然たるものであった。

44 **intelligence**＝information, news.

46 **conformed**＝adapted.

47 **Milton** ジョン・ミルトン（John Milton）1608-1674年。イギリスの詩人。ルネッサンス的な美的感覚と清教徒的な信仰とを兼ね備えた人物で、幅広い文化意識と鋭敏な感受性によって、聖書を題材としながら人間の悪と善の相克を描写し、強烈な個性によって調和的な理想世界を模索して、苦闘する不屈の精神を見事に表現した。

47-8 **frantic novels** 当時一般に流行していたschool of Terror の一派の人々の作品。Mrs.RadcliffeやMatthew Gregory Lewis といった人々がいた。

48 **sickly and stupid German Tragedies** 1797年から1801年にかけて、ドイツの通俗劇作家August von Kotzebue の作品の翻訳が熱狂的に受け入れられた。ワーズワスはこのような大衆の卑俗な趣味に迎合する演劇をきびしく批判した。

48 **deluges**＝great flood.

4- 1 **stories in verse** Gregory Lewis編纂の*Tales of Terror* や *Tales of Wonder* などに収録されている韻文物語。

3 **counteract**＝defeat, frustrate.

6 **the great and permanent objects** この詩集が目標としたような雄大なる山岳の光景や、洋々たる大河など大自然の営みや神聖なるものなどを指す。

11 **apprise**＝inform.

17 **regular**＝usual, customary.

18 **a figure of speech** ＝ personification, metaphor.

21 **prescription** 「長年の使用や慣行によって公認された権利」

22 **flesh and blood**＝living person.

25 **poetic diction** 「詩語」イギリス18世紀の古典主義の詩壇において流布した詩的作法としての言葉遣い。日常的言語の卑俗さを極端に避けようとして洗練された用語を高い教養の表現と考えた。 birdsは airy nations であり、spring flower は vernal bloom といったごとくである。また詩作上において、韻律を正確に整えるために、言葉を長くしたり短くするために形式を重んじる古典主義文学の立場からは必要なものとして高く評価されたが、時と共に後にはマンネリズムに陥って衒学的なものとなり、初期の必然性や自然らしさを失ってしまった。

27 **alleged**＝asserted positively.

30 **culpably particular**＝reprehensibly detailed.

36 **friendly**＝serviceable, propitious.

39 **abstained**＝refrain.

46 **stumble upon**＝come upon, discover.

46 **prosaisms**＝prose style. 「散文的な語句、表現」

47 **exult over**＝triumph.

48 **canon**＝criterion. 「（倫理。芸術上の）規律、規範」

5- 4 **in no respect** 「いかなる点においても全然～でない」

5 **but likewise**＝but also.

9 **adduce**＝cite as proof. 「（証拠として）引用する」

10 **Gray** トマス・グレイ（Thomas Gray）1716-1771年。イギリスの詩人で『墓畔の哀歌』の作者として有名である。

14 **In vain to me～** グレイのソネットで ' On the Death of Richard West' という題名である。

15 **Phoebus**＝sun.本来、ギリシャ神話に出てくる太陽神としての Apollo の名前である。

16 **amorous descant**＝melody of love.

17 **resume**＝take back.

22 **race**＝group.

24 **wonted**＝habitual.

25 **complain** 《詩》「小川や風などが）さびしい音を立てる」

29 **rhyme** 「raim」《詩学》「押韻」 *cf.* greet : deceit, quality : frivolity.

39 **typify**＝represent, exemplify.

40 **the same organs**＝the organ of speech and that of hearing.

41 **kindred**＝similar, congenial.

44 **celestial**＝heavenly, divine.

44 **ichor** [áikɔ:] 「(ギリシアやローマの神話の中で)神々の脈管を血液のように流れると想像された霊液」

6- 1 **overturns**＝overthrow.

2 **paves the way for** 「〜のために道を開く」「〜を容易にする」

6 **distinction**＝individuality, excellence.

13 **ornaments**＝decorations.

16 **figures**＝figures of speech. 《修辞》「詞姿」「文彩」表現効果を増すために用いるさまざまな語句や文章の形式のこと。

16 **incongruity**＝disagreement, discordancy.

20 **abound**＝be plentiful.

20 **due**＝proper, adequate.

22 **subdued**＝repressed, mastered.

24 **just**＝right.

26 **detached**＝unconnected.

33 **censure**＝blame, reprove.

45 **disposition**＝turn of mind, natural bent.

47 **conjuring up**＝calling up, raising.

7- 4 **readiness**＝easiness.

10 **fall short of** 「(〜にまで)達しない」「〜に不足する」

13 **exalted**＝noble, dignified.

18 **delusion**＝illusion.

18 **confound**＝confuse.

24 **trick out**＝adorn showily.

27 **emanations**＝efflux.

32 **scruple**＝hesitate.

35 **submit**＝surrender, give in.

39 **Frontiniac** 「(フランス)フロンティニヤン産のぶどう酒」

40 **Sherry** 「シェリー酒」スペイン南部で産出する白ぶどう酒。

40 **Aristotle** アリストテレス(前384-322年)ギリシアの哲学者。『詩学』は彼の言語芸術論として、文学論の古典となり作劇法における古典的な典拠となった。

42 **operative**＝working.

43 **competence**＝legal capacity, authority.

44 **tribunal**＝court of justice. 「法廷」

46 **fidelity**＝loyalty, exactness.

8- 3 **natural philosopher**＝physicist.

11 **homage**＝reverence, respect.

11 **the native and naked dignity of man** ワーズワスの詩論.1.1の特性を表すものとしてよく引用される有名な語句である。

13 **propagated**＝spreaded, extended.

26 **deductions** 「(一般に)推論」

35 **properties**＝attributes, characteristics.

41 **cleaves**＝is attached, is faithful.

42 **unalienable** 「譲渡できない」

45 **benefactor**＝kindly helper, patron.

48 **impassioned**＝ardent.

9- 2 " **he looks before and after.** " ハムレット第4幕4場 33- 9行。

7 **empire**＝vast domain.

11 **the first and last**＝the beginning and end.

12 **material**＝important, essential.

14 **sleep**＝be inactive.

21 **manifestly**＝evidently.

21 **palpably**＝obviously.

25 **genuine inmate**＝true inhabitant.

28 **pictures**＝mental images.

30 **assumed**＝supposed.

33 **authorize**＝justify.

42 **referring**＝directing the attention of.

44 **conducing**＝contributing.

46 **promptness**＝quickness.

10- 11 **impossible** 詩人の言葉が、ものをいきいきと感じ、はっきりと見る他のあらゆる人間の言葉と、それ程ひどく相違するはずがないこと。

12 **supposing that this were not the case** 仮に、詩人がひろく人間の熱情の本質の即して考えたり、感じたりしないと想定するならば。

15 **advocates**＝supports, plead for.

15 **subsists**＝continues to exist, is extant.

24 **arbitrary**＝capricious.

26 **respecting**＝concerning.

44 **injudicious**＝unwise.

11- 2 **numbers**＝verses.

5 **underrate**＝underestimate.

6 **observe**＝comment.

6 **poems are extant,** … 『抒情民謡詩集』というこの書物の題名が示す通り、ワーズワスは古くからイギリスに伝わっているバラードを常に念頭に置いている。したがって、かりに詩人が単に自分自身や詩人という特別な人種のことを表現するにすぎないとしても、常に詩人は詩人仲間だけでなく、一般大衆の人々のために書いているのだという彼なりの信念が表明されている。

9 **affords**＝gives.

10 **presumption**＝assumption.

17 **supposition**＝assumption.

21 **undue**＝improper, unsuitable.

24 **efficacy**＝effectiveness.

29 **unsubstantial**＝visionary.

35 **perused**＝read thoroughly.

37 **Clarissa Harlowe** イギリスの作家サミュエル・リチャードソン(1689-1761)によって書かれた書簡体の小説。全7巻の長編小説である。薄命の女主人公の生涯を取り扱った不幸の物語。

38 **The Gamester** 1753年にエドワード・ムーア(1712-57)によって出版された悲劇作品。ワーズワス自身による次の様な註がある。

' A domestic tragedy by Edward Moore, first performed in 1753 by Garrick, who contributed some passages to it. '

40　**ascribed**＝attribute, impute.

43　**incommensurate**＝inadequate.

12- 3　**effect**＝achieve, accomplish.

4　**maintained**＝asserted, affirmed.

7　**reckoned**＝regarded, consider.

20　**emotion recollected in tranquillity**　ワーズ
ワスにとって、詩の成り立ちは単に力強い情緒の自発的流
出ではなく、静謐のうちに回想された感情にその起源を有
する。歳月を通して脳裡にしまっておかれた過去の感動が
反芻によって、円熟して詩想を形成するに足るだけ十分に
浄化されるのを待って、はじめて彼は筆をとるといった詩
人であった。この様な彼独自の詩作態度は、ひろく詩人た
るものが取るべき心がまえであると彼は考えたのである。
現実の機縁から得た感動と、長い歳月の後に回想された静
謐の感動との間の深淵が彼独特の哲学性を詩に与え、第三
の情緒を生み出すことを可能にしたのである。

26　**qualified**＝moderated, tempered.

29　**being**＝human being.

30　**held forth**＝offered by Nature.

33　**blind**＝concealed.

45　**executed** [éksikjuːtid]＝performed, accom-
plished.

13- 2　**pleading**　「抗弁する」「弁じる」

8　**apprehensive**＝anxious, worried.

12　**ludicrous**＝absurd.

21　**debilitated**＝enfeebled, weakened.

23　**presumption**＝effrontery, impudence.

29　**detained**＝kept back, delayed.

32　**parodies**　「こっけいな作り替え詩文」作風や
文体を風刺や嘲弄的に模倣する。

32　**Dr.Johnson**　サミュエル・ジョンソン(Samuel
Johnson) 1709-84年。イギリスの詩人、批評家。

32　**stanza**　「連」通例4行以上から成る詩の単位
で韻律的構成を有する。

33　**I put my hat … in his hand.**　ある日の夕方
のレイノルズ夫人宅での茶会の席で、トマス・パーシーが
古いバラードの素朴な美しさを賛美したことをからかうた
めに、ジョンソン博士が即興的に作り出したという逸話に
出てくる語句である。

34　トラファルガー広場（当時はなかった）から東北
に向かってティムズ河と並行しているロンドンの大通りで、
ジョンソンの時代も繁華街であった。

38　"**Babes in the Woods**"　トマス・パーシー編
集の『イギリス古詩拾遺』(Reliques of Ancient English
Poetry) の中の「森の中の子供たち」と題するバラード
にあたる (SeriesⅢ. Book ii. 18)。パーシーはイギリス
の宗教家であったが、主として中世の古い詩歌176編を集
めたこの詩集の編者として知られ、収録された詩の素朴さ
や率直な表現は多大な関心をよび、次代のロマン派の詩人
たちに大いに影響を与えるものとなった。

39　**These pretty babes … from the town.**　ノー

フォークの裕福な両親を失い、後に残された3歳程の息子
と妹は奸悪な叔父に託される。しかし、彼は財産を奪おう
として2人の殺害を悪漢に依頼する。しかし、子供を不憫
に思った悪漢の一人が他の悪漢と闘って、子供を森の中に
置き去りにしてしまう。この悪漢は他の悪漢を殺してしま
うが、あどけない幼児たちを殺すにしのびず、空腹を訴え
る彼らをパンを買いに町へ行くと森に置き去りにして結局
餓死させてしまう。大人を信じて空しく帰りを待つ幼児の
姿をこの一節は簡潔に表現したものである。

14- 3　**contemptible**＝despicable, mean.

6　**parallelism**＝resemblance, similarity.

7　**wants**＝lacks.

12　**genus**　《生物》「属」

15　**genuinely**＝truly.

19　**unadulterated**＝pure, genuine.

20　**abide**＝remain.

21　**affected**＝influenced.

21　**conjectures**＝guessworks.

31　**Sir Joshua Reynolds**　サー・ジョシュア・レ
ノルズ（1723-92）イギリスの肖像画家でジョンソン博士
らとも親交があった18世紀イギリスの屈指の画人である。
これは美術講話を集めた『講話集』の第七講の中で精確な
鑑識眼の基準を論じた部分で述べられている。すべてイギ
リス王立美術院の研究生に彼が講じたものである。1768年
に彼は初代院長となっている。

35　**temper**＝moderate, mitigate.

39　**further**＝advance, promote.

45　**furnish**＝provide, supply.

48　**endearing**＝attractive, caressing.

15- 1　**bigotry**　「がんこな信仰」

9　**the reader assisted**＝the reader might have
been assisted.

23　**approbation**＝approval.

THE THORN

1798年の作品で偶然に嵐の日、クォントックの丘の茨か
ら受けた強烈な印象を詩中に永遠のものに創造しようとい
う意図の下に書かれた。中、下層階級の使用する日常語が
詩の言葉としてどの程度まで詩的快感を与え得るものであ
るかという意図の下に書かれた点で、『抒情民謡詩集』の
中でも、この詩は最も典型的な実験的作品の一つと考えら
れるが、コールリッジはあまり高く評価しなかった。しか
し、ワーズワス研究家のダービシャーはこの詩を優れた作
品として高く評価し、見捨てられた乙女の愛の苦悩や子供
への愛に狂気した母親のみじめな魂が自然に救いを求めて
いる悲痛な姿を如実に描くことによって、人間の根本的な
感情を真正に取り扱っていると言っている。

16- 1　**Thorn**＝hawthorn　《植》「サンザシ」この木
は狂気の女が人生において受けている苦難を暗示している。
この詩の語り手は隠居したり退職した初老の全く普通の人

物と想定すれば問題はない。土地になじみのうすい田舎町に引っ込んだおしゃべり好きの人物である。

11 **lichens** [láikenz] 「地衣」
15 **crop**＝the top part of the thorn. 「（樹木の）てっぺん」
24 **gale**＝strong wind.
28 **espy**＝catch sight of.
43 **cups**＝calyxes. 「（花の）がく」本来、被子植物の花冠の一部を意味するが、ここでは、さんざしの赤い実を指しているのであろう。
44 **vermilion**＝cinnabar.
17- 46 **olive green** 「黄緑色」
47 **spikes** 《植》「穂状花序」
63 **cloak**＝mantle.
68 **wretched**＝miserable.
78 **wherefore**＝why.
88 **doleful**＝mournful, sad.
18- 96 **hut**＝hovel.
104 **rack**＝strain. 知恵を絞る。
110 **trace**＝discover, find.
119 **blithe** [blaið]＝joyous.
125 **oath** [ouθ]＝「誓い」
131 **cinder** 「燃え殻」
132 **tinder** 「ほくち」火打ち石で打ち出した火花を捕らえるために麻布を焦がしたものに硝石を混ぜて作ったもの。
19-140 **sober**＝moderate.
150 **wrought**＜work.
153 **time** 「分娩期」
169 **seek**＝go.
173 **many**＝a large number of people.
180 **sworn**＝pledged.
184 **Ere**＝before.
193 **jutting crag**＝projecting steep rock.
196 **as I am a man**＝truly. 「まったく、まぎれもなく」強調する言葉。
20-226 **view**＝beholding.
227 **trace**＝come upon, see with difficulty.
21-240 **aver**＝declare to be true.
245 **strive**＝endeavour, try hard.

WE ARE SEVEN

1798年オールフォックスデンで書かれた。ワーズワスは実際にこの詩の主人公にあたる少女に1793年グッドリッチ城の庭で出会ったと言っている。ワーズワス兄妹がワイ川の近くのこの城を訪れたのは、ワイト島からソールズベリ平原へ出てさらにブリストルからワイ川をさかのぼる旅行中のことで、「ティンタン僧院」でもこの旅行のことが言及されている。
2 **draws its breath**＝breathes.

9 **air**＝appearance, manner.
10 **clad**＜clothe
14 **may you be**＝do you have.
17 **I pray you**＝please.
19 **dwell**＝live.
22- 42 **kerchief**＝handkerchief.
42 **hem** 「折り返してへりを縫う」
46 **fair**＝sunny.
47 **porringer** 「（ポリッジやスープ用の）深ざら」浅いどんぶりのようなもの。
23- 67 **throwing words away** 「いくら言っても無駄」 throw away＝waste

HART－LEAP WELL

1800年初頭にグラスミアで作成。前年末に妹ドロシーと共にグラスミアに徒歩旅行した時、土地の老農夫から教えられた逸話が素材となっている。
勇ましい狩猟の姿はスコット的な外観を持ち、心ない騎士の単純な喜びと動物殺害による呪いを取り扱ったこの詩のテーマは、コールリッジの「老水夫の歌」と合い通じるものがある。そこに内観的なワーズワス一流の思想が述べられている所に独特の味わいを生んでいる。

hart＝stag 「雄じか」
well＝natural spring. 「泉」
chase＝hunting.
1 **The knight**＝Sir Walter.
1 **Wensley moor** ヨークシア北西部の村の荒野で狩猟場。
3 **vassal**＝feudal tenant.
6 **steed** 「（乗馬用の）馬」
7 **he**＝the horse
9 **prancing** 「踊りはねる」
9 **courser**＝swift horse. 「駿馬」
12 **doleful**＝mournful.
13 **rout** [raut]＝company, assembly.
14 **That** 関係代名詞で先行詞はrout。
15 **one and all** 「皆ことごとく」
16 **Such race** 急激な追跡を意味する。
17 **veering**＝changing direction.
19 **Branch, Swift, and Music** 三頭の猟犬の名前。
20 **strain**＝exert to the utmost.
21 **hallooed** 「大声で呼んで（猟犬たちを）励ました」
21 **chid**＜chide＝scold.
22 **suppliant**＝entreating.
22 **upbraidings stern**＝harsh reproaches.
24 **fern** 「しだ」 *cf.* heath.
24- 26 **bugles** 《古》「（狩用の）角笛」 where is the buglesとなる。

27　**not like an earthly chase**　サー・ウォルター唯一が鹿を必死になって追う姿は常軌を逸するまでに至り、一種異様で奇怪とも思える光景を現出するのである。it はchase と同格である。

29　**toils**＝goes along with effort, moves laboriously and pantingly.

35　**smacked**＝cracked 「(むちを) ぴしゃりと鳴らす」

36　**spoil**＝prey 「(狩りの) 獲物」

38　**his dumb partner**　彼の駿馬のこと。

39　**the hour that it is yeaned** 「生まれたばかりの」 yean＝bring forth.

40　**cataract**＝waterfall.

43　**fetched**＜fetch＝utter. 「(うめき声を) 出す」 fetch a groan.

50　**roods** [ru:dz] 「ルード」長さの単位でおよそ6 ヤードから8 ヤードに相当する。正確には地方によって異なっている。

51　**several**＝different, separate.

52　**verdant**＝green.

55　**brow** [brau] 「(額のように突き出た) がけの上端」

61　**cunning**＝skilful.

62　**basin** 「石盤」「水ばち」 cf. l.82. A cup of stone.

25- 65　**gallant brute**＝brave beast.

68　**grazed**＜graze＝touch or rub lightly in passing.

70　**paramour**＝mistress.

71　**minstrel**＝singer, poet, musician.

72　**bower** [báuə]＝leafy nook.

73　**Till the mountain……fail** 「この山嶽のいしずえが揺るぎない限り」

75　**The joy**＝My mansion with its arbour. 同格である。

75　**till**＝cultivate, plough.

75　**Swale**　ヨークシアのウーズ河の支流。

76　**Ure** [juə]　同じくウーズ河の支流。

77　**stone-dead**＝quite dead.

78　**nostrils** 「鼻孔」

80　**whereof** 「そのことについて」

81　**Ere thrice…………steered** 「月が三たびその港へと航行しないうちに」月が船にたとえられており、三ケ月と経たないうちにという意味。

82　**living well** 「湧き水を出す泉」

85　**stature**＝height.

86　**trailing**＝creeping, straggling.

87　**sylvan**＝wooded.

95　**rhyme**＝verse, poetry.

97　**moving**＝pathetic.

101　**Hawes to Richmond**　ホーズはユア河畔にあってウェンズレーの西方のあり、リッチモンドはスウェール河畔にあってウェンズレーの北方である。

103　**aspens**＝trembling poplars.

26-105　**ill divine**＝not guess, not conjecture.

109　**neither arms nor head** 「枝もなければ梢を飾る葉もない」

110　**Half-wasted**＝was half-wasted.

110　**tawny** [tɔ́:ni] 「黄褐色の」

112　**the hand of man has been** 「人の手が加わっていた」

117　**in various ～** ＝lost in various ～

118　**garb**＝costume.

119　**accost** 「近づいて言葉を掛ける」

122　**rehearsed**＝narrated in detail.

129　**The arbour……tell**　そのあずまやは在りし日の昔の様子を偲ばせている。

131　**lodge**＝mansion, pleasure-house.

131　**you might……dream** 「半日捜しまわっても、忘れ去った夢のように跡かたも見つけ出せない」

133　**heifer** [héfə]＝young cow.

134　**Will wet**＝who will wet.

135　**fast**＝soundly.

136　**dolorous**＝mournful.

138　**blood cries out for blood**　血が血を求めて呼び叫ぶとは、殺された者が呪いをもって復讐を求めているということ。

27-149　**asleep he sank**＝he sank asleep＝he sank into slumber.

150　**summer-tide**＝summertime.

154　**carols**＝songs of joy 「(楽しくさえずる) 鳥の声」

155　**for aught we know**＝perhaps. 「もしかすると」「よくは知らないが」　aught＝anything.

156　**half a furlong**＝110 yards.

162　**creed**＝set of opinions.

163　**not unobserved**　その死を自然は見守っていた。

165　**The Being**　自然の万物に遍在する神。

170　**no common**＝unusual.

173　**She**＝nature

174　**That**＝in order that.

174　**what we are, and have been** 「人間の現在と過去」

177　**divide**＝share.

178　**what she shows, and what conceals** 「自然が荒廃の跡を示し、またそれを自然の美によって覆いかくすこと」

180　**the meanest thing that feels** 「たとえどれ程つまらないものにせよ、いやしくも生命のあるもの」

' THERE WAS A BOY '

1798年10−12月にドイツで書かれた。この詩は後に1805年の原稿の『序曲』第5巻、389−422行に入れられている。

この詩のテーマについてワーズワスは1815年版の序文の中で次の様な説明をしている。（1845年版では削除された）

Guided by one of my own primary consciousnesses, I have represented a commutation and transfer of internal feelings, co-operating with external accidents to plant, for immortality, images of sound and sight, in the celestial soil of the Imagination. The Boy, there introduced, is listening, with something of a feverish and restless anxiety, for the recurrence of the riotous sounds which he had previously excited; and, at the moment when the intenseness of his mind is beginning to remit, he is surprized into a perception of the solemn and tranquillizing images which the Poem describes.

28- 2 **Winander**＝Windermere. イギリス湖水地方の大きな湖。

    6 **glimmering**＝flickering.

    9 **instrument**＝musical instrument.

15-6 **concourse wild Of mirth and jocund din**「わきかえるような陽気な騒ぎ」concourse＝confluence. din＝loud noise.

    18 **hung**＜hang 「じっと見守る」

    21 **torrents**＝rushing streams. 山の急流の響きが少年の心底に不思議な声となって語りかけてきて、その予期せぬ驚きが彼の胸にやさしい衝撃を与えたのである。

    23 **solemn imagery** 突然に少年の心に浮かんできた自然の厳かなたたずまい。

    29 **hangs**＝overhangs

THE BROTHERS

1799年12月に執筆を始めて、翌年に完成された。ワーズワスの自注によれば、この詩の背景は、カムバランドとウェストモーランドの山中であり、彼の一連の田園詩の結びの詩として製作された。したがって、詩の書き出しが、いくぶん唐突になっているのはこのためであると彼は述べている。また、ワーズワス自身の解説によれば、この詩の構想はエナデールの谷で実際に聞いた実話にもとづいており、岩の上で寝こんだある羊飼が落ちて死亡し、彼の杖が岩の途中でひっかかっていたという事実から発想を得たという。

    1 **needs**＝necessarily. mustと共にneeds must またはmust needsとして用いる。「きっと～にちがいない」「～せざるを得ない」

    4 **wheel about** 「（蝶が）ぐるぐる回って飛ぶ」「旋回する」

    5 **as wise**＝as wise as before. 「相変わらず」

    6 **jutting**＝projecting.

    7 **sit perched** 「（高くてあぶなそうな所に）すわる」

29- 11 **moping**＝dejected.

    12 **tarry** *yonder*＝linger over there.

    21 **teasing**＜tease＝comb, card. 「（羊毛・麻などを）すく」

    21 **matted**＝tangled 「もつれた」

    22 **cards** 「梳毛機」紡績で繊維の毛並みをそろえる工程中に用いるもの。

    23 **spindle** 「紡錘（ぼうすい）」「つむ」昔手紡ぎに用いたもので、両端を細く削った棒または糸車に用いた鉄の針。

    24 **round wheel** 「紡ぎ車」

    27 **Girt**＜gird＝surround.

    30 **ridge** 「隆起」

    33 **locked** 「組み合わせた」

    39 **calling**＝occupation, profession.

    40 **fared**＜fare＝get on. 「暮らす」「やって行く」

    44 **shrouds** 《海》「横静索」マストの頂上から両船側に張った支索。

    50 **main**＝high sea 《詩》「大海」

    55 **employment**＝use.

    56 **overcome**＝overpowered.

    58 **bosom of the deep**＝surface of the ocean.

30- 60 **verdant**＝green.

    61 **clad**＜clothe.

    63 **perils manifold**＝various dangers.

    66 **resume** [rizjú:m] ＝take up again.

    69 **borne**＜bear＝entertain.

    71 **foul**＝stormy.

    75 **Failed**＝grew feeble, diminished in strength.

    76 **Tidings**＝news, report.

    80 **the file** 「（墓の）列」

    99 **short**＝suddenly.

    99 **at leisure**＝deliberately.

    100 **scanned**＜scan＝scrutinize, look at closely.

    100 **complacency**＝quiet contentment.

    101 **vicar**＝priest.

    102 **needs must** *cf.* p.28. *l.*1

    105 **creep**＝walk stealthily.

    106 **Following his fancies** 「気のむくままに」

31-112 **The good man** 牧師のこと。

    112 **communed with himself** 「沈思内省した」

    116 **Leonard** [lénəd] 男の名前。

    117 **ensued**＝followed in order, came after.

    126 **mortality**＝liability to die.

    127 **threescore**＝sixty.

    131 **cleft**＝chasm.

    132 **wear**＝exhibit, display.

    133 **for aught I know.** *cf.* p.27. *l.*155.

135-6 **a friend That does not play yon false** 記憶が確かで間違っていないこと。

    136 **pike**＝peaked hill.

    138 **bubbled**＝gurgled.

    142 **rent**＜rend＝split.

    145 **water-spout** 「川の氾濫」

146　feast＝exquisite gratification.

150　loads＝heaps, plenty.

32-151　score＝set of twenty.

152　**To feed the ravens**　「大鴉の餌にする」

153　untoward＝unlucky.

156　christened＝baptized.

157　web＝cobweb.

158　decked＝adorned, arrayed.

160　chronicle＝egister.

162　fire-side＝home.

164　**Commend me to**＝give by choice　「(〜なら) …が一番よい」「…に限る」

165　freedom＝frankness, excessive familiarity.

166　heedless＝careless, inattentive.

168　**head- nor foot-stone, plate of brass**　「墓石もなければ台石もないし真鍮の名札もない」

169　type＝symbol, emblem.

171　fellow＝equal.

178　**immortal part**　死後の魂。

179　plain＝evident.

183　**second life**　「死後の人生」

185　past＜pass.　187行目の I might に続く。

188　nook＝corner.

189　**turning o'er**＝turning over　「思いめぐらす」「熟考する」

189　hillocks＝mounds.

190　round　「一巡り」

191　**broad highway**＝comprehensive ordinary course.　「この世の中の普遍的な常道」

33-196　**you ridge**＝yonder mound.

201　Engendering＝producing.

201　hale＝robust, sound.

203　bounds＝territory on a boundary.

206　sire《詩》＝father.

207　yielded＝produced.

210　burthens＝burdens＝obligations.

212　**buffeted with bond**＝battled with debt.

213　mortgages [mɔ́ːgidʒiz]　「抵当」

214　**before his time**　「まだ死ぬには早いのに」

215　spurred＜spur＝drive.

217　**lightest foot**　「一番足が早い」

219　tripping＜trip　「速く軽快な足取りで歩く」

221　**be your host**　「君を泊める」

228　**Two fathers in one father**　「一人で二度も父親の役目を果たした」

230　hauntings＝obsessions.

230　infirmity＝disease.

237　**bear looking**　「見るに耐える」「見るだけの価値がある」

34-240　darlings＝favourites.

242　kinsman＝male blood relative.

243　spare＝dispense with.

252　rivulet＝brook.

254　fords　「浅瀬」

256　stray＝sporadic.

262　**the great book of the world**　「この世の中という偉大な書物」

263　piety＝admirable act.

264　**break English bread**　「イギリスの食べ物をたべて生きる」

266　mealy＝farinose.

268　**sabbath breach**　「安息日を破ること」

269　**I warrant**＝I assure you.

273　roebucks　「のろじかの雄」

276　betters＝superiors.

279　**wager**＝stake　「賭ける」

35-286　**is left among you**　「あなたがたのところで生存している」

299　thriving＝prosperous.

299　trafficked＜traffic＝trade.

290　**but for**＝if it had not been for.

291　**never handled rope or shroud**　「決して船乗りにならなかっただろう」

293　**stripling**「strípliŋ] ＝lad, mere youth.

296　**torrent**＝the storms of life, the rough dealings of the world.

297　estate＝landed property.

298　**for aught I know.** cf. p.27. l.155.

300　**destitute**＝in extreme want and misery.

303　tidings＝news, report.

306　**Great Gavel**　カムバランドの山岳地域で最高峰の山である。

306　**Leeza** リーザ川はエナデール湖に注ぎ、エナ川はエナデール湖から流れ出ておりエグレモントから少し下流で海に注いでいる。

313　**Moors**　「ムーア人」アフリカの北西部モロッコ地方の回教徒でバーバリ人とアラビア人との混血人種。

314　**Barbary coast**　アフリカ北部のバーバリー海岸。

315　**bring down his spirit**　「彼の意気を消沈させる」

317　crossed＝thwarted, opposed.

322　needs＝necessarily.

36-324　**As any**＝as happy as any　「誰にも負けない程幸福である」

327　fellow＝same.

330　offices＝services, assistance.

333　checked＝hindered, arrested.

343　blithe＝cheerful.

346　practice＝habit.

354　new-dropped　「生まれたばかりの」

355　**it chanced**＝it happened.

356　further＝additional.

357　dale-head　「谷間のはずれ」

37-363　**Whence**《詩》=from which.

365　**purposed**=intended.

367　**comrades**=companion, mate.

370　**heed**=notice, careful attention.

372　**learned**　主語は370行目の one である。

378　**mangled**=spoiled.

382　**Ay** [ai] =aye=yes.

384　**one**=home.

389　**unhallowed**=wicked, profane.

390　**Nay**=no.

390　**God forbid**　「そんなことがあってたまるものか」「とんでもない」

390　**recollect**=remember.

392　**brought upon**=caused, induced.

396　**margin**=edge.

38-398　**perished**=suffered death.

402　**mouldered**=decayed.

404　**rushing in**　「（涙が）急に出てくる」

409　**entreated**=asked earnestly, implored.

410　**fare**=food and drink.

411　**fervent**=ardent.

413　**pursue**=continue.

416　**reviewed**=recalled and considered.

418　**cherished**=fostered.

423　**relinquished**=abandoned.

434　**thence**=from there.

EXPOSTULATION AND REPLY

この作品は、次の「反論」と共に、ワーズワスの思想の精髄を明確に表現したものとして有名である。1798年の春、オールフォックスデンで書かれた。会話体のこの詩は、その頃オールフォックスデンにワーズワスを訪問していたウィリアム・ハズリットを相手としたものである。当時、ハズリットはゴッドウィンの哲学書に没頭していた。「趣意書」によれば、この時の会話から詩が生まれたとある。また、詩中のハズリットに相当する相手をマシューと呼んでいるのは、ワーズワスが好んで使用する架空の人物名で、さまざまな人物の性格を複合させた素朴で思索的な人格を有し、詩人自身の思想を代弁するものである。

39-　6　**beings else forlorn and blind**　書物の光が片時でもなければ、何も理解せず、何も見えない盲目のような人々。

8　**their kind**　同じく死すべき運命にある人間。

10　**As if she for no purpose bore you**　「まるで何の目的もなく、大地が君を生み出したかのように」

13　**Esthwaite lake**　ウィンダミアの西で、ホークスヘッド小学校の南にある湖。

14　**I knew not why**=I knew not why life was sweet.

17　**cannot choose but**　《古》「～せざるをえない」

18　**bid**=command.

20　**Against, or with our will**　「意志に何ら関係なく」

21　**Nor less**　「しかも」

21　**deem**《古》=think.

22　**of themselves**=of their own accord　「ひとりでに」「自発的に」

22　**our minds impress**=impress our minds.

24　**a wise passiveness**　「賢明なる受動性」この言葉はワーズワスの思想を特徴づけるものとして有名である。

25-6　**mighty sum Of things**　「荘厳なる森羅万象」

27　**of itself**=of its own accord.

29　**wherefore**=why.

30　**Conversing as I may**=as I may be conversing.

THE TABLES TURNED

前編の詩「諫めと答え」と対になっている作品であり、相手の諫めに対して反論して逆にやりかえすという意味である。すなわち、詩人とマシューとの問答の関係が局面一変して、詩人が相手マシューに対して諫め勧告する立場になったことを指す。 turn the tables on 「～に対して形勢を逆転させる」

40-　1　**my friend**=Matthew.

1　**clear**=take away =quit.　本の虫の様になって陰気な顔をするなということ。

4　**grow double**　「腰が曲がる」

6　**lustre mellow**=rich radiance.

8　**His first**　太陽が沈み始める頃の。

9　**endless strife**　書物にばかりかじりついて空理空論のはてしない議論に明け暮れること。

10　**linnet**　「べにひわの類の美しい鳴鳥」

11　**on my life**　「確かに」「命にかけて」

13　**blithe** [blaið] =cheerful.

13　**throstle**=song thrush　「うたつぐみ」

14　**no mean**=considerable.

17　**She**=Nature.

17　**a world of**=great quantity or extent　「無数（量）の」

17　**ready**=immediately available, easily secured.

19　**Spontaneous wisdom**　前出の「賢明なる受動性」と深く結びついており、健全なる心身による受動状態の中で、自然は人間にどんな書物もおよびつかない英知を与えてくれるということ。

20　**Truth**　心身共に快活であれば自然発生的に賢明なる考えが湧き出て、自然界が人間に無量の英知を与えて、事物の真理への到達へと導いてくれるのである。

21　**One impulse**　春の緑の森を眺めて鼓吹される

ようなある感動。

21　**vernal**＝of spring, fresh.

25　**lore**＝learning.　特殊な職業又は題目に関する知識で、特に科学的根拠を必要としない、民間伝承的な性質のものを指す。

27　**Mis-shapes**＝misform, deform.

28　**We murder to dissect**　人間のおせっかいな知性の分析や解剖によって、美しい事物のありのままの生命が害なわれる。

31-2　**a heart That watches and receives**　「諫めと答え」の中の「賢明なる受動性」を説明する言葉。　*cf. ll*.23-4.

LUCY　GRAY

この詩は1799年、ドイツのゴスラー市滞在中に書かれたもの。ヨークシアで実際あった出来事をドロシーが語った話に基づくもので、所謂ルーシー詩集のルーシーとは別である。寒くて快適でもなかったこのドイツの宿で、ワーズワスは「木の実取り」のような回想詩も書き上げ、そして自伝的哲学詩『序曲』をも書き始めている。遠い異国の地にあった孤独な心が自然に故郷を懐かしむ心的態度を生み出すと共に、自らの過去を距離を置いて回想することを可能にしたのであろう。

2　**the wild**＝desert＝wide moor.

3　**break**＝dawn 「夜明け」

9　**fawn** [fo:n] 「子じか」

10　**hare** 「野うさぎ」

10　**the green**＝glassy land.

15-6　**light Your mother**　カンテラ（堤灯）を持って町まで行って、母親のために雪道の案内をすること。

18　**'Tis scarcely afternoon**　「まだお昼をすぎたばかり」 'tis [tiz] 《古》＝it is.

19　**Minster clock**＝church clock.

20　**yonder is the moon**　昼間の月を見つめる少女の孤独な境涯が示されている。

21　**hook** 「三日月形のかま」

22　**snapped a faggot-band**　「まき束の縄をぷっつりと切った」

23　**plied**＜ply 「（まきなどを火に）盛んにくべる」「（仕事に）精を出す」

25　**roe** 「のろじか」

26　**wanton stroke** 「気まぐれな足どり」

29　**before its time** 「尚早に」「時ならずして」

33　**wretched**＝miserable.

40　**furlong**　長さの単位で約201.17メートル。

42- 57　**some maintain**　不思議に消息を絶った人間は、特に片田舎では村人達によって一種の迷信的な伝説となる場合がある。ことに行方知れずの美しい少女などは噂の対象になることが多い。この詩の基になった実際の出来事では、少女の死体が水路の中で見つかったらしい。

61　**trips along** 「軽快に跳びあるく」

64　**whistles**　荒野に吹きすさぶ風のぴゅーと鳴る音と、今は亡き少女の寂しい歌とが渾然一体となっている様子。その鋭く凄惨な音色は一種怪異な感慨を与える。

POOR　SUSAN

1797年頃に書かれた。後に「哀れなスーザンの幻想」という題名に変更された。ウッド街、ロスベリ街、チープサイド街などの地名はいずれもロンドンの街の名前である。スーザンをさすらいの女と呼ぶのは不適当というラムの意見に従って、1802年以後の版では第5節の詩は削除されている。

5　**note**＝sound, tone.

5　**ails**＝troubles.

7　**volumes**＝considerable mass or quantity.

10　**pail**＝bucket.

16　**passed away**＝vanished.

RUTH

1799年、ドイツで書かれた作品であり、ワーズワスによれば、サマセットシアを放浪していたある人物について実際に聞いた話に基づいている。1802年の第3版と1805年の第4版で改訂されたものが出た。

43- 2　**mate**＝spouse 「配偶者」「連れ合い」

4　**slighted**＝ignored 「無視された」

8　**oaten pipe** 「麦笛」からす麦の茎で作った。

10　**the green**＝grassy place.

19　**Georgia**　米国南東部の州

20　**casque**＝helmet 「かぶと」

22　**Cherokees** 「（北米土人の一種族）チェロ一族の土人」

24　**gallant crest**＝decorative apex , showy plume.

26　**tongue**＝language.

29　**jeopardy**＝risk, hazard.

31　**genius**＝natural capacity, inherent aptitude.

44- 48　**perilous**＝hazardous, dangerous.

49　**rout** [raut] ＝disorderly crowd.

50　**fold**＝pen

53　**choral song**＝chorus.

59　**stand** 「〜の状態にある」

61　**ambush** 「待伏せ」

61　**siege** 「包囲攻撃」

70　**Encompassed**＝surrounded.

72　**main**《詩》＝high sea.

74　**banner**＝flag.

74　**unfurled**＝spreaded out, unrolled.

45- 88　**break** 「突然見えて来る」

91　**magnolia** 「もくれん」

92　cypress [sáipris]　「いとすぎ」

92　spire＝spear, shoot.　「若枝」

93　flowers　バートラムの旅行記の中に、これらの真紅の花が北アメリカ南部の山岳地帯に群生していることが言及されている。

95　leagues　距離の単位で約3マイル。

97　savannahs　「サバナ」熱帯又は亜熱帯寡雨地方の無樹の大草原。

106　Still《古》＝always, continually.

108　glade《米》「草の生えた低い湿地」

113　woe《古》＝bitter grief.

122　helpmate＝spouse　「つれあい」

124　adopted　「正式に娶った」

125　sylvan　「森に住む」

46-133　fitting＝suitable.

134　plight　「誓う」

138　more than human life　「人生における最高の日であった」

141　floods《詩》＝lake, river.

143　lawful　正式の夫婦としての。

143　bear＝have　「（名前を）持つ」

146　stripling＝lad.

149　roamed＝wander.

149　vagrant bands＝nomadic party.

152　tumult＝uproar.

153　food　「精神のかて」

156　impetuous blood＝furious temperament.

157　climes《詩》＝country, region.

158　Irregular　「異常な」

160　kindred＝similar.

163　voluptuous＝sensual.

164　wrought＜work. wrought to feed と続く。

166　languor＝sentimental dreaminess.

166　lent＜lend＝impart, add.

47-169　worst pursuits　「不道徳な行為に耽ること」

169　ween《古・詩》＝believe, think.

170　intervene＝come in, interfere.

172　forms　大自然の事物。

178　undeceived　「迷わずに」

180　his own＝his own vice.

181　moral frame＝moral character.

187　no feigned＝genuine, sincere.

191　nature＝inherent character, disposition.

191　played＝worked.

195　stirred＝instigated, roused.

199　fared＝turned out, happened.

203　Deserted＝abandoned.

207　housed　「収容された」

208　exulting in her wrongs　「悲運に放心して」

210　caroused　「泣き騒いだ」

48-213　pastimes＝diversion.

214　cell　「（刑務所の）独房」

217　lain＜lie＝remain, be kept.

218　respite＝temporal cessation.

220　took thought＜take thought of　「思いやる」

224　master-current of her brain　「頭脳中枢」

226　Tone　「トーン川」サマセットシアに流れる川で、美しいクォントックの山岳地域からもそう遠くない。

229　engines of her pain　「苦悩を生み出すもの」

232　vernal＝of spring.

233　taxed＝accused, reproved.

241　astray＝out of the right way.

242　day　「（人の）一生」「盛りの時代」

244　needs must＝necessarily.

247　pressed＝oppressed.

249　Repairs＝goes, makes her way.

49-253　mute＝silent.

256　hemlock《英》　「どくにんじん」

261　spouts　「水のほとばしり」

262　small machinery　「玩具」

263　Ere＝before.

266　hallowed [hǽlouid] mould　「神聖なる土地」

267　corpse＝dead body.

NUTTING

1798年、ドイツで書かれた作品。ワーズワス自身が少年の日のなつかしい思い出を回想して書いたと述べているように、彼が少年時代に木の実取りに行った時の感想を回顧して作られた詩である。したがって彼独自の自然観への心理的崩芽というべきものが表現されている点で、詩人としての原点を示す興味深い一編であると言える。

2　singled＝selected.

3　cannot die　「決して忘れられない」

4　sallied＜sally＝rush out.「（勢いよく）出かける」

5　wallet　「ずた袋」「物入れ袋」

6　nutting crook　木の実取りに使う曲がった手鉤。

8　Tricked out＝adorned showily.

8　weeds《古》＝clothing.

10　frugal＝economical, sparing.　当時、ホークスヘッド小学校へ老婦人の家に下宿して通っていた。

11　Motley accoutrement [əkú:təmənt] ＝heterogeneous dress.　珍妙なボロ服をまとった身支度をいう。

11-2　smile At＝show scorn or indifference to　「冷笑する」「一笑にする」

12　brakes＝thicket.　「やぶ」

12　bramble《英》＝blackberry bush　「西洋やぶいちご」

15　nook＝recess.

17-8　ungracious sign Of devastation　「殺風景な略奪の跡」木の実を取るために他の誰かが来て荒らしまわっ

たしるしのない格好の場所を見つけたのである。

18 hazels 「はしばみ」

21-2 Breathing with……delights in 「嬉しさのあまりに、ことさら躍る胸を抑えて息をしながら」

22-3 with wise restraint Voluptuous 「賢明に抑制しながらも官能的に」

50- 26 A temper 木陰に坐って花とたわむれている気持ち。

29 bower [báuə] ＝leafy nook.

32 water-breaks＝small springs. 「川瀬」「水の瀬」

35 fleeced 「（羊毛状の物で）一面をおおう」こけむした石の様子。

38- 9 pleasure loves …… ease 快楽を貪るのではなく、適度に安逸とまじり合っており、しばらくの間、呑気な気分に身を任せるという態度。

40-1 The heart……kindliness はしばみの実をたくさん手に入れることは確実なので、喜びの心はしばらくの間、あたりにある何でもない事物に心を通わせて楽しみ、心地よい思いの中で温和な悦楽に浸ること。

41 stocks and stones 「樹木や岩石」

43 branch and bough [bau] 「大枝小枝」大きさの順序は、bough, branch, twig となっている。

44 ravage＝destructive action.

46 Deformed and sullied＝disfigured and defiled.

46-7 patiently……being 「静かな身体を投げ出して、なされるがままにしていた」静かな緑の木陰を人間であるかのように描写して、人間的感情さえも与えているところにワーズワスの自然観の特色が現れている。

52 intruding sky 折り取られてなくなった枝のところに、顔を出すように割り込んできた青空。

53 dearest maiden 妹のドロシーのこと。

55 a spirit ワーズワスの汎神論的自然観。自然を霊的存在として捉える彼の態度は、この様な幼年時代の経験から発展したものである。

THE ANCIENT MARINER

1798年3月にコールリッジによって完成されたイギリス・ロマン主義の代表的名作である。1797年11月にワーズワス兄妹と共にリントンへ徒歩旅行をした時に計画されたという。1798年の『抒情民謡詩集』初版の巻頭を飾って以来、1800年の再版では改題され、詩句にもかなりの推敲がなされた。さらに1817年のコールリッジの詩集では、おびただしい改訂の個所が見られ、注釈やラテン文の題詞まで加えられた。この詩の主題や発想は、友人ジョン・クルックシャンクの幽霊船の夢、シェルヴォク著『南海経由の世界周航』の中の船員があほうどりを射殺する話、死人が船を動かすというワーズワスから出た話などの貢献に負うところもあるが、やはり詩作の根本的源泉となったものは、コールリッ

ジ自身の個人的経験や詩的体験であり、現代のフロイトやユングの深層心理学的解釈も可能な深遠な象徴性を持つものである。単に怪奇な物語として読むのではなく、老水夫のあほうどり殺害によってひき起こされる罪、罰、祈り、救済の一連の過程には、人間の原罪、堕落、煉獄、再生という詩的イメージの原型が示されているのである。この詩は聖書的含蓄や夢の論理と象徴性を適合させながら、人間のモラルの問題を厳しく取り扱っており、詩人の内的体験を語る寓意的物語詩である。

コールリッジが『文学的自叙伝』で述べているように、ワーズワスの目指す詩が日常的事物に新奇の感を与えて、習慣という無気力な状態から人心を覚醒させるものであったのに対して、彼自身の抱いた意図は、超自然的な少なくとも浪漫的な人物や事件を想像力によって描き、その幻想世界が、一時疑いを挿むことを中断するような詩的信仰を読者の心の内的本性から生じせしめることであった。また、1817年につけ加えられた傍注は、当時の無意識的な幻想詩に哲学的思索や形而上的探究との関連をさらに深めるものとなった。なお、テクストには初版のものを採用した。

1 It 古風なバラッド形式においては、書き出しの導入的 it は there と同じ用法で使用されることがある。

2 stoppeth《古》3人称・単数・現在形動詞の語尾－eth の短縮形。

2 three 3は7とか9と同様に神秘を暗示する数。

3 thy [ðai] 《古》「汝の」 thou の所有格。

4 stoppest《古》-est は2人称・単数・直説法・現在形の動詞語尾。

6 next of kin＝nearest relative 「最近親」

8 May'st hear＝thou mayest hear＝you may hear. 婚礼の祝宴と異様な老水夫の姿との対置の妙があり、突如とした話の展開にもバラッド的な素朴さとおもしろ味がある。

51- 10 quoth《古》＝said. 通例主語の前に置かれる。1人称、3人称の直説法過去形。

13 skinny＝lean, emaciated.

15 get thee hence 「ここから立ち去れ」 cf. go hence＝die. Hence！＝Depart！

15 Loon《スコット・北英》＝worthless fellow, fool.

16 make thee skip 「（杖で）追い払う」

20 hath his will＝gets what he desires. 「望み通りである」

21 sate《古》＝sat

25 cleared＜clear 「（船が港を）離れる」

26 drop 「（風と潮の流れに乗って）進む」

27 Kirk《スコット・北英》＝church.

29 the left＝the east. 船は南方へ向かっている。

35 beat his breast 胸をたたくのは悲嘆などの身振りを意味する。

36 bassoon＝fagott 「バスーン」二重の舌のある低音大縦笛。

40 Minstrelsy 「楽人たち」「楽士たち」

52- 48 **Chaff**＝husks of grains 「もみがら」

53 **drifts**＝floating ice 「氷山」

53 **clifts**＝cliffs

54 **dismal sheen**＝dreadful brightness.

55 **ken**《スコット・北英》＝recognize.

62 **Thorough**《古》＝through.

69 **sprung**＝sprang.

73 **shroud**《海》 「横静索」「帆綱」マストの頂上から両船側に張った支索。

74 **vespers**《詩》＝evenings. nine は神秘を暗示する。

76 霧の中の白い月の微かな光は不気味な不吉さを予感させる。

79 **crossbow** 「いし弓」中世時代の武器。

53- 89 **an hellish** 1834年版では a hellish となっている。

90 **woe**＝misfortune, calamity.

91 **averred**＝asserted positively.

94 **uprist**《古》＝uprose.

97 **slay**＝kill.

100 **furrow**＝track 「航跡」

101 **burst**＝broke forcibly 「突然に入る」

104 **sad as sad could be** 「この上もなく悲しい」

107 **All**＝quite.

112 **stuck**＜stick＝be at a standstill.

119 **deeps**＝sea.

123 **reel and rout**＝dance and riot.

124 **Death-fires** 「鬼火」死体にみられる燐光。

129 **fathoms** 「尋（ひろ）」水深を計る単位で1メートル83センチに相当する。

54-131 **drouth** [drauθ]《スコット》＝drought [draut]＝thirst.

133 **no more than**＝as much as.

135 **well-a-day！**《古》＝well-a-way. 悲哀を表す感嘆詞。

140 **glazed**＜glaze 「（目が）どんよりする」

143 **speck**＝spot 「しみ」

146 **wist**＜wit《古》＝know.

149 **dodged a water-sprite** 水の精をよけるかの如く。

150 **plunged** 船が縦に揺れて、船首と船尾をかわるがわるに浮き沈みさせている。

150 **tacked** 間切る。すなわち帆船が風を帆に斜めに受けて進むこと。

150 **veered**＝turned round 「進路を変えた」

157 **Agape**＝open-mouthed with wonder.

158 **Gramercy！**《古》＝Thanks 「有難い！」感謝や驚きの声。

162 **Hither**＝she comes.

162 **weal**《古》＝happiness, good fortune.

164 **steddies**《古》＝steadies＝moves steadily 「着実に進んでくる」

55-166 **well-nigh**《古》＝very nearly.

171 **straight**《古》＝imediately.

172 **Heaven's Mother**＝Virgin Mary 「聖母マリア」

172 **grace**＝mercy.

178 **gossameres** [gósəmiəz]＝gossamers. 「蜘蛛の糸のようにうすいもの」

180 **as**＝as if.

182 **Mate** 「つれあい（夫）」

186 **mouldy**＝musty 「かび臭い」

186 **charnel** 「ぞっとする」

186 **crust**＝scab 「かさぶた」

188 **free**＝bold, or unreserved.

193 **Hulk**《古》 「大型で扱いにくい船」

194 **Twain**《古》＝two apparitions.

197 **sterte up**＝start up 「急に起きる」

56-203 **clombe**《古》 climb の過去。

203 **bar**＝horizon.

204 **The hornéd** [hó:nid] **Moon** 「三日月」月に星がまとわりついている様子は、水夫の間では凶兆と考える迷信があった。

209 **ee**《古》＝eye.

215 **to bliss or woe** 「天国あるいは地獄へと」

216 **it** 同格として every soul をうけている。

221 **ribbed Sea-sand** 波のあとがついて肋骨のように見える海岸の砂。

239 **or ever**《古》＝before.

57-243 **balls** 「眼玉」

247 **their limbs** 前行の the dead を受ける。

257 **The moving Moon** 凶兆を予告する月の動き。詩中において太陽と月は、重要な役割を果たしており、激しい陽光の下で罪と受難がおこなわれ、月光の下で究極的な救済が訪れている。月光は詩的想像力のシンボルでもある。

260 **beside**＝close to the moon.

261 **bemocked**＝mocked.

261 **main**《詩》＝high sea.

264 **charméd** [tʃa:mid] **water**＝phosphorescent sea.

264 **alway**《古》＝always.

277 **might**＝could.

279 **I blessed them unaware！** 月光の下で海蛇を無意識のうちに祝福し、讃える老水夫の行為を契機として、あほうどり殺害の罪と受難に対する救いが訪れることになり、第5部では天から慈悲の雨が降りそそぐ。

280 **Sure**＝surely.

287 **from pole to pole** 「世界中で」

288 **Mary-queen**＝Virgin Mary.

291 **silly**《廃》＝simple, homely. 「粗末な」「用をなさない」

292 **so** 前行の silly である状態をいう。

304 **anear**《詩》＝near.

306 **sere**＝sear＝withered. 「ぼろぼろの」

308 **fire-flags**＝meteoric flames 「流星の光」

308 **sheen**＝bright, shining.

59-319 **with never a jag**＝with no zigzag at all. 「一直線に」

327 **It had been**＝it would have been.

331 **'gan work the ropes**＝began to set the ropes in motion. 「帆綱をひいて働き始めた」

342 **corses**《古》＝corpse

354 **that are**＝that exist.

356 **jargoning**＝twittering, warbling.

60-362 **noise**＝melodious sound（Now rare）

363 **like**＝as

379 **'gar stir**＝began to stir.

386 **swound**《古》＝swoon.

388 **I have not to declare**＝I have not the power to declare.

390 **discerned**＝perceived, detected.

393 **By** 「～の名にかけて」

394 **laid full low**＝killed, slew.

396 **The Spirit**＝the Polar Spirit.

396 **bideth**＝dwells.

61-402 **penance** 「（罪業消滅の）苦行」、「（罪滅しの）難行」

412 **If he may know**＝asking.

413 **she**＝moon

413 **grim**＝fierce. 「時化（しけ）」

415 **him**＝ocean.

417 **or…or**《古》＝either…or.

429 **charnel-dungeon** 「死体安置所」

430 **stony**＝motionless.

62-435 **them** 前行の eyes を受ける。

436 **spell was snapt** 「呪縛が解けた」

439 **what had else been seen**＝what would have otherwise been seen.

446 **a wind**＝the holy spirit.

451 **meadow-gale**「牧場に吹く風」

453 **felt**＝was felt.

461 **countrée**＝country.

462 **drifted**＝were driven along.

462 **Harbour-bar** 「港口の砂洲」

464-5 これが夢でないことを願う気持ちと、もし夢ならばいつまでも眠らせて欲しいという気持ちを絶妙に表現している。

467 **strewn**＜strew＝overspread.

469 **shadow**＝reflection.

472 **steeped in**＝pervaded, saturated.

472 **silentness**＝silence.

63-475 **the same**＝the bay.

476 **shadows**＝spirits, ghosts.

477 **colours**＝dress.

482 **corse**＝corpse

483 **by the Holy rood** 「十字架に誓って」「確かに」 rood＝cross.

484 **seraph-man** 「光輝く男の天使」

496 **perforce**＝of necessity 「必然的に」

501 **blast**＝blight, shatter. 行の最初に that を補って読む。

506 **shrieve**《古》＝shrive 「懺悔（ざんげ）を聞く」

510 **rears**＝raises（rare）「（声を）張り上げる」

64-514 **plump**＝well-rounded 「ふっくらとした」

517 **Skiff-boat**＝light rowing boat 「軽舟」

518 **trow**［trau］《古》＝suppose, think.

519 **those lights** 492 行以下に出現した seraph-band のこと。

520 **but now**＝just now.

521 **by my faith** 「確かに」「誓って」

524 **sere**＝sear＝withered.

525 **aught**《古・詩》＝anything.

526 **perchance**《古》＝by chance.

527 **skeletons of leaves** 「筋だけになった枯葉」

527 **lag**＝float, liger.

529 **Ivy-tod**《古》＝ivy-bush.

530 **Owlet**［áulit］ 「梟の子」

534 **a-feared**《古》＝afraid.

539 **straight**＝at once.

540 **it**＝a sound.

544 **Stunned**＝astounded, dazed.

551 **spun**＝span.

553 **telling of**＝echoing.

65-557 **sit** 跪くのでなく坐ったままで。

564 **all**＝quite, wholly.

572 **Forthwith**＝immediately.

572 **wrenched**＝distorted, wrest.

574 **tale**＝confession.

576 **uncertain**＝unexpected.

578 **ghastly**＝horrible.

580 **like night** 婚礼の客や祝宴が昼と光の世界であるのに対して、漂泊する老水夫の住む世界は夜と闇の世界である。

588 **bride-maids** 花嫁の付き添う若い処女。

66-616 **He**＝wedding-guest.

617 **forlorn**《古・詩》＝desolate, abandoned.

618 **sadder**《古》＝more serious, graver.

THE TWO APRIL MORNINGS

この詩と次の「泉―対話」も1799年の作であり、同じモチーフを取り扱っている。揺るぎない幸福が、傷つきやすい人間の心と、その奥に秘められた悲哀によって、かき乱される様子を描いており、陽気な男であるマシューの内奥の悲しみは、読者に予期せぬ心の琴線に触れる思いを抱かせる。

10 **steaming rills** 「陽炎（かげろう）の立っている小川」 Heat waves are shimmering.

67- 13 **work**＝excursion.

28 **brother**＝same.

30 **plied**＜ply＝work at, follow diligently.

36 **nightingale** 「美声の持ち主」

37 **Emma** マシューの娘の名前。

40 **e'er**《詩》＝ever.

43 **blooming**＝beautiful.

44 **points**＝drops.

48 **pure**＝unqualified, complete, sheer.

54 **ill confine**＝not suppress.

68- 68 **Methinks**《古・詩》＝it seems to me.

60 **wilding**＝crab tree 「野生りんごの木」

THE FOUNTAIN

後出のサイモン・リーなどと同じように、日常的な出来事に新奇な感動を与えることを意図した詩である。若者と老人マシューとの間の素朴な会話が示され、通常の穏やかな幸福感が漲っているかのようである。しかし陽気な平静さの背後にある人間の孤独や利己心を描いてみせて、この詩は読者に不意打ちを与える。時の流れの無情の前に、人間の無力さがさりげなく強調される。二人の友情は変わらず、いつもながらの幸福感は維持されているが、詩の終わりに近づくにつれて、最初と同じ陽気さの中にまったく異なった感慨がひき起こされるのである。

7 **broke**＜break＝gush out, spring.

9 **match**＝harmonize with, correspond with.

11 **catch**《音楽》 「輪唱」

14 **Sing** 前行の of に続く。「詩（歌）にして賛美する」

15 **rhymes** [raim]＝verse, poetry.

21 **steers**《詩》＝direct the course. 「（ある方向に）向かう」

23 **'Twill**《詩・古》＝it will.

26 **cannot choose but think**＝cannot help thinking.

27 **a vigorous man** 前に when I was を補う。

28 **brink**＝margin.

30 **idly** 「いたずらに」「ただわけもなく」

33 **fares**＝happens, turns out.

69- 39 **carols**《詩》「（楽しくさえずる）鳥の声」

41 **wage** 「（闘争を）する」

42 **see**＝experience.

46 **glad no more** 前に though we are を補って読む。

47 **wear**＝display, exhibit.

48 **of yore**《古》＝long ago, formerly.

49 **bemoan**＝moan over, lament.

51 **hearts** 「大事な人達」

57 **he** 次行の The man を受ける。

57 **wrongs**＝misunderstands.

60 **plains** 「野原」

67 **glide** 「静かに歩く」

MICHAEL

『抒情民謡詩集』第2版の出版直前の1800年10月11日から12月9日に書かれた作品である。この頃ワーズワス兄妹はダヴ・コテッジから北西1マイルにあるグリーンヘッド渓谷を訪れていた。コールリッジの「クリスタベル」を掲載する予定であったが、未完であることや、詩風や内容的にも民謡詩集の意図に合致しないため、急遽この詩と差し替えることになったらしい。主人公マイケルは強い意志力と鋭敏な感受性を持った人物である。この男が親としての愛と住みついた土地への愛着という二重の強烈な感情によって揺り動かされる姿を描くのが作者の意図であった。副題として「田園詩」と加えられているが、古典文学のいう「田園詩」のつもりはなく、素朴に羊飼いについての話を物語るといった意味である。おそらく、当時の産業革命の波によって、新たな経済発展の中で脅かされ、取り残されていくカンバーランドやウェストモーランドの羊飼いたちの生活ぶりを何らかの形で詩として記録しておきたいというワーズワスの望みがあったのであろう。羊飼いマイケルの心情を素朴な威厳をもって見事に描写したこの作品は、ワーズワスの代表作の中に数えられている。

70- 2 **Gill**《英方言》＝wooded ravine 「樹木の茂った峡谷」

4 **bold**＝steep, abrupt 「けわしい」

5 **pastoral mountains** 「羊飼いの住む山やま」

7 **opened out**＝spreaded, extended.

11 **kites** 「とび」

15 **But for**＝if it had not been for.

17 **unhewn**＝rough.

18 **appertains**＝pertains.

19 **ungarnished**＝not decorated.

22 **spake**《古・詩》 speak の過去形。

24 **verily**《古》＝certainly, truly.

26 **abode**＝dwelling place.

27 **hence**＝for this reason, therefore.

27 **this tale** 主語で動詞は30行目の led である。

34 **history**＝story.

35 **the same**＝a history.

36 **natural**＝genuine.

37 **fonder**＜fond＝foolishly credulous, sanguine.

39 **second self**＝alter ego 第2の自分、すなわち志を継いでくれる者。

39 **gone**＝dead.

46 **calling**＝occupation, trade.

71- 49 **blasts**＝sudden gusts of wind.

49 **oftentimes**《詩・古》=often.
51 **noise**=sound.
52 **bagpipers** 「風笛吹奏者」
52 **Highland hills** 「スコットランド高地地方」
54 **Bethought**<bethink=recall. 前行の of に続く。
55 **devising**=contriving, thinking out.
62 **grossly**=excessively.
66 **common**=usual, familiar.
66 **oft**《詩・古》=often.
76 **blood**=consanguinity. 「血縁」
81 **comely matron** = good-looking married woman.
83 **stirring**=active, busy.
86 **flax** 「亜麻」
88 **pair**=married couple.
90 **telling o'er**《古》=count. o'er=over
91 **phrase**=mode of expression.
93 **tried**<try=put to a severe test.
96 **proverb**=precept
72-102 **a mess of pottage** 「一わんのあつもの」 mess=mixture. pottage《古》=soup, broth.
102 **skimmed milk** 「脱脂乳」脱脂乳の入ったスープの一さらという意味。
106 **betook**<betake《再帰動詞》 「(ある行動)に身を入れる」
108 **card** 「(羊毛・麻などを)すく」
110 **injury**=damage.
114 **projection overbrow** 「(大きな)庇が覆っていた」
115 **duly**=punctually.
116 **hung a lamp** 112行目の Down from へと続く。
117 **utensil**=implement.
133 **chanced**=happened.
134 **plot**=plat.
140 **limits**=boundary.
143 **must needs**=necessarily.
144 **help-mate** 「つれあい(夫または妻)」
148 **spirit**=mental attitude, ardour.
73-149 **gifts**=boons.
151 **inquietude**=uneasiness.
152 **tendency of nature** 「自然の成り行き」
156 **bare**《古》bear=entertain の過去形。
160 **dalliance**《詩》=sport, trifling.
160 **use**《廃》=ordinary occurrence or experience.
166 **Albeit** [ɔːlbíːit]《古》=although.
166 **unbending**=obstinate.
167 **To have** 165行目の love を受ける。
172 **shearer's covert** 羊毛刈りの日除け」
174 **bears** 「(名前を)持つ」

177 **exercise his heart** 「気をつかう」
178 **fond**=tender.
184 **coppice** 「雑木林」
187 **Due requisites** 「然るべき必要条件」
191 **called** 前の to に続く。 call to 「(ある地位に)つかせる」
192 **urchin**=mischievous boy.
192 **divine**=guess.
195 **hire of praise**=word of compliment.
74-202 **went** 200行目の to the heights に続く。
206 **emanations**=spiritual effluence.
212 **fashion**=manner, mode.
215 **tidings**=news
216 **bound**=under obligation.
217 **surety**=pledge, guaranty.
218 **means**=resources.
221 **discharge the forfeiture**=pay out the penalty.
223 **substance**=means, resources.
223 **unlooked-for claim**=unexpected demand.
227 **gathered so much strength** 「大いに元気を取り戻して」
229 **refuge**=reliance.
230 **patrimonial**=hereditary 「先祖伝来の」
232 **heart failed him** 「気がくじけた」
239 **lot**=destiny.
247 **'Twere**《詩・古》=it were の短縮形。
249 **remedies**=legal reparation.
75-250 **shall** 「～させよう」 話者の意志を表す。
254 **friend**=helpful person.
257 **thrift**=prosperous growth, or frugality.
258 **repair**=make amends for.
265 **parish-boy** 「教区の世話になっている子」
266 **gathering**=charitable contribution.
268 **wares**=goods, articles of merchandise.
272 **overlook his merchandise**=superintend his commodities.
274 **estates**=landed properties.
277 **like**=similar.
280 **resumed** [rizjúːm] =began to talk again.
281 **meat and drink** 「何よりの楽しみ」
286 **more** 前行の of the best に続く。
292 **with her best fingers** 「念入りに」「手をつくして」
294 **glad** 次行の To stop に続く。
76-305 **jocund**=cheerful.
307 **heart**=spirit, fortitude.
308 **bring forth**=produce.
311 **ensuing**=following.
315 **utmost**=best.
316 **forthwith**=immediately.
325 **at such short notice** 「そんなに急いで」

123

335 **thitherward**《古》=thither=there.

337 **spake**《古・詩》 speak の過去形。

338 **wilt**=will.

340 **wert**《古・詩》 be の二人称・単数・直説法および仮定法過去形。

340 **promise**=hope.

343 **do thee good** [お前のためになる」

346 **befalls**=happens.

77-354 **a feeding babe** 「乳飲み子」

358 **brought up**<bring up=rear, foster.

368 **herein**=in this way.

375 **their time**=time of death.

375 **loth**=loath=reluctant.

376 **mould**《古・詩》=ground, or earth=grave.

380 **burthened**《古》= burdened = mortgaged [mɔ́ːgidʒid]

398 **resigned**=handed over, yielded.

401 **wont**=accustomed.

402 **Before I knew thy face** 「お前が生まれて来る前は」

78-409 **corner-stone** 「基石」「隅石」

416 **fathers**=forefather.

418 **Bestir**=stir up, rouse to action.

420 **covenant**=contract, compact.

426 **first stone**=corner-stone.

427 **broke**<break=burst forth.

432 **put on**=assume, pretend.

443 **went about**<go about=busy himself about.

449 **dissolute**=licentious, debauched.

450 **ignominy**=disgrace.

79-458 **heavy**=lamentable.

466 **repair**=go, frequent. 前行の to that 以下に続く。

474 **old** 年老いた犬のこと。

482 **ploughshare** [pláuʃɛə]=blade of a plough. 「すきべら」

LOVE

1799年にコールリッジがサラ・ハッチンソンと出会った後に書かれ、同年の12月21日の『モーニング・ポスト』に最初「黒髪美人の物語の序章」という題で掲載された。現在の形のものは『抒情民謡詩集』の1800年第2版に「囚人」の代わりとして入れられた。

3 **ministers**《古》=servant, attendant.

4 **feed**=sustain, nourish.

7 **mount**《詩》=mountain.

10 **eve**《詩・古》=evening.

13 **arméd** 「鎧を身につけた」

21 **air**=melody, tune.

23 **rude**=artless, natural.

24 **hoary**=ancient.

25 **flitting**=slight. faint.

30 **burning brand**《詩・古》=blazing sword.

35 **another**=the knight.

36 **my own**=my own love.

40 **fondly**=lovingly.

81- 45 **den**=cave.

47 **starting up** 「急に現れる」

48 **glade** 「林間の空地」

51 **fiend**=evil spirit.

53 **unknowing what he did** = like one in a delirium, or an absolute altruism.

58 **tended**=looked after.

59 **strove**<strive=endeavour.

66 **strain**=note, melody.

66 **ditty**=short simple song.

72 **balmy** [báːmi] =refreshing.

80 **breathe**=whisper.

86 **meek**=mild.

' STRANG FITS OF PASSION I HAVE KNOWN '

1799年、ドイツのゴスラーで書かれた。次の3編も含めて、いわゆる「ルーシー詩群」と呼ばれているものである。月と恋人とが無意識裡に同一視されていく過程は、神秘的であり、ワーズワス特有の不意の意気阻喪と深い喪失感が表現されている。ルーシーは想像上の人物と考えられるが、妹ドロシーの存在やフランスでのアネット・バロンとの恋愛、ケンブリッジ在学中の初恋などが詩作に大いに影響を与えたといえる。

82- 3 **the lover's** 恋を経験した人。

2 **to tell** 4行目の What 以下に続く。

7 **bent**<bend=turn.

10 **lea**《詩》=grassland.

11 **trudged**=plodded.

11 **nigh**《詩》=near. we 「馬と私」

13 **plot**=plat.

14 **cot**《詩》=cottage.

24 **the planet**=the bright moon. 輝く月が急に見えなくなるので、怪訝の念と共に、深い喪失感が詩人の胸に去来する。

25 **fond**=foolish.

'SHE DWELT AMONG TH' UNTRODDEN WAYS'

83- 1 **untrodden ways** 「人の通わぬ山里」

2 **Dove** 「ダヴ川」ダービシアのバクストンのあたりに源を発して、南に流れてトレント川に合流する。他にヨークシア、ウェストモーランドにも同名の川あるいは

泉が存在する。

    5 **A violet** 山里に生きる美しい乙女の清らかな姿のこと。

    7 **Fair as a star** 乙女の孤独と精神的な美しさから生まれる孤高を強調している。

    10 **ceased to be**＝died.

    12 **The difference to me.** ルーシーを喪失することに対する無限の痛恨の心情を簡潔に表明したものである。

' A SLUMBER DID MY SPIRIT SEAL '

    1 **seal** ＝ keep shut from facing the actual reality of life and sleep in a sweet dream.

    2 **human fears**＝that she might die.

    4 **The touch of earthly years** ＝ growing old and dying, as every mortal does under the influence of time.

    7 **diurnal** [daié:nəl] 《古》＝daily.

' THREE YEARS SHE GREW IN SUN AND SHOWER '

    6 **A lady of my own** この女性を自然と同化した優美な自然の愛児として立派な淑女にしようという「自然」の意図。

    8 **Both law and impulse** 心身共に自然の法則や精神と融合調和すること。

    11 **an overseeing power** 岩山や平原、大空と大地など自然界のあらゆる事物が、彼女を励まし、あるいは節度を与えて見守り導く力として作用すること。

    16 **breathing balm** 「かぐわしいそよ風」

    19 **state**＝dignity, pomp. 漂い浮かぶ雲によって、その威容を彼女に与えようということ。

    20 **bend**＝shall bend.

    28 **rivulets**＝small streams.

    28 **round**＝round dance.

    30 **pass into her face** 小川の流れの美しい音が、彼女の顔に融け込んでいくこと。

    33 **swell**＝shall swell.

    38 **race was run** 「一生が終わった」「寿命が尽きた」

    41 **The memory** 39行目の left の目的語。

LINES

ワーズワスの会心の名作と称される作品。妹ドロシーと共にワイ川を渡ってティンタン僧院を出発する時に作りはじめて、4、5日の逍遥の後、ブリストルに入ったおりに完

成したものである。作者自身も述べているように、この詩ほど理想的な状況の下で書けた詩は他になく、ブリストルに到着するまで一行も変えなかったし、書きとめることもしなかったらしい。したがって、この160行ほどの詩を逍遥しながら頭の中だけで完成させたのである。この詩の完成後、2カ月ほどしてからワーズワス兄妹はドイツへ旅立った。ティンタン僧院は11世紀に建立されて、廃墟になっている寺院である。ワーズワスはウェールズ東部のワイ川沿いにあるこの僧院を、1793年に唯一人でセイルズベリ平原からウェールズに徒歩旅行した時に訪れている。過去の経験と現在の状況を彼の人生の持続的一貫性の中で捉えながら、自然そのものに内在する感化力、自然からの深い感銘を受けて深遠な内省と瞑想に入るという体験などが語られており、天来の霊感と感興によって試作した彼の特長がよく表現されている作品である。深い思索力と深い感情とが見事に融合したワーズワスの代表作とするにふさわしい秀作である。

84- 1 **Five years** 最初に一人で訪れてから現在に至るまでの1793-8年の期間をいう。

    4 **a sweet inland murmur** ワイ川はティンタンの上流数マイルでは海潮の影響を受けない。外洋の影響を一切受けない内陸のしとやかな川のさざめきを意味する。

    7 **connect** 荒涼隔絶の断崖から天空に眼を移すと、大空の静けさが幽玄なる絶壁の光景と融合調和して、大自然の営みがひしひしと感じられるのである。

    10 **dark sycamore** 葉が繁って黒ずんだ楓。

    11 **tufts**＝clump, bush, thicket.

    13 **lad**＝clothed＝covered.

    14 **copses**＝coppice 未熟の果物が他の緑樹と融け合って、唯緑一色に見えている。まだ青々とした果樹は森や雑木林と区別がつかない様子。

  16-7 **little lines Of sportive wood** 気ままに生い茂っている灌木（低木）の列。

    17 **pastoral**＝rustic, rural.

    18 **wreaths**＝curls, rings. 渦巻く煙。

    20 **With some uncertain notice.** 定かでないが次のような感じを与えるという意味。

    23 **Through**＝throughout.

    25 **As is……man's eye** 眼前にしなければ、盲人のように見ることができないのとは違って、その景色のあらゆる細かな点をはっきりと思い浮かべることが出来る。

    28 **sensations** 前行の owed の目的語。

    31 **tranquil restoration** 血肉で感じ心躍らせる快い感覚的感興から、さらに精神的慰安をもたらし、心を清新ならしめることによって、喧騒に疲れた詩人に平静なる再生の気運を与えて、落ち着いた健全なる状態を再び取り戻すこと。

    32 **unremembered pleasure** あるいは、また忘れられた過去の歓びが漠然として現在に与える快感。

    34 **best portion** 善良な人の生涯の最良の部分には、このような歓喜の情が影響を与えており、日常生活の中で自分でも忘れてしまうような親切な心温まる行為となっ

て現れる。

38 **blessed** ［blesid］ この世の不可解な種々の問題、苦痛や不幸、憂鬱な気分から解放された状態。

50 **the life of things** 一見して矛盾と偶然に満ちたこの世の不規律も、深い精神的歓喜を伴った心眼をもってすれば、清く澄み渡った調和統一の世界におのずと触れることになり、事物の不滅の生命の真理を洞察するに至る。

53 **joyless daylight** 52行目の darkness と対照する。俗世間の無味乾燥の不快な白昼の事物。また、夜の闇では熱狂する浮世の焦慮から煩悶悔恨して心安まることがない。このような世俗の重圧が詩人の心臓の鼓動さえも威圧するのである。

57 **sylvan**＝of the woods.

59 **half-extinguished thought** 遠い過去の光景が心眼に現出するにつれて、かって抱きながら半ば消えかかっていた思想があざやかに輝き始める。

61 **sad perplexity** 幾多の歳月の故におぼろでかすかな回想には、なにか物悲しい当惑を感じさせるものがある。

66 **For future years** 詩人の天啓の瞬間は霊感に満ちており、単に現在の歓びばかりでなく、未来に対する生命的糧と精神的展望すら得られる歓喜極まるものである。

68 **roe**＝roe deer 「のろじか」

72 **Flying from something** あたかも何か怖いものから逃げるかのように、熱狂的に自然の衝動に身を任せた。

74 **The coarser pleasures** 少年時代のもっと荒くて感覚的な衝動の快楽。

76 **all in all**＝everything, of paramount importance.

78 **like a passion** 轟き渡る瀑布が恋の情熱かのようにつきまとって詩人を悩ませた。

81 **An appetite** 若き日のワーズワスの自然に対する態度が、非常に感覚的で激しいものであったことを示す。前出の passion と共に当時の詩人の自然に対する直接的感応力を物語るもので、自然の外観の美しさだけで十分満足を感じていた時期で、後年に至ってこれに思想の深さが加えられて円熟味を増すのである。次の a feeling and a love も当時の自然に対する態度を簡潔に表明したもの。高遠な魅力をもつ思想や、肉眼によって受容しない精神的な興味ともまったく無縁であり、必要ともしなかった一種本能的といえるような激しい感情であったことがわかる。

85 **aching joys** 次行の dizzy raptures と共に、本能的衝動にのみ支配された原始的な歓喜を指す。精神的成熟が思考力の鍛練と思索による抑制を通して生み出されて後に、はじめて深い思想と感情の融合調和が可能となり、あらゆる自然の事物が十全なる意味を持ち得るのである。詩人はより高度な次元に立つ自分を自覚する。

92 **sad music of humanity** よく引用される有名な語句。長い人生経験を経て、人間性に内在する静かな悲哀に満ちた音楽を聞くことができるようになった現在の自分は、おのずと自然に対する以前の態度を変えて、その

中により深遠な意味を探ろうとし、人間や人生の悲しみが心を焦ら立たせるのではなく、心を清め厳粛なものにする力を有することを十分に理解すると述べている。

95 **A presence** ワーズワスの詩心に深く関わるもので、自然宇宙に存在する不可視の霊的存在。

97 **something** 自然界と人間性とを深く交わり合わせる何か一貫した存在。

101 **A motion and a spirit** あらゆる思考と、その対象となるものを押し動かし、万象に一貫してめぐり流れている霊的な動き。

107 **what they half create** 心のあり方によって見る対象もさまざまな印象を与える。したがって、見ることは半ば見る人の心が創り出す行為である。つまり、肉眼による観察ばかりでなく、心の眼による観照によって自然の美は把握され得る。

109 **the language of the sense** ワーズワスの最も純化された思想も、その根底となるものは感覚を通して訴えてくる自然現象に他ならない。自然によって教化されることを望んだ彼は、感覚的経験が自然界に秘められた深い意義を把握し、心を深め精神を培養して、より洗練された人間的徳性の核心となることを自らの信念としていた。

113 **If**＝even if.

115 **thou**＝dear sister＝Dorothy.

117 **in thy voice** 今のお前の声や眼は、かって私が自然に対して抱いた狂おしい喜びと同じものだという意味。

121 **May I behold** 「見たいものだ」

123 **Nature never did betray** 自然を愛する者を絶対に自然は裏切らないし、十分に報いられるというワーズワスの信条の表明。

126 **inform**＝inspire, enlighten.

127 **impress** 次行の feed と共に The mind を目的語とする。

129 **evil tongues** 「悪口」

130 **Rash judgments** 軽率に他人を批判すること。

131 **greetings where no kindness is** 「うわべだけのお世辞」

133 **prevail**＝be victorious.

135 **Therefore** 私が経験したように、自然の感化力が人間の精神に与える無上の歓びをお前も今から身をもって体得するが良い。

140 **sober pleasure** 以前の私のような、そして現在のお前のような狂おしい歓喜が円熟味を増して抑制のきいた落ち着きのある歓びになるということ。

141 **a mansion for all lovely forms** 「すべての美しい形象を受容する館」

142 **Thy memory be**＝when thy memory shall be.

144 **solitude** 孤独は必ずしも詩人にとって否定的な要素ではなく、内省や熟考を通しての心の眼を開かせる機会ともなる。

148 **where I no more can hear** 詩人の死後を暗

示する。

150 **wilt thou** 147行目の Nor と連結する。

152 **and that** 150行目の forget にかかる。

154 **rather say** むしろもっと温かい愛情を抱いて、といってもよい気持ちで。

156 **Of holier love** 少年時代の未熟で官能的な愛情ではなく、より純化された精神による聖なる愛情にかられて。

160 **for themselves and for thy sake** それ自体懐かしく、親しみ深いものであるが、妹のお前がいてくれるために、かっての過去の自分の姿を見る思いがして、なおさら、この緑の田園の美景を愛する念が強くなってくるという意味。
ワーズワス兄妹が精神的にいかに深く影響を与えあっていたかが察せられるような結びである。

GOODY BLAKE AND HARRY GILL

1798年早春の作品。当時、ワーズワスはエラスマス・ダーウィンの『生物の法則』の中で、貧困に苦しんでいる若い小作農民の話を知り、自分が計画している詩作に適した素材であると認識するに至った。ワーズワスは老婆グディ・ブレイクに心から同情し、一部の地主階級だけが裕福な生活を続けていることを批判するのである。詩人は単に感傷的になるのでもないし、面白がったり皮肉ったりするのではなく、老婆の困窮に心からの理解といきどおりと示している。

2 **ails**＝troubles.

3 **evermore**＝always.

6 **duffle** 「ダッフル」厚いけばを立てた粗織りラシャ。

8 **smother**＝cover, wrap up.

17 **drover** 「家畜商人」

20 **the voice of three** 「三人分の声」

22 **clad**＜clothe

29 **Dorsetshire** イングランド南部の州。

31 **dear**＝high-priced, costly.

32 **by wind and tide** 風向きと潮の流れしだいの(帆)船で運ばれてくる。

39 **canty**《スコット・北英》＝lively, cheerful.

40 **linnet** 「べにひわ」

50 **made a rout** 「ざわざわ騒がしい音をたてた」

55 **wood or stick** 「まきや枝木」

66 **trespass**＝intrusion, sin.

73 **rick**＝stack.

76 **stubble**＝stump. (麦などの)刈り株。

83 **elder** 「西洋にわとこ」

85 **turned about**＝faced to the rear.

99 **never out of hearing** 「いつも聞いてくれた」

110 **not a whit**＝not at all.

111 **Another** 寒いのでもう一着着た。

114 **pinned**＜pin＝bind.

117 **fell away**＝grew thin.

122 **Abed**《古》＝in bed.

SIMON LEE, THE OLD HUNTSMAN

1798年春の作品。ワーズワス自信の言葉によれば、この老人はオールフォックスデンの郷士の猟犬係であり、実話に基づいて詩作したらしい。45年を経た後でも、この老人の姿が昨日のようにいきいきと眼に浮かんでくるという。『抒情民謡詩集』序文で述べられた計画を完全に果たした詩は、実際には比較的少ないと言わねばならないが、日常の言葉で田園生活から素朴な出来事に取材するという方針は、このサイモン・リーにおいて最もよく成功した例を見ることができるであろう。

6 **burthen**《古》＝burden.

26 **awry** [ərái] ＝twisted, distorted.

30 **husbandry**＝farming.

36 **stone-blind**＝utterly blind.

39 **chiming**＝barking.

41 **feats**＝surprising performance.

48 **common** 「(村の)共有地」

54 **wean**＝estrange, distract.

59 **scrap**＝shred, fragment.

85 **mattock** つるはしに似た根掘りぐわ。

85 **tottered**＝faltered.

92 **proffered**＝offered.

94 **severed**＝cut, cleaved.

LINES

ワーズワスの学生時代の彼自身の体験に基づいて書かれたもので、ホークスヘッドで書き始められ、1798年頃に完成したものである。作詩に長い期間を要したので、この詩にはさまざまな想念が反映されている。後年に至って、人間と自然との結びつきを新たな視点から見るようになって、初期の自分の体験を再考しているのである。積極的に政治問題に関心を示した時期もあった彼であるが、ここでは孤独に隠棲する人間の瞑想や観照を描写して、当時の合理主義的啓蒙思想への反感を表明している。

3 **verdant**＝green, fresh-coloured.

7 **saved from vacancy** 「虚空から開拓した」「無から生み出した」

16 **A favoured being** 「才能のある人物」

17 **hallow**＝reverence, make holy.

21 **Owed him no service**＝Owed no service to him.

27 **stone-chat** 「のびたき」

27 **sand-piper** 「いそしぎ」

28 **juniper** 「杜松」

29 **thistle** 「あざみ」
36 **sustain**＝endure.
44 **lost man** 40行目の labours of benevolence と対照する。
51 **disguised**＝intoxicated, or hide.
58 **holds**＝regards.
63 **revere**＝venerate.
64 **lowliness**＝humility, modesty.

THE FEMALE VAGRANT

この詩は、最初『ソールズベリ平原』と題された長編詩の一部であり、ワーズワスによれば、1791-2年に書かれたものらしい。もとの原稿では、平原を旅する者が嵐の夜に放浪する女に出会い、彼女の物語を聞くというものであった。ワーズワスはこの詩を1795-6年にかけて、改訂しており、今度は旅人自身が流浪する水夫であり、貧苦の果てに絶望し犯罪者となって逃亡の身となっている設定である。「放浪する女」はもとの詩の改訂の一部である。全体としての詩は、さらに手を加えられて、「罪と悲しみ」と改題されて、1842年に出版された。「ソールズベリ平原」製作の6ケ月前に、ワーズワスはフランスから帰っており、熱烈な人道主義者となっていたので、当時の戦争や社会的不正に対する抗議として書かれたものと考えられる。ワーズワス自身、この詩の内容や用語に不満で、たびたび改訂が加えられており、次第に最期の激しい怒りや陰気な気分はやわらげられた。

12 **hall**＝manor house.
13 **sway**＝dominion.
15 **took** 13行目の No joy に続く。
16 **gainsay**＝contradict.
18 **brook**＝tolerate, endure. 初めの ill にかかり否定文となる。
21 **traversed**＝opposed, thwarted.
26 **Seized**＝confiscate.
29 **sire**《詩》＝father.
42 **prize**＝esteem, value highly.
47 **repaired**＝went, made his way.
47 **ply**＝work at, follow diligently.
47 **artist**《古》＝artisan, handicraftsman.
55 **blest**＜bless＝favour.
61 **Thrice**＝extremely, very.
62 **loom**＝weaving machine.
68 **strain**＝hug.
72 **drew**＝moved, approached.
74 **weighed**＝hoisted, raised.
77 **Ravage**＝devastation, ruin.
81 **streamed** 「（旗が）吹き流された」
83 **equinoctial deep** 「赤道付近の海」
89 **rue**＝regret.
90 **devoted**＝doomed.

97 **ravenous**＝famished.
102 **main**《詩》＝high sea.
110 **racking** 「身を苦しめる」
111 **festering**＝rotting.
114 **mine**＝land mine 「地雷」
120 **bayonet** 「銃剣」
127 **gulf**《詩》 「（海の）深み」
129 **resigned**＝abandoned.
152 **stung**＜sting＝rouse, stimulater.
155 **crowd's resort** 「盛り場」
159 **vitals** 「生命の維持に絶対必要な器官（内臓）」
168 **no part** 「何の関係もない」
175 **Dismissed**＝discharged, expelled.
183 **paint**＝describe, represent.
187 **wain**《詩》＝wagon, cart.
188 **stowed**＝packed compactly.
190 **panniered** 「荷かごを背負った」
200 **theft**＝stealing.
212 **incline**＝direct.
216 **moping**＝dejected.
219 **bounty**＝generosity.
222 **ruth**《古》＝pity, compassion.
224 **home**＝convincing.
227 **tend**＝move, lead.

LINES

1798年5月に書かれた作品で、後に「わが妹へ」という題名に変えられた。春の自然の再生の姿を豊かな感受性によって素朴に描写している。自然の秩序は調和と慈愛を示すもので、人間が自然に学ぶべきだというワーズワスの信条を、この作品は率直に表現している。

3 **larch** 「からまつ」
6 **yield**＝give, grant.
11 **resign**＝give up, relinquish.
28 **the season**＝spring.

THE FOSTER-MOTHER'S TALE

コールリッジが1797年3月から書き始めた悲劇『オーソリオ』から取った作品である。1800年の第2版で「恋」と入れ換えられた「囚人」もこの悲劇から取ったものである。この劇は最初ドルリー・レイン座で上演を拒否されて後、1813年に『悔恨』という題名で上演された。しかし、「乳母の話」の部分は劇から削除された。

6 **beam** 「梁（はり）」
10 **thistle-beards** 「あざみの冠毛」
11 **brambles** 「黒いちご」
15 **nor told a bead** 「（じゅずをつまぐって）祈りを唱えることもしなかった」

21 **simples**《古》　「薬草」
28 **his brain turned**　「頭がおかしくなる」「頭がぐらぐらする」
37 **well-nigh**《古》=almost, very nearly.
50 **doted**=loved blindly.

LINES WRITTEN IN EARLY SPRING

1798年の作品。この一見素朴な詩にワーズワス的な重要な主題がいくつか取り扱われている。早春を眼前にしての詩人の歓び、自然と人間との深い結びつき、挫折した博愛主義、ハートレイの哲学、植物に関するダーウィンの学説などである。クームからオールフォックスデンを通って流れる川のほとりで坐って作った作品である。

9 **primrose**　「さくらそう」
10 **periwinkle**　「つるにちにちそう」
14 **measure**=estimate, judge.
19 **do all I can**　「どう考えてみても」

THE NIGHTINGALE

1798年の４月に書かれたコールリッジの作品。この詩は「エオリアの琴」、「真夜中の霜」など一連の会話体詩のひとつであり自伝的要素の強いものである。ワーズワスの詩における実験と同じく、これらの詩も伝統的な詩の用語や修辞法を排斥しようとしたものである。いずれも、高尚な思索を伝えながら、直截的で親近感を与える効果を模索した結果である。

2 **slip**=slender piece.
7 **verdure**=grass, green vegetation.
16 **pierced**=moved.
18 **distemper**=illness.
22 **strain**=tone, melody.
23 **conceit**=whim, conception.
27 **influxes**=inflows.
32 **venerable**=hallowed.
39 **Philomela**《詩》=nightingale.
41 **lore**=learning.
41 **profane**=violate.
44 **precipitates**=urges forward.
50 **hard by**　「すぐ近くの」
54 **king-cups**=buttercups　「きんぽうげ」
59 **skirmish**=short contest.
60 **jug**　「（ナイティンゲールの）じゃっじゃっという鳴き声。
75 **minstrelsy**《詩》=song of birds.
79 **blosmy**=blossomy.
86 **fain**《詩・古》=gladly.
88 **Mars**=spoils, injures.

THE LAST OF THE FLOCK

1798年の作品。オールフォックスデンの近くのホルフォードの村で起った実話である。ワーズワスは1795年後半までウイリアム・ゴドウィンの思想に強い影響を受けていたが、この詩では私有財産を諸悪の最大の根源とする彼の考え方に反対している。財産の所有が人間に善をなし得ることを少なくともこの作品は暗示している。それは所有者に喜びと誇りを与えて、自尊心を植えつけ、高貴な感情と結びついて家族愛を生み出す。

13 **essay**=attempt.
14 **briny**　[bráini]　=very salty.
17 **lusty**=lively, stout.
24 **ewe**　[juː]　「雌羊」
29 **a full score**　「多数」
34 **grazed**＜graze=eat growing grass.
42 **a time of need**=crisis, emergency.
50 **due**=that should be given.
72 **crossed**《古》　「（考えなどが）胸に浮かぶ」
86 **sore distress**=grievous affliction.
93 **wether**　「（去勢した）雄羊」

高瀬　彰典

学歴：東洋大学、甲南大学大学院
職歴：日通商事、熊本商科大学教授、京都外国語大学教授、
　　　富山大学教授、島根大学教授

著書一覧

〈単著〉

小泉八雲の日本研究：ハーン文学と神仏の世界

小泉八雲の世界：ハーン文学と日本女性

小泉八雲論考：ラフカディオ・ハーンと日本

コールリッジ論考：付録 詩と散文抄（英文）

コールリッジの文学と思想：付録 ミルのコールリッジ論（英文）

イギリス文学点描：
　　第Ⅰ部 ロレンスとエリオット、第Ⅱ部 ラムと前期ロマン派訳詩選

抒情民謡集：Lyrical Ballads, 序文と詩文選, 注釈解説

A study of S.T. Coleridge：コールリッジ研究（英文）

D.H. ロレンスの短編小説と詩（英文）注釈解説

〈共著〉

ロレンス随筆集：フェニックス（英文）注釈解説

ロレンス名作選：プロシア士官、菊の香（英文）注釈解説

教育者ラフカディオ・ハーンの世界：主幹

想像と幻想の世界を求めて ―イギリス・ロマン派の研究―

国際社会で活躍した日本人 明治～昭和 13 人のコスモポリタン

リリカル・バラッズ
ワーズワス・コールリッジ
抒情民謡集（英文）
序文と詩文選

2021 年 8 月 8 日　初版発行

解説・註釈　　高瀬　彰典

発　　行　　ふくろう出版
〒700-0035　岡山市北区高柳西町 1-23
　　　　　　友野印刷ビル
TEL：086-255-2181
FAX：086-255-6324
http://www.296.jp
e-mail：info@296.jp
振替　01310-8-95147

ISBN978-4-86186-832-0 C3098
©TAKASE Akinori 2021